The Paths of the Sea

By Pierre Schoendoerffer

FAREWELL TO THE KING
THE PATHS OF THE SEA

The Paths of the Sea

PIERRE SCHOENDOERFFER

Translated by Patrick O'Brian

Coward, McCann & Geoghegan, Inc.
New York

First American Edition 1978

First published in France under the title *Le Crabe Tambour*
© 1976 Editions Grasset et Fasquelle
© 1977 in the English translation William Collins Sons & Co Ltd.
SBN: 698-10903-1

Library of Congress Cataloging in Publication Data

Schoendoerffer, Pierre.
  The paths of the sea.

  Translation of Le crabe tambour.
  I. Title.
PZ4.S363Pat 1977 [PQ2679.C38] 843'.9'14 77-18148

Printed in the United States of America

For Ludovic
and
for my friend Pierre G.

The wild geese flew lower and Akka of Kebnekaïse called out, 'Come with us! Come with us! We are leaving for the Fjells.'

The tame geese could not help lifting their heads to listen. But they were full of common sense, and they replied, 'We are quite happy here, we are quite happy here.'

Selma Lagerlof: *Nils Holgersson's Wonderful Journey*

———◆———

The Sun

Of course you may be too much of a fool to go wrong –
too dull even to know you are being assaulted by the powers
of darkness.

J. Conrad: *The Heart of Darkness*

Clouds fleeing aimlessly; and right ahead of us, very low, just clearing the horizon, the sun: a pallid sun, with neither rays nor warmth.

Sunday, 18 December 11.30
The short-lived lashing downpour of a squall that swept in over the starboard quarter blinded us. The half-smothered lookouts, their oilskins shining in the rain, huddled against the wing-bulwark for shelter. They rose and fell with the rolling of the ship, hanging there, exposed to the cruel beating that blotted out both sea and sky. When the punishment came to an end, as suddenly as it had begun, they turned their reddened faces to the sun once more.

The ship was ploughing due south at ten knots, rolling gunwales under. The radar-screen showed the unseen coast of one of the Lofoten Islands about fifteen miles to the east, and much closer to it had picked up the echo of a big ore-carrier bound for Narvik. In the waste of waters a nasal voice on the radio was preaching the Sunday sermon: '*But the fearful, and unbelieving, and the abominable, and murderers, and whoremongers, and sorcerers, and idolaters, and all liars shall have their part in the lake which burneth with fire and brimstone: which is the second death.*'

The edge of the next squall rose in the west, throwing darkness over the grey swell and its long streaks of white. Up on the bridge, leaning forward with our elbows on the brass rail, our unblinking eyes wide open, we gazed straight ahead: the sun!

A month and a half, fifty-seven days precisely, in the night. We had just spent fifty-seven days in darkness . . . The night, the triumphant night, our certitude, the ultimate night that no dawn would ever follow. And since the darkness first fell it poisoned all delight in living. Maybe . . .

But at this moment all that was nothing but a pack of lies. I should have liked the voice to chant an Alleluia rather than go on and on about those eternal truths to do with the wretchedness and vanity of mankind and with the betrayal of the best among them. 'Did not Peter himself on the road to Gethsemane cry, *Though all men shall be offended because of thee, yet will I never be offended.*' At this moment my whole being was strength, new birth, and wonder. In the gust the ship quivered beneath my feet. This pitiful sun, pale and cold like the kiss of death, was as splendid as the creation of the world: *God saw the light that it was good . . . and the evening and the morning were the first day.*

It was a rough beginning to the winter that year in the high latitudes, north of North Cape, in the waters around Bear Island, and in the Barents Sea. Tirelessly, one after another, the depressions on the far side of the Atlantic, south of Cape Hatteras, built up over the Newfoundland Banks and off Cape Farewell to strike us even more ferociously in our appalling night.

Always the same dreary sequence. The barometer falls: the south-wester strengthens: the officer of the watch, clinging to the chart table, writes in an unsteady hand, 'Heavy seas. Wind SW, force 7 to 8. Temperature −8°C.'

The busy trawlers, shining like so many Christmas-trees with all their lights ablaze, vanished: squalls that we could not see covered them, wiped them out, melted them. The glass dropped. The wind strengthened. Hail rattled on the plating. Amidships, the blinded lookouts, overwhelmed and useless, crept secretly under the lee of the bridge: they could be heard blowing on their fingers. Far out over there –

and only the radar could tell just where – the trawlers were still fishing.

The glass dropped. The darkness howled: the darkness moaned. We were entirely alone. Nothing was left in the world apart from the voice of the darkness, the clatter of the steering-gear, eyes gleaming in the red light of the watch-lamps; and beyond the sightless glass the beginning of what could not be seen.

The wind grew even stronger, veering north-north-west. A crueller wind. A more broken sea. A still colder night.

(The log-book: 'Very heavy seas. Wind NNW, force 9. Temperature −12°C.')

The glass dropped. The hail gave way to snow. One after the other the trawler-skippers angrily reported their defeat over the radio: 'Coming up to the wind to lie to,' or more briefly, 'Lying-to, lying-to.'

The glass dropped. (Log-book: '980 millibars . . . 970 millibars . . .') The wind hauled due north and then north-east. (Log-book: '75–80 knots with gusts of 85. Temperature −21°C.')

Still the same wind; but the night had changed. Now it was a gleaming black diamond. There is nothing like a storm under the mineral clarity of the far north for giving the sensation of dread, of awe before the horror and the splendour of the world.

The Northern Lights flashed and shimmered. The ship, overburdened with ice, rolled, rolled, and rolled again under the huge seas, heaving sullenly to the rise. One felt oneself being sapped by an insidious longing for quietness and rest, for oblivion.

The glass steadied. The ice-bank was coming closer. The swell died away to a flattish smoking sea – the first throes of an enormous death-agony.

The trawlers started fishing again. The men, labouring awkwardly in their crackling shells of yellow oilskin, toiled under the blaze of their lights and the twinkling of the stars, moving like crustaceans out of water.

Slowly the barometer began to rise. The wind slackened, wavered, and died away. The silent sea, oily, motionless and so very cold, seemed to have died.

Then in the south-west the night darkened once more, the forerunner of the next depression. And everything began all over again . . . Always this same crushing monotony. And the darkness: the night, the night, the everlasting night.

Of course we did see it grow paler sometimes at noon when we ran down to Honningswag or Hammerfest to land the sick and wounded from the trawlers. When a north-easter was blowing the sky would take on the colour of dead ashes; while with a south-wester we could see something like a great smear of blood behind the racing black clouds, and then we knew that far away down there the sun had risen upon the world.

Yes, it was a rough winter in the north. In the fishing-fleet there was a murder, a man killed with a cod-knife: drunkenness, desperation, loneliness, insanity? And four losses that could not be explained; four men overboard. Suicides? Hands reaching up that no one could seize, that no one wished to seize? Who could tell?

Night! Who is talking about the night?

A modern warship is a hermetically sealed tin can – no openings, no portholes – made to stand out just a little longer against the atomic radiations of some unlikely apocalypse. Only a handful of specialists have access to the bridge, the deck, the wind and the sea. All the others feel perfectly safe as they work, eat and drink by the unmysterious light of electricity and sleep in the carefully-regulated atmosphere and the gentle warmth of a maternal womb, protected from all the powers of darkness by stout armour-plating. A bunk, settled habits, accustomed noises, a steady, unchanging job, an invariable routine, and the slow, even days flow by, blunting curiosity and uneasiness.

14

Yet every time we put to sea a few men lingered on the bridge. A short stay seemed to be enough for them, however; for coming to the conclusion that the secret was not worth the trouble, they would resign themselves to incomprehension, turn their backs on the sea, and dive down to the warm and humming regions below.

The propellers spun with never a pause, unfaltering; the turbines snarled, time slipped by. Tomorrow would be like today, and like tomorrow. There would be no sharp smell of powder, no promise of glory; neither hope nor fear. Death would not come storming in. But it was there for all that, an infinitely patient thief lurking in the corner.

The days flowed past, slow and untroubled, vanishing one by one into oblivion. The ship rolled and pitched; tedium dulled the eye; what had seemed new was new no longer, and colours lost their freshness. Trifling pleasures, trifling irritations: a vague boredom with no particular cause. The morning bugle sounded: time to get up once more and begin it all over again. On and on beneath the flying masses of uneasy clouds, the ship followed her given course: what did it matter to us?

We carried out our allotted tasks and then we played cards or read detective stories or listened to songs on the radio: sometimes, with a bottle on the table, we would wrangle for hours on end, going on about our rights, our chances of promotion, our privileges, our pensions . . .

Who is talking about night? There was no night.

The voice on the radio: *'Verily I say unto thee, That this day, even in this night, before the cock crow twice, thou shalt deny me thrice.'*

The Captain was gazing at the sun and at the flying clouds, his forehead pressed against the glass screen. He had not stirred. I watched his face, a face drawn and parched by years of service: for some considerable time I had been trying to make him out by its fleeting shades of expression.

Every captain, sole master under God, sets his mark on his ship. Ours, grey, cold, crippled by old wounds and shut up in a Trappist's silence, ruled us with an enigmatic authority that no one ever dreamed of disputing, an authority that made itself felt even from the other side of his steel cabin door. I knew that his proud solitude and his severity contained a certain element of contempt, bitterness, and despair; but the ship's company did not choose to see it as anything other than a stiff-necked refusal to accept the least weakening or slackness. I believe that in their depths, half-consciously, men do not so much want to be free as to be led.

'And they all forsook him, and fled . . .'

The western squall had covered half the sky. Low storm-wrack veiled the sun. The sea was green. All at once the Captain jerked his forehead from the glass and moved towards the radio.

'And Peter followed him afar off . . .'

His right hand was no more than iron and plastic covered by a black leather glove, so he used his left to switch off the sermon. Then, speaking over the internal circuit, he said, 'Captain to ship's company: for the first time we can see the sun. We have come out of the darkness.'

He looked up: his washed-out eyes usually made me uneasy, but this time they avoided mine. I saw him suddenly redden, as though he had just shown me a hidden weakness, and with a feeling of embarrassment I turned away.

He switched the radio on again.

'And when they had kindled a fire in the midst of the hall, and were set down together, Peter sat down among them.'

He moved off, stiff and upright, turning his back to the sun and leaving me as incredulous as though I had seen a figure in a station of the Cross shed tears of blood.

And the miracle happened! Like crabs emerging from their holes the men below came up on deck, silent, awkward, all staggering together with the roll: the men from below, for whom day and night had no existence, rational, satiated men, knowing neither hunger nor thirst nor anxiety; and here they were swarming up from the depths by every hatchway and spreading over the deck, sheltering behind the forward gun, behind the deckhouse, and under the bridge. The wind filled their eyes with tears. They lurched into one another like blind men. They gazed at the dying sun, sensing or rather guessing at its warmth; and they shivered with cold. There were a score of them huddled together behind the gun on the more accessible afterdeck, craning their necks for a better view, and the splendour shone upon their pallid faces.

The wind and the spray soon sent most of them below again, but there were some who stayed on, as though it had suddenly come to them that the thick armour-plating of the hull was no longer a shelter but a prison.

'. . . *Thou art also of them. And Peter said, Man, I am not. But he began to curse and to swear . . .*'

The cold breath of the squall reached us before the rain struck the glass, pouring down it like a waterfall and shooting off on to the backs of the lookouts. Beneath us, on the deck, the startled crabs crept back to their holes. Only one remained, a man who still gazed hungrily towards the south. Then he too gave in.

The squall passed, leaving the ship clean and glistening in the sun.

'. . . *the cock crew . . . And Peter remembered the word of the Lord . . . And Peter went out, and wept bitterly.*'

That evening the engineer officer, the Chief as we say, inveigled me into one of those games of draughts in which every man is a glass of whisky, and I never saw the sun again until we reached Amsterdam, our first port of call.

PART ONE

THE NIGHT

Ships that pass in the night and speak each other
in passing,
Only a signal show and a distant voice in the darkness.

H. W. Longfellow: *Tales of a Wayside Inn*
(The Theologian's Tale)

CHAPTER I

The Scarecrow

How I had longed to go back to sea! Twenty years and more had passed since I was last afloat.

Twenty years ago I turned my back on Europe for good. 'Goodbye, old Europe,' the Foreign Legion used to sing, 'Goodbye old Europe, and you can go to Hell.'

I had chosen my country, 'somewhere east of Suez': untroubled forests, vast clay-coloured rivers, high mountains blue in the quivering heat, the mingled smells of mud and spices, the warm monsoon rain, the blaze of a white sky that drains the colour from the earth and weighs down upon its inhabitants.

I had chosen my people: yellow, brown, copper-coloured, with black hair and black eyes. I wanted to belong to them...

I had chosen my life. Twenty years! Close on a quarter of a century of toil, faithfulness, submission, revolt; close on a quarter of a century of love . . . and of fear, of efforts at trying to . . . What does it matter? I am taking myself altogether too seriously.

Then six months ago I walked down a gangway one morning, alone, with no baggage, shivering in my tropical clothes, battered. I had come back.

A door had closed (or had I slammed it behind me as I left?) and behind me I had distinctly heard the rattle of the chains and the lock. Now I had to cast about in search of some fresh illusion that would make life bearable.

I wandered aimlessly about the town, and it seemed to me that I was moving in a dream. Stray sheets of newspaper bowled along before the west wind. Some people were running; others stood motionless, waiting: for a sign? For a bus? Still others were drinking in the ghastly light of bars. It gave me the strangest feeling – these people did not look as though they were alive. They were ordinary men and women going about their business: some were sad, some were happy, clinging to one another; others were merely concerned with satisfying their hunger, their thirst, or their desires; but they all seemed to me much the same as the grey cardboard dummies in the glaring shop-windows.

Under the huge cinema posters, nearly always showing half-naked women, other glum crowds stood still or slowly advanced, just as silent, just as dreary as the rest.

I had come back. Old Europe had not changed much. Life was going on, harder still and still more grim. I merged with the general herd, my brothers in denial, men whose nameless faces were lit from time to time by the implacable glare of advertisements.

One night I chanced upon a scarecrow that rose up from my past. I had not spoken to anyone since my return and I had no intention of doing so. He pinned me, a man with bleary eyes and a puffy, swollen face, and talking fast he insisted upon drinking to our young days and our former comradeship. Between two gulps of brandy he grew maudlin, tearful: he clung on, his hoarse drunkard's voice going over and over the same stupid memories in an attempt to keep me: all he succeeded in doing was to strip the last shreds of beauty from the youth we had shared.

'Ah, Doc, it's not like it was in '49 any more – we were real men in those days, right? – we showed them a thing or two, you remember? On that fucking river – the little midshipman with the black cat, the guy that had them blow the bugle. You know, the tall fair-haired guy in charge of the flotilla, all skin and bone with a Kraut name – the Drummer-Crab they called him – the guy that made me haul down the black skull and crossbones I had aboard my sampan – haul it down and stuff it up. Oh, the sod! Give me a cigarette, will you? The daughter of the Chink that kept the little eating-joint by the landing-stage, Christ, she was sweet on him. Pierrot, the same again. Yes, yes: it's not every day that . . . no, don't bugger off. Stay with me. And you remember the time they cut the old guy into little slices?'

His voice changed, and as the drink gave him back his self-confidence I saw him look round with a patronizing air while at the same time he gave me a knowing wink. 'Fucking hell, we were real men.' Sitting there full of brandy, pleased with himself, he was a pitiful sight.

I stayed with him, fascinated and horrified: there are mornings when you stare into a looking-glass and there on your own face you see the undeniable mark of a weakness you had always suspected. It was just like that.

He had been my friend. He had been a 'real man'. That was true enough. At least once he had done something I should have been proud of doing. Yes, we had been happy, serving together under the sun and the rain . . .

Time passed and the bird in the ludicrous Swiss chalet hanging over the bottles cuckooed three times. Pierrot, the boss, yawned and put out some lights. 'Closing time.'

My grisly clown got to his feet, staggering. His eyes were filled with extreme unhappiness. 'Fucking hell, it's as dreary as death here.'

There were whores on the pavement, looking out for customers. He lurched along like a sleepwalker, indifferent to their smiles. I paid, caught him up and took his arm. 'Leave me alone,' he growled. 'I know very well you were fed to the teeth with all my fucking anecdotes. And to tell you the truth I'm fed to the teeth with them myself. That's all over and done with: ancient history.' He broke into an unexpected, stupid, pathetic laugh, wrenched his arm away, took a few steps, came back and stopped, looking ghastly. 'Bugger off, bugger off, cock. Get out before it's too late. Bugger off quick, or you're fucked for good and all.'

He ran off along the street, wide-legged like a sailor. I

tried to remember his name. Dubourg? Babourg? Lebourg? He vanished.

That same morning I stood for a long while in front of the bathroom mirror before I shaved. What I saw there in my face decided me: I asked to be taken back into the Naval Health Service.

I was coming back. Now I had come back: for good and all. The wheel had turned full circle.

I was no longer either innocent or carefree. I was afraid. All at once I had caught a glimpse of the unknown depths of weakness and mediocrity in human nature: in my nature. I was afraid. I had thought I was made of bronze and marble: I was only flesh and blood. It is not man who wins; it is life. O ye scribes and Pharisees who knew it all the time, why did you never call out and tell me? I knew what heroic feats, what endurance, what acts of baseness we were capable of, merely for the sake of keeping alive. I knew the smooth inveigling voice of cowardice, I knew it very well, with its deadly persuasive power. I was afraid . . . not of death, but of the atrocious road I still had to travel before coming face to face with it.

I ran away, just as a crab runs for its hole.

I had seen my friend's signal of distress clearly enough. (Dubourg? Babourg? But what did it matter what the ghost was called?) I had seen his hand stretching out for mine as the current swept him away and I had done nothing. There was nothing I could do. The ground was giving way under my feet as well and the filthy ever-flowing river was drawing me under. I felt I was losing my grip – it was like an anchor dragging on a foul bottom – and slowly drifting on to a lee-shore.

I was afraid of myself. I went back into the service; I returned to the fold.

The colonel in charge of the health examination had been through medical school with me. He took my arm and said,

'Don't be a fool. Surely you're not going to sign on for another stretch at this point?' I nodded. 'We could find you a job in a clinic. Private practice is booming.' I shook my head.

'You're an old fool. You'll end up as a captain, with nothing but a captain's miserable pay.'

I made no reply, but took off the rest of my clothes.

Night. Rain. A red sky – the reflection of the city's lights – criss-crossed by the masts and aerials of warships. The putrid reek of the river lapping along their sides.

A few women lingering there under umbrellas, feebly lit by the quayside lights that swung in the October wind, flashing off and on.

The trembling of the ship. The warm, slightly sickening waft of fuel oil from the turbines. The muffled hooting of a tug in the commercial port: it was like the trumpeting of a lone elephant in the forest I had lost.

What was left for me to do, I should do in the service, aboard this ship or aboard another.

The headlights of a cab. A sailor in uniform ran through the puddles towards the gangway. Someone called out 'Goodbye, goodbye!' The cab drove off. A train crossed the iron bridge with a thunder like artillery, drowning the sharp voice of the master-at-arms and the seaman's muddled explanation of his lateness. The watertight door screeched open: a rectangle of sudden light, as sharply-defined as if it had been cut out, lit up the sentry, all hoary with the rain. A voice: 'All aboard, sir.' Another voice: 'Right.' Two shades. The steel door slammed, abolishing everything. Night.

What had happened to the wonderful, sleepless nights of the eve of battle?

———◆———

CHAPTER 2

I Take Over

At 00.30 the bugle sounded 'Hands unmoor ship'. The red light of the watch-lamps made the bridge seem as if it were deep under water, a submarine impression strengthened by the smell of night and marsh, and by the squalls of rain swirling at the open side doors. The Captain remained silent, his forehead against the glass. A young sub-lieutenant was officer of the watch, and his anxiety and delight were almost tangible: the Captain had left him the responsibility of getting under way.

On the glistening quay, all streaked by the waving of the lamps, little lights hurried to and fro, busy about our mooring-bollards.

'Can I let go the cross-line, sir?'

'Yes. And single the hawsers fore and aft.'

The sub-lieutenant's voice was sharp and clear, almost harsh; yet I could feel an anxious tension mixed with the confidence. For some hours this young fellow was going to live through a great adventure.

The manœuvre that had to be carried out was by no means simple. The fairly strong wind was bearing the ship against the quay, but the ebb-tide should help to move her clear. Then she would have to turn in a narrow channel, cluttered with mooring-buoys, beacons, and lighters: and the darkness, the cross-wind and the current would make it none the easier.

'Ahead zero. Helm starboard fifteen. Cast off forwards.'

'Ahead zero signalled, sir.'

'Right.'

'Helm starboard fifteen it is, sir.'

'Right . . . Stand by to cast off aft.'

The fury of that damned cross-wind seemed to double. The fenders squeaked and cracked. The Captain stood there with his forehead against the glass, still and motionless, wrapped in his duffel-coat, silent, as though the manœuvre had nothing to do with him. His silence weighed upon the sub-lieutenant.

In spite of the wind the ship, helped by the current, slowly began to move away from the quay. I felt the young man's relief. His eyes gleamed in the watch-lights and there was a fine smile on his face. His clear voice became even more detached.

'Ahead two.'

'Ahead two signalled, sir.'

'Right. Helm amidships.'

'Amidships it is.'

'Right.'

'Ahead two carried out, sir.'

'Right. Cast off aft.'

The thick hawsers splashed into the oily water and the party on the afterdeck hauled them aboard.

The brief orders, echoed by anonymous voices, followed one another like the raises in a game of poker. What needed saying was said, and nothing more: but beneath the brusque efficiency lay the dumb rapture and the tension of this twenty-four-year-old who surely had no need to shave more than once a week – and who was responsible for 1500 tons, 10,000 horsepower, launched into all the perils of the night: I could hear the thumping of his heart.

The ship's head was making an open angle with the quay. Her stern was a little way from it, too (the fifteen degrees of helm at the beginning had had its effect).

She gathered headway and moved clear. The stronger current in mid-channel took her forwards and increased this turning movement. A little man on the quay waved a lantern by way of farewell and ran for the shelter of one of the arsenal sheds.

'Hard a-port.'

'Hard a-port it is.'

'Right.'

Right ahead and close, very close on the other side the letters of an advertisement blazed over a warehouse. The pitch-blackness of the sea was streaked with red lines, cut across and across by the rain-squalls. The ship was head-on to the wind: the current, now on her beam, was carrying her with it. The lookout on the port wing cried, 'Buoy two hundred yards on the beam.'

'Right. Astern two. Helm . . .'

'I take over. Astern four. Helm as she lies.' The Captain's voice. He had barely moved, merely standing back from the glass; he had not raised his voice, but his words had such authority that the sub-lieutenant leapt.

'Astern two signalled. Astern four signalled, sir.'

'Helm hard a-port it is, sir.'

The tone of the responses had changed, growing more intense. The turbines' throb increased: we felt a prolonged tremor underfoot.

'Two astern it is. Four astern it is.'

'Right Bosun!'

'Yes, sir.'

The boatswain, a cheerful old gnome, sprang from the darkness. The Captain did not stir: he did not even move his head; and the stone-like immobility added still more to his air of command. 'Go out on to the wing and tell me when she has sternway. And keep an eye on that buoy.'

'Aye-aye, sir.'

The buoy was dragging at its chain, and in the rain-squalls it seemed to be rushing towards us. The boatswain picked it up in the beam of a searchlight: it was a cruiser's mooring, huge, black, all agleam. It was now no more than fifty yards away and coming nearer every moment, coming sideways, as though it were looking for the best place to strike. Our screw turned furiously, churning up the water.

'Sternway, sir, sternway,' roared the boatswain: and in spite of the wind and the thundering turbines his voice must have reached both banks of the river.

'Right. Hard over. Hard a-starboard.'

The steering-gear clattered madly.

'Hard a-starboard it is, sir.'

'Right.'

The buoy stopped; it rocked in the wash from the screw, and began to fall back: we could hear the grinding of its chain. It moved off forwards and then suddenly vanished as the boatswain switched off the beam.

'Ahead one.'

'One ahead signalled, sir.'

The letters of the advertisement were now on our starboard beam. Wind and rain swirled into the bridge. The ship had carried out her turn and she was now heading for the mouth of the river and the sea.

'Helm amidships.'

'Helm amidships it is, sir.'

'Right. Carry on, Lieutenant.'

I had forgotten the little sub-lieutenant. 'Thank you, sir,' he murmured, adding very quickly, 'I'm sorry, sir.'

'An officer never thanks his superior nor begs his pardon. Never! That is one of our privileges.'

The Captain too had spoken in a low voice, and apart from a slight emphasis on the *never*, quite objectively. He had not moved from his favourite position, with his forehead against the glass.

'Yes, sir.'

Right ahead lay a little wooden pier, its seaward end half fallen: and the whole stood out against the diffused light of the commercial harbour like something in a Chinese shadow-play.

'Port five.'

'Lieutenant, when you take command of the bridge, you say "I take over".'

'Yes, sir. I take over. Port five.' His voice was clear and frank. He had tripped but he had got to his feet again at once.

Somewhere along the bank a dog was barking. The water slipped by, spreading outwards from the hull. There was the smell of paint and hot oil, and the wind brought a whiff of jungle-scent to mingle with it: we were running past stacks of teak or randam logs piled on the wharves. They brought to my mind my forest and its death. The sub-lieutenant kept his eye firmly on the river, blacker than the storm-clouds: never worry, boy; you have a long road before you still, and presently you will step out faster. Later on you will falter; you will trip again, and then one night you will fall, like all the rest of us.

'Steady.'

'Bearing 210, sir.'

'Right.'

I felt almost happy, and my fear was dying away. We were putting to sea, turning our backs on the weeping and wailing and gnashing of teeth; we were leaving the lamentations, the wrangling and the miserable excuses behind us: here, on board, it would be required of us that our yea should be yea and our nay nay, that and nothing more. There would therefore be no room for the wiles and seductions of the Evil One.

'I take over.'

The last buoys, the last low spits of land. We passed so close to one villa that looking through a broad lit window with my binoculars I could see a couple in front of a wood fire. The man was slumped in an armchair; he was smoking, and he had a drink in his hand. The woman, dressed all in black, was on her feet: she was talking, and as she talked she made sweeping, irregular gestures. In spite of the distance and the veil of rain her vehemence and her desperate unhappiness touched me. She walked towards the window and gazed out into the night. I could still see her, slim and upright, a prey to strong emotion. She seized something on the mantelshelf – a vase, a little ornament? – and flung it down. Then I lost sight of her.

A gust of wind and rain swept over me: we had just passed through the channel. The ship pitched and rolled in a black swell from the offing: I had not been ready for it and I staggered right across the bridge before recovering my balance and getting hold of a door.

'Stay with us, Doctor,' murmured the young sub-lieutenant.

On the far edge of the horizon a solitary buoy was winking. Nausea wrung my stomach. I was sick. I leant over the side to vomit. Flying spray slashed me in the face. I fought to get my breath back, and then furtively I left the bridge.

CHAPTER 3

The Deaf-Mutes

The *Eole* headed westwards.

The modern Navy lives under the protective shadow of glory won in earlier centuries by its success in battle and the self-sacrifice of its men. The *Eole* was the seventh of her name. The first of them gained her reputation in the reign of Louis XIV, at the battle of Sole Bay in 1672. She was sent out to reconnoitre far offshore, and at dawn she came flying in, her guns blazing to signal the presence of the Dutch squadron under Admiral Ruyter; and this saved the anchored Franco-British fleet. The other five made less mark in history. One *Eole* was a store-ship in the days of Napoleon; then came an elegant corvette, said to be a fine sailer; then a gunboat, a guard-ship in the Yangtse-Kiang, that took part in some brisk engagements; then a six-funnelled torpedo-boat attached to the Mediterranean squadron; then an auxiliary belonging to the Atlantic flotilla. And the latest, the present *Eole*, was a little general-purpose sloop of 1500 tons built in the 'fifties: she had a fine hull with a graceful cutwater, a sturdy bridge-unit, a large funnel raked aft, a tripod mast covered with complicated aerials, two automatic hundred-millimetre guns in turrets, and a handful of oerlikons and grenade-throwers. The Admiralty had not seen fit to refashion her, nor to install missile-launchers; but before assigning her to high-seas fishery-protection and other less obvious missions, they had perfected her electronic equipment.

The *Eole* headed westwards.

Running by the Eckmühl light and the Penmarc'h, she

altered course to the north and passed through the Raz de Sein, the Iroise, and the Chenal du Four.

It was the season for storms, and that night the heavy weather did not spare us: twice I was flung out of my bunk. I could not sleep; I was seasick (the mere idea of the wardroom with its smell of food and coffee turned my stomach); so I made my way up to the bridge again.

I stayed outside with the lookouts. A wet wind was buffeting the ship: the beam of the Creac'h light swept the low clouds like a feeler: the monotonous fog-horn hooted from Le Conquet. My nausea faded and once again I felt a kind of happiness.

The steady rolling heave, the cold, and my tiredness kept me hanging there in a state somewhere between a clear-minded daydream and a doze. The feeling of guilt and of distress at merited punishment for some unknown though perhaps dimly suspected crime which had haunted me ever since my return died away. I felt detached, unconcerned by anything that might happen to me. Long ago the Venerable Huong, the one-eared prophet, had told me a legend, a fable: it drifted into my mind, and now all at once I was struck by its truth.

One day a cruel king, or a war-lord, ordered the poorest and most wretched of his subjects to go off into the forest that surrounded his realm, to live there, and to give him warning of any enemy armies or dangerous beasts that might approach.

The unfortunate creatures plunged deep into the forest. They had understood nothing of the orders that had been given them, because they were all deaf and dumb. All they had seen was the outstretched sword and their lord's cruel eye: it was wiser not to disobey. Some believed he merely wished to be rid of them; others thought they had read something on their ruler's lips, but none of these agreed about the meaning of what they supposed they had read.

33

They travelled far into the dark forest. For months and years they dragged along, full of doubt, bent low, almost never seeing the sun, contending with the wild beasts for their food. They suffered; they groaned; sometimes they even laughed. At nightfall they huddled around their fires, assailed by all the terrors of the darkness. They questioned the flames, the stars, and the wind; they were waiting for a sign, since for their own part they were unable to find any meaning in their banishment to this forest.

They increased and multiplied. Some died of weariness, despair, and misery. Many of those who lived forgot that the king had given an order; they supposed that they were there by chance and that there was nothing to expect nor to hope for; but they were none the happier for that.

However, one morning three dragons made their way into the dark forest (*or were these in fact the four ill-omened horsemen of death?*). At dawn one morning three dragons made their way into the forest: fire, smoke and brimstone issued from their mouths. And the host of deaf-mutes, both those who believed that the king had given an order and those who believed it no longer, fled in horror towards the kingdom, preferring to face the cruel tyrant's rage rather than the three atrocious monsters.

The king heard their terrified gruntings and the sound of their headlong flight. He knew that some danger was approaching. At once he caused the gates of his ramparts to be locked and barred.

It seemed to me that I too – that all of us – had been given orders and instructions in an incomprehensible tongue. (Do men hand down a little tune from the heart of the everlasting night – hand it down unknowingly, together with their chromosomes?)

At times it seems that some of us can make out a few words, and guess at broken sentences, much as the deaf-mutes supposed they had read the king's lips: these men then reveal new philosophies, beliefs, and religions. They speak of Truth, Justice, Freedom, Brotherhood, and Love; and the strangely convincing words they use in speaking of these things cause the mysterious little tune to echo in one and all. Others again seem to have been given warnings and to have seen omens that they can neither utter nor describe; and of them we say that they have premonitions, or just that they are gifted with second sight.

For my own part, did I not feel the distress of that unknown woman I saw for a moment at the window of her villa?

I should never know whether I had carried out my mission or not (was I too one of those deaf-mutes, sacrificed dawn-watchers?), but the mere thought that I had one was curiously heartening.

A strident bugle-call brought me back to earth. There I was again with the dank breeze, the night – a little less dark now – the Creac'h light farther astern, the lookout, black and motionless against the side, and the cold. My certainties faded, just as those strong, clearcut notions born of fever or insomnia always fade, so that next morning they are gone beyond recall. I took shelter behind the glass screen of the bridge.

'There's hot coffee in the chart-room,' said the officer of the watch.

Below me, in the brilliantly lit 'tween-decks, the men were getting up, queasy, unwilling, half asleep; and those who had not turned in fully-dressed, wearing their shoes, were laboriously putting on their dungarees, clinging to the stanchions with one hand.

I had passed a sleepless night; I had seemed to detect a meaning in life; the coffee was good, and I was no longer seasick. The breeze on the open sea had something of that exalting quality which made the monkeys in my forest utter their cries just before the dawn.

The lookouts: 'White fixed light, three points on the port

35

bow. Green light one point on the starboard bow.'

'Right,' answered the officer of the watch each time.

The bugler, who had just sounded the reveille in front of the interior-circuit microphone, was spitting into his mouth-piece: from time to time he made the bugle speak, as all performers do before they launch into a piece. He was waiting the regulation ten minutes before blowing the men's breakfast. I remembered another bugler, a bugler of long ago. Was it perhaps my meeting with the unfortunate Babourg that had revived long-sleeping memories?

———◆———

CHAPTER 4

The Bugler

'In '48 I once took part in a bugle-charge,' I said. I gave a slighting kind of laugh to take away from the romantic aspect of my words; and it seemed to me that I heard a murmur of approval or of interest.

'I was a young doctor then,' I went on, 'stationed at the naval base on the river. One night a small infantry post was attacked – it often happened. One of those absurd little posts with a tower made of bamboo and dried mud. It was on the bank upstream, in the middle of the reeds and of nothing else at all: not a tree, not a hut. Nothing else at all, except for the mosquitoes. By what they said over the radio it seemed they were having a rough night of it. There were some wounded – you could even hear one of them in the earphones – and a good deal of rifle-fire. A young sub-lieutenant named Willsdorff – you've heard of him? He was twenty-two at the time. A maniac! They called him the Drummer-Crab – he was in command of the flotilla. The flotilla! A very grand word for it. Two LCVPs, those little American landing-barges: before sending them out, the Navy had heaved them off Omaha Beach and had patched them up, more or less. Less rather than more, since they only held together by the paint. Two LCVPs then, and two motor-sampans, strengthened with sandbags. They had tremendous names, all duly registered: *Magnifique, Glorieux, Tonnant,* and *Dévastation.*

'Willsdorff knew the man in charge of the post that was being attacked, a sergeant in the Marines. "We can't let him down," he said in that careless tone of his. "Otherwise we'll never drink his revolting pastis again." The sergeant brewed his own, a very bad pastis with an aftertaste of rice-spirit. As there were some wounded I decided to go too. Of course, we had strict orders not to go out at night, because of the ambushes, but – '

'Red and white fixed lights. Five points on the starboard bow,' roared a lookout.

'Right.' The officer of the watch leant over the radar-screen. A great many echoes were beginning to show. 'It must be her,' he said, pointing to a bright patch, a big tanker. 'We are getting near the tramline.'

Silence once again, the voice of the sea ripped by the cut-water, and the hum of the wind in the rigging. The Captain was there, with his iron hand in its leather glove, but I did not know it: I did not see him, a dumb shadow against the glass, a little darker than the night.

Too much taken up with myself, like that wretched Babourg, I carried on with my tale. 'The river was as smooth as glass. Willsdorff sat there in his armchair on the roof of the LCVP with his cat on his knees. The sergeant was not coming in on the radio any more, and ours was playing up – another piece of equipment saved from the European battlefields – but still we had heard the wounded man howling. A Frenchman by the sound of it: the Viet-namese creep into their holes and die in silence, like cats.

'Willsdorff had a cat called Monsieur Dégouzzi, a black cat with a white bib – a little triangle of white fur under his neck. When the flotilla came back in the evening, the hands, Bretons, Cambodians, Vietnamese and a man from Anjou, used to pipe up to the tune of one of those children's counting-songs:

> *Dégouzzi has a little prick*
> *It's hardly more than a matchstick*
> *He uses it when he wants to pee:*
> *God save the prick of Dégouzzi.*

'A filthy brute! No respect for God or man, always asleep by day and on the prowl by night; and if you trod on him in the darkness – a coal-black cat in a coal-black night for God's sake – he bawled you out like a fishwife.

'Monsieur Dégouzzi was lolling on Willsdorff's lap, and Willsdorff himself was sitting up straight in his chair, a severe blackwood mandarin's armchair. Its back was white-veined grey marble with red ideograms carved in the stone, and it had some collector's seal. I don't know where he had found it, but he had had this museum-piece bolted to the tin roof of his old tub.'

The bugle's brassy voice again. The ten regulation minutes had gone by: all hands to breakfast.

Down below, some of the men had crowded into the cafeteria with its folding tables and metal stools, and they laughed and swore every time she rolled, amidst the din of rattling tin plates, their mouths stuffed with the food they washed down with great gulps of coffee. The others were surely hanging over buckets and washbasins, green in the face, shivering, dripping with cold sweat.

I looked at the distant lights of the merchantmen entering and leaving the Channel, the tramline, as the sailors called it. I no longer felt much wish to tell my tale.

Yet there are times when little pieces of your life come to mind with brilliant clarity: lines by forgotten poets do the same. So do some songs: you are not very sure of the words, but you cannot help humming the tune ... Willsdorff in his chair. The warm darkness. All those stars, and the crescent moon! The glass-smooth river: the banks covered with quivering, threatening reeds. The smell of mud and fever. There are no words to convey the feeling of moving into battle. I should have liked to smoke a cigarette, but we were running with all lights out. It is as strong, as urgent, as a boy's tormented sexual longing.

The warm night, the river like glass. Willsdorff sitting there with his cat on his lap ... You feeel mpty: never an

39

idea nor a word nor an image in your mind. Empty: as empty as you must have been before being born. And all the time you are on the watch, your wits are tensely alive . . .

We have two brains inside our skull. The Greeks already had some notion of it. Now the biologists and neurologists have gone much further: we are all thorough-paced schizophrenes. We have two brains: the smaller one, which Broca calls the limbic cortex, is that of a mammal or even perhaps of a reptile, haunted at times by all the terrors that come from the remotest ages: the larger, the neo-cortex that envelopes the first, is an astonishing gift of nature, being the seat of reason and thought, and of speech which is thought's expression. The trouble is that there are few links between these two brains and no chain of command. The neo-cortex seems to exercise an intelligent rule over men until fear, hatred, and love too, the visceral emotions of the limbic cortex, flood them with chaotic, inarticulated passions.

I no longer felt much wish to tell my tale: after all, only a few hours before I had congratulated myself on refusing any display of emotion whatsoever. I was angry with myself; but since I had begun I either had to go on or feel a fool.

'We heard the firing from a good way off. The radio was no longer working, and there was no way of telling the poor sergeant that we were coming to the rescue. Willsdorff called his bugler. "Sound the charge. They'll hear us, and it will keep their hearts up."

'"Never learnt it, sir," said the bugler.'

True enough: you don't often have to sound the charge in the Navy.

'"Then just play something, never mind what. Something cheerful."

'Bocheau, the bugler – he came from Anjou – was a very good player. He spat into his bugle for a moment and then went at it heart and soul. Monsieur Dégouzzi leapt into the air, fur all on end, and vanished: it seems that cats so hate

40

being startled by a noise that it makes them lose their wits. Willsdorff lit a cigar and beat on his belly with both hands for the drum. So there we were, advancing at full speed – not that that amounted to much – with the other LCVP and the two sampans stuffed with sandbags in our wake: the entire squadron in line of battle, the *Magnifique*, the *Glorieux*, the *Tonnant* and the *Dévastation*. The night, the moon, the smooth river, the threatening banks – watch out, there can always be an ambush – and Bocheau standing on the roof sounding the reveille like a maniac.

'When he paused for breath, Willsdorff said to him, "Can't you think of something else?"

'"Well, sir," said Bocheau, "it's more inspiring than 'Come to the cookhouse-door boys' or 'Lights out'."

'Willsdorff burst out laughing and said, "You're right. Carry on."

'"I could do you a pot-pourri, sir, if you'd rather."

'"Yes. Go ahead, go right ahead: you're magnificent."

'And it was true: our bugler was magnificent, blowing away there in the warm darkness – a great musician. He made us shiver: a massive secretion of adrenalin, a quickening pulse, strong heartbeat and everything else; in short, all the phenomena related to a good hearty visceral emotion. Monsieur Dégouzzi too: not that he cared for it.

'His pot-pourri had everything – action stations, defaulters, all hands on deck, everything. And always the reveille as a leitmotif. The finest bugling that any Marine sergeant had ever heard. We reached the post just as . . .'

'Red and white lights on the port beam, sir.'

'Right.'

'The tanker is coming close, sir.'

'Right.'

'Fixed light three points on the port quarter, sir.'

'Right.'

The new officer of the watch studied the radar-screen and muttered, 'There we are, right on the tramline. At least fifteen ships within a radius of twelve miles.' He stepped out on to the wing to look at the tanker. 'Starboard five.'

Dawn: a steel blade between clouds so low that you could almost touch them and a wild extent of grey waves, a shifting plane whose motion nearly made you throw up as you watched it. The huge tanker astern of us looked as motionless as a sea-swept cliff.

'Steady.'

'Forty-six . . . forty-seven. Course forty-seven, sir.'

'Right.'

The officer of the watch checked his position on the Decca and transferred the new course to the red-lit chart. It was then that I first saw the Captain – a premonitory shiver had already warned me. A vague, dumb, unmoving shadow: a crucified face leaning against the glass.

I was even angrier with myself. I had the feeling that his silence judged me. What was the matter with that mummi-fied old image? He had elected to be mute, to say nothing, nothing at any time: nothing but 'Helm amidships' or 'ahead two' or God knows what else of the same order.

Nothing heightens authority like silence. And then, what is there to say? We live alone and we dream alone. There is nothing to say, you hear that, poor old Babourg? Nothing, nothing that can be said. Nothing, unless you are an artist, a musician, a painter, a poet. Maybe when you uttered your lame, silly 'fucking hell' anecdotes you were trying to be a poet, a populist poet. An indifferent, a very indifferent poet, my unhappy friend.

Bocheau was a good player, one who could really make a bugle say something. The pallid dawn: the bugle's song! (We got there just at break of day.) The sun suddenly flooding the world with colour; and still the bugle's song! The ancient mud-coloured river, its green banks as tender as springtime, its marshy smell; and the bugle sang on and on. The vast light-filled sky, and then all at once, round the last bend, the little French flag flying so gaily in the quivering air over its crumbling tower: and the bugle's song!

Our Marine sergeant was alive all right. We had to drink his pastis: and that at seven in the morning! First I saw to a quite badly wounded Vietnamese auxiliary and the Frenchman – he was still howling. The post's double palisade of sharpened bamboos had been half destroyed. There were bodies too, the buzzing of flies, the smell of death.

At ten, when the day had begun to warm up, we all went and splashed in the river like so many ducks, and then we drank more pastis. The sun beat down like a club, and the insects' stridulation made the overwhelming silence seem even heavier.

It was no doubt the mysterious little tune of the limbic cortex which had led me to call that pitiful Babourg to mind: the little tune of our old crab's – no, rat's or adder's – brain that can only express itself by jets of adrenalin, jets that the brilliant neo-cortex, with its thousands of millions of neurons, is incapable of translating into articulate speech.

Bocheau was a wonderful player. And a great hunter, too. In civilian life he played the horn, or more precisely the hunting-horn. He made a good living, but . . . a longing for escape? The Far East had made him too dream dreams. Willsdorff found him a hunting-horn in Saigon (or did he perhaps have it sent out from France?), a move hardly calculated to please Monsieur Dégouzzi, who liked the horn no more than the bugle.

In the evening when my day's work at the hospital was done, I often used to go down to the landing-stage and wait for the flotilla to come in. A little eating-place stood on the wooden pier, a few planks and pieces of old Japanese tents, and I liked to linger there, nibbling *cá long tôngs* and drinking beer with my Vietnamese friend and colleague Cao Giao among the sailors and the coolies squatting on their stools. A little coolness rose from the apparently unmoving river. The setting sun sent enormously long shadows over the sleepy plain: it was not the gold and crimson blaze that may be seen at sea, but a slow, calm smothering, a farewell with no colour, no passion, no regret. A haze rose up, as grey as dust: we considered the barking of the dogs, the flight of the great black birds that glided high with never a movement of their wings; and then far away, from nowhere, came the sound of the horn.

The seamen and the coolies listened in silence. The daughter of the eating-house lifted a flap of canvas and gazed at the river. She gave Willsdorff Vietnamese lessons, and I believe she loved him.

The old song of the European hunters, sad and noble, seemed to fill the emptiness of that plain, that sky, that dust; it seemed to echo from the rampart of the night itself.

One after the other, lights appeared: the little vessels rounded the last bend and came alongside, Willsdorff sitting in his kingly chair. Bocheau standing on the roof and sounding away so as to break your heart.

Sometimes the cry of the horn was sadder than usual, and then I knew there would be wounded aboard, to take to the hospital.

One evening I was not on the pier, and that evening there was a shot. Just one shot. Then after a long pause, the answering fire: then nothing at all, only the dull throbbing of the motors. Bocheau was already dead when they brought him to me.

'Course forty-seven. We are right in the middle of the tram-line; there are about fifteen ships in the area. A big tanker astern, at least two hundred thousand tons.'

The watch had changed. The new officer received the orders, studied the chart and the radar-screen, ran his fingers over the complicated instruments with professional skill. The wind had veered northwards, and the gauge was showing thirty-five knots; the barometer was steady with perhaps a slight tendency to rise; the sea was still running high. The *Eole* lurched heavily in the hollow of the waves.

It was more or less daylight, and a lightening behind the clouds gave some foretaste of the sun.

'I take over,' said the new officer of the watch.

The light of dawn dispels ghosts, chimæras, and dreams: one has to get back to work to earn one's daily bread. In my forest this was the time when the monkeys stopped their pathetic din, as though their anxiety and distress had been suddenly relieved. Now I had to go down into the warm and well-lit 'tween-decks again, put some order into the chaos of my cabin, shave as usual, and go to my proper place, the sick-bay.

The Captain still stood at his window, a dawn sentry, deaf and dumb: though deaf is an overstatement, since he did after all make a gesture in reply to the 'Good morning, sir,' of the officer of the watch. He stayed there, as though he were patiently waiting for a sign in the flying clouds, a clue to some hitherto unanswered question in the crash of the waves.

Of course, he could do what he liked without any earthly person saying him nay: he was sole master under God.

You've got the better of me, old crab. Your silence has taught me a lesson. Right! (To use your own vocabulary.) There'll be no more hunting-horns on the twilit river, no more Willsdorff, no more armchairs: I shall confine myself to diagnosis. That is what I said to myself as I staggered along the white alleyways to my cabin.

I was wrong.

CHAPTER 5

The Junk

I was wrong. That same day the old crab invited me to luncheon. Those were his steward's very words: 'The Captain invites you to luncheon, sir. At twelve-thirty.'

There we are, I thought, he has decided to give me a dressing-down. 'If you really have to tell the story of your life, do so in the wardroom over a bottle of whisky, *not* on my bridge.' I was not a little sub-lieutenant just out of his mother's womb; I was the ship's surgeon, and I was almost as old as the Captain. So he was going about it delicately: 'I invite you to luncheon.'

One second after half-past twelve I knocked on the door of his day-cabin.

'Come in, Doctor . . . Will you have a drink?'

He was standing up, holding on to the side of the book-case with his left hand. He was newly shaved, and a few nicks on his chin were still bleeding on to the knot of his tie: severe in his blue uniform. I wondered how he managed it with this roll; two hands were scarcely enough for me, even when it was only a question of putting on my trousers.

'If you please, sir.' I might just as well fortify myself: I had not slept that night and what was in store for me here made me feel sick. I had not been idle in the sick-bay either – a cheerful Negro with a deep cut in his forehead that needed stitches and two young hands who were so ill with sea-sickness that they were on the verge of syncope: faltering pulse, eyes showing only the whites. Solucamphor injections, etc. And they had been sick all over the place, the creatures.

The ship began a fresh series of even wilder capers. The

46

Captain let go the bookcase and sat heavily on the couch. 'We are changing course. She rolls a little – such slim lines – too much top-hamper. But she's a good sea-boat.'

I clung to the door, too busy keeping upright to reply; then, taking advantage of a favourable lurch, I flung myself into an armchair. We drank in silence. A generous tot of whisky for me, a finger of sherry for the Captain. The ship's persistent gyrations angered me. Still in silence we sat down at the table. He is waiting for the steward to leave, I thought.

Every moment the slope of the table changed. A bottle of mineral-water was wedged into its fiddle by a large book, and I made out its title: *Ulysses*. By way of breaking the silence, a silence hitherto sprinkled with no more than please, thank-you, and other civil formulas, I casually observed, 'I don't think Joyce would be very flattered.'

'I beg your pardon?'

'Your bottle, sir. It is Joyce that holds it up: he must be turning in his grave.'

The old crab sent me a glance that seemed to strip me of all personality. 'Why, as to that,' he said, 'it is not such a contemptible fate for a book that has been read and re-read to be used, still used for something . . . positive.'

'Yes. But the point is the water. Irishmen, you know . . .'

The Captain spoke to his steward. 'Bring me *Lord Jim*. In the bookcase. A big white book.' Then he turned to me with something like mockery in his grey eyes. 'It is about the same thickness. Conrad never drank. A good ship's commander does not drink. And I think he'd have liked to see his Jim there, in this cabin, in the chops of the Channel . . . homeward bound.'

When the steward had changed the books he went on, 'Did you know that the Polish merchantman *Josef Conrad* was the only ship burnt in the last American raids on Haiphong harbour two years ago? He mentioned Haiphong once or twice in his novels, but I don't think he ever went there.'

A long silence.

To keep the conversation alive I spoke about my patients: the cheerful Negro – 'Your *Nigger of the Narcissus?*'

The old crab condescended to smile. 'Bongo Ba,' he said. 'He used to work on the chain in a Citroën factory. Before that he collected dustbins and swept the streets. Naturalized French. In his own country he had thumped a compatriot on the head, a compatriot who has since become a minister; so Bongo Ba can't go home – a political refugee, as it were. Like all good French citizens he has to do his military service. What miracle brought him into the Navy I cannot think. He must have told them he was a canoeman on the Ogoué. He's rated ordinary – completely illiterate – and one of our conscripts, a school-teacher rather far out on the extreme Left, is giving him evening lessons.'

'At all events he swears wonderfully,' I said. 'Most of them words I had never heard before.'

The Captain nodded. 'He has a splendid voice, don't you think? He came to see me before we left and said, "I like it here, sir, and I want to sign on again." I believe he feels happy and in his place aboard. He has friends – French friends for the first time – and they go to dance-halls together. With them he belongs, he's one of us. Only . . . the Navy doesn't want him any more: too old, and illiterate.'

That was about the whole of our conversation until the dessert appeared.

'You may leave us now,' he said at this point. 'I'll ring for the coffee.'

The steward quietly left the cabin. I poured myself out a last glass of wine: I was neither Conrad nor the captain of a ship, and I felt that now we were moving on to serious matters.

'I heard you on the bridge last night . . .'

The words hung up there in the air. I lit a cigarette and looked him right in the eye: I was not going to make things easier for him.

'I knew your friend well,' he went on, to my astonishment. 'I knew him towards the end of 1955. I had the *Cap Saint-Jacques*, a logistic support ship. It was we who found him – he had been put down as lost with all hands. We were bound Diego-Suarez from Saigon by way of Trincomalee, for evacuating French military equipment to Madagascar. He was thirty-five or forty days behind his given time, and everyone thought he had foundered. There had been that cyclone in the Bay of Bengal . . . Indeed, I believe the Navy had even told his family the . . . the news. A very bad cyclone. I lost almost all my boats, and the forward forty-millimetre gun had come unbolted; it – ' with his dead, leather-gloved hand the Captain made a gesture of one sweeping things away – 'did a great deal of damage. Two days of lying-to. Barometer at 750: never seen the like. After that I decided to go and anchor in the Maldive Archipelago to give the hands a rest, to let us swim in the lagoon, and to have a look nevertheless, although the Navy had decided to abandon the search. And that was where he was found. He still had both his masts, mind you; but there was no rudder left, just a makeshift oar to steer with. We made him another with heavy irons . . . He lost that too, a little later.' The Captain gave a meaning shrug. 'His junk was too old, rotten . . . He came in at night. The radar did not pick him up – maybe the lookout was asleep. Anyhow, first thing in the morning there he was. The sand, the line of surf, the coral, three or four palm-trees – you know the Maldives – and there in the middle, gently rocking, this . . . this thing, white with salt, and seabirds screaming all around it. Not a wreck, oh not by any means; the junk still had her two masts. I took my only sound boat to go and have a look. I came up under his lee – Lord, what a stench! It was as though that . . . that thing were crammed with putrefying corpses – appalling. I hailed the junk. No reply. Only a black cat's head that instantly vanished down the hatchway. And, of course, all those vile birds with their deafening

49

noise. I came alongside. There's just no describing the deck
. . . Lord, the stench! I dived down the hatchway and it was
enough to make you sick. Would you like some coffee?'

'No thank you, sir.'

'There he was, stretched out on a mat, bare to the waist in
his sarong, thin and sunburnt. And the black cat too, sitting
by him and washing its paws: black all over, except for a
white bib. It was not . . . what did you call him? Monsieur
Dégouzzi, of course. This one had a different name. Its
green eyes shone in the darkness. It was dark down there,
with no other light than the hatchway and . . . the little
lamp. "What do you want?" he growled, holding up the
needle.

'I sent the boat back. I stayed with him the whole morning.
My fine white uniform was ruined – the reek – and the huge
indelible yellowish stains of *nuoc mam*. The cat licked its
paws, delighted: two jars of Phu Quoc *nuoc mam* broken by
the cyclone, and dried fish everywhere. It purred and licked
its paws. After a while you forget the smell, you know. I
stayed there with him smoking, my head on a sack of rice. I
had already . . .' He raised his dead hand. 'It was he who
prepared the pipes for me. He talked about you a great deal,
Doctor. You were his friend . . .'

CHAPTER 6

———◆———

Mad-Head

Hell, I had a very good notion of what Willsdorff might have told the old crab. He must still have been terribly angry with me: I had let him down.

In 1948 we had both of us decided to go back to Europe under sail. The idea had come to him one night, one of those spongy nights of the south-west monsoon. The eating-house girl had cooked us a *hu tieu*, a soup with Chinese vermicelli, slices of buffalo-meat, herbs and red pepper, a soup that warms your heart as well as your throat. We drank beer straight out of the bottle as we lay there, wearing sarongs, at the feet of the mandarin's chair on the roof of the LCVP, the *Magnifique* or the *Glorieux*, I don't remember which. Babourg was swearing and cursing at one of the seamen, mixing Vietnamese and French. (He was already drinking too much, the poor brute.) His bawling disturbed the serenity of the river, and Willsdorff shut him up; but for some time after that you could still hear him snorting and grumbling. The day before, Willsdorff had been invited to dinner by the Venerable Huong, a Cambodian half-caste he was very fond of, the leader of a religious sect some way up the river. A formidable pirate, that old Huong. They say he cut off his enemies' heads himself with a jungle-knife and then licked the blood from the blade. He had come over to the French a year before, stripped almost naked to prove his innocence and the poverty of his disciples; there were about a hundred of them, equally naked and armed with spears, jungle-knives and a very few rifles. As a pledge of everlasting alliance he cut off one of his ears and offered it to a fat,

51

astonished colonel. Then he asked for machine-guns for his
gang of ruffians. I saw the ear myself at the district capital;
it was in a bottle of formol on the top of a shelf.

The Venerable had invited Willsdorff to a ceremonial
dinner in his fief to thank him for having come to his rescue;
a feast, a banquet with the rarest dishes, cognac, rice-spirit,
and all the rest of it. He had never been given his machine-
guns, and Willsdorff, with one of those famous bugle-
charges, had extricated him from a battle just in the nick of
time. The rebels had fled *mau len*, leaving weapons and a
good many people behind them; they fled without having
managed to slaughter all the old prophet's followers.

Willsdorff told me about the dinner: 'I'm very fond of
that bearded old maniac. He makes me laugh. He'd lit a
huge fire on the river-bank, and there was a whole mob of
his crabs, a guard of honour with torches, waiting there to
escort me. I was wearing my white Sunday uniform, and
Monsieur Dégouzzi was in a good mood, even when Bocheau
sounded his horn to announce me: splendid! They wanted to
carry me in a kind of chair. Then there was old Huong in
black pyjamas in front of his temple (a straw hut among the
reeds) surrounded by fourteen or fifteen mute disciples,
buried up to the neck in holes and smoking cigarettes: he
had made up a poem for me:

The Drummer-Crab came beneath the southern sky:
he has washed his armour in our stream.
Since his coming our enemies stare at him with a
blinded gaze, as though they looked into the sun.

'Get on with your drink, instead of laughing. It was
something along those lines: I'm not sure of my translation.
Then I had to produce an effort of my own . . .'

Willsdorff recited in Vietnamese and the daughter of the
eating-house burst out laughing. They argued for a moment
and then he explained. 'I said *nhā thô* instead of *nhā thò*,
brothel instead of church: that's why she is laughing at me.
Yes, my poem had a church in it. After all, the old sod did

invent a religion. Anyhow, *he* didn't laugh. Pass the beer . . .
What puzzled me was these fourteen or fifteen dumb crabs
in their holes: there was an old witch with a shaved head
who went round, drawing on their cigarettes and putting
them back in their mouths. The dinner began: *cha gio*,
buffalo – absolutely delicious. Too much cognac, as usual.
But these motionless crabs in their holes made me feel very
queer, watching me eat and letting their cigarettes be taken
without a word. And the mosquitoes didn't seem to worry
them, either.

'Monsieur Dégouzzi went over to sniff one, gave an
awful howl, and I got the point. There were no holes,
brother. Ha, ha, ha! No holes at all, only heads plonked
down on the ground. The old witch was keeping their
cigarettes on the go to make it more realistic. Ha, ha, ha!
Huong and all his followers laughed until they cried. The
sod! Now I understood what his poem meant with its "his
enemies stare at him with a blinded gaze". Blinded gaze, all
right. Well, anyhow, the dinner was prodigious. There were
little cubes of liver swimming in a sharp, peppery sauce, but
I let them go; the old crab pressed me too hard, and I had
no real wish to become a cannibal.'

And it was then, after a long silence, that Willsdorff told
me about his plan. 'You know, Pierre,' he said, 'one of
these days we'll have to go. Go for good. Leave all this . . .
leave it for ever. I'd like to buy a junk and go back under
sail. Four months at sea. Things will be better after that.
Here, take the bottle . . . Would you like to come with me?'

That was how he spoke of it the first time. I remember
everything. The maddening barking of a dog in the night
and the answering barks far away like so many warnings,
calls, or lamentations; the smell of the river and the sandal-
wood burning in the eating-house; the silent lightning and
the enormous clouds. We shared out the tasks: I should
take care of the victuals, Willsdorff of the navigation. He
said we should have to take advantage of the north-east

monsoon and run for Singapore and the Sunda Strait. 'It's longer, but it cuts the line. And then I want to see the Thousand Islands. That's something not to be missed.' (I went there not so long ago. Willsdorff had been right: they were indeed something not to be missed.) Then with the trade-winds to Ceylon, 'the course of the Macassar schooners and the Arab dhows'. At Colombo we should make up our minds whether to go on by the Cape and the South Atlantic or by the Red Sea; it would depend on the weather and the state of the junk.

Towards midnight there was a puff of wind and the rain started, a very heavy downpour. Almost at once Monsieur Dégouzzi reappeared, blaspheming at the top of his voice because he had been soaked, the filthy brute.

Willsdorff was twenty-two at the time. We were both young; we were both trying to find ourselves, dazzled by the idea of being men at last, no longer children. We measured life by the yardstick of our dreams, and life seemed richer and more fiery than even the wildest of those dreams, more wonderful than any book. We felt that time, the dreadful Time that fades, wears, erodes and gnaws away, always killing in the end, had no power over us. We were children.

Asia!

When the *Pasteur* was sailing to Saigon and Haiphong in 1946, she put into Colombo. The English would not let us land because they were searching the town for a dangerous Irishman who had escaped from one of their troop-carriers. They told us that the fellow in question was mad, that he had carved himself out a kingdom in some remote part of Borneo, that to save his people he had made war against the Japanese and then against the English, and that he had been betrayed and given up for three bags of salt. At dawn I found myself in a damp cell together with three red-headed Legionaries, guarded by truncheon-bearing Sikhs. It took the French consul and the master-at-arms hours to prove that we were only French soldiers, not mad Irishmen. Back on board I was put under cabin-arrest for having landed without permission and for having delayed the ship's sailing (the three red-headed Legionaries were in irons, at the bottom of the hold), but I did not care; I had known the smell of the Colombo nights, the nights of Asia, heavy with promises, threats, and madness. They had gone to my head: never again should I be able to forget them.

Asia!

Since then I have seen the elephants of Luang Prabang, the tigers of Ban Me Thuot, the opium-fields of Xieng Kuang, the princes of Johore and the beggars of Calcutta; Angkor and Borobodur; in Borneo I have sailed up the Sembakung river and heard the tale of the grey-eyed Irish king ('He had a red flame in his blood and it came out of the top of his head in the shape of hair'); I have swum in the grey, green or violet China Sea: there are names that ring for me alone – Tao Tsai, Thule, Ban-pha-Dinh, Tomani, Long Aka, Hoa Binh, Phu Lang Tuong, Kubaan Bario, Tandjungpriok ... Yet when I close my eyes it is this first caper in the Cingalese night that I see, the prison walls running with damp, the bearded Sikhs, and the very dreams in which I too should carve out a kingdom. Everything was possible.

We were children.

Willsdorff did not become a king, either; but he was the master of a fair stretch of the river and the protector of the mad prophet, the one-eared poet, the inventor of a new belief. Of Huong, who still played ever more amusing pranks on his protector before being thrown into the river by a disciple, cut into very small pieces so that no one should ever find his body.

In 1950, without having bought his junk, Willsdorff went back to France, taking Monsieur Dégouzzi. He spent two years in a fast escort-vessel of the Atlantic squadron and then volunteered for a second spell in Indo-China. I met him again at Haiphong in 1952, and he was carrying another absurdly-named black cat, Mimi.

The war had changed a great deal. The days of casualness, of bugle-charges in rotten old tubs, and of prophetical poets, were over. The French expeditionary force in the Far East was killing and getting itself killed amidst a universal indifference.

We had elected to believe in simple things – a cigarette, a canteen of clean water, a good pair of jungle-boots, a bowl of rice or a tin of rations, a strong drink shared in the evening after the march. And the comradeship! (Never since have I known such a feeling of brotherhood.) We had chosen our princes: lean great captains, leaders of men. And we often saw them die. They would raise their eyes – eyes that were already dull – with a look of supreme weariness, making a gesture as though to tell us that it did not matter, that all this was only so much foolishness.

Goodbye, old Europe, and you may go to Hell.

1953 separated us again. Willsdorff stayed on, making war in the Delta, and I went off to the Thai country, Laichau, and the upper Rivière Noire. It was there that Asia had the greatest thrill in store for me: after the hot, teeming plain with its rice-paddies, I discovered the great forest and the Mountain tribes . . . Muong Lay, the Valley of Love, so beautiful after the morning rain . . . the Hundred Thousand Hills, where clouds and legends have their birth . . .

I was coping with an outbreak of typhus in a Meo village lost in the mists on a ridge close on ten thousand feet up when my radio-operator told me the news: 'Lieutenant-Commander Willsdorff is reported missing, presumed dead' – the stock administrative phrase. An ugly business, a night-engagement on the Dai, one of the Red River tributaries; it made a great deal of noise and a great many casualties. Several boats blown to pieces by mines or bazooka fire. An ambush.

I wrote to Willsdorff's brother, a colonial warrant-officer in command of an isolated little post in northern Laos. I told him . . . Oh, I must have been very sentimental, very conventional: I told him that his brother was one of those princes we had chosen for ourselves . . . I have no idea whether he ever received the letter, by the way: things were not so good in Laos, and his post really was at the back of beyond.

Mimi was not aboard during that spectacular night on the Dai. Willsdorff was always convinced that the filthy brute had had some premonition. When he was released from his prison-camp at the end of 1954, after the Geneva agreement, he found Mimi calmly installed in the kitchens of the naval base and he called him Mimi the Rat – the rat that leaves the sinking ship. (He also used the terms vile bumpkin, thief, father of the Devil, bastard, or just old soul.)

Like many other released prisoners, Willsdorff showed no wish to be sent home. He could be seen strolling about the Chinese-Vietnamese quarter of Saigon, in the rue du Grand-Bouddha, the rue des Balances, the rue des Voiles: he used to squat on the food-pedlars' stools and eat a bowl of rice; and in the evenings he would dream beside the Grand Lac or on the banks of the Red River, with Mimi. He did not talk much; and almost never about his captivity. He was in fairly good shape. Some anaemia, some malaria, a little avitaminosis and the beginnings of beri-beri, but no amoebas – in short, nothing serious. He used various ploys to draw out his sick-leave, and I helped him a little; though it must be admitted that both the administration and the military security left the former prisoners very much to their own devices – let them do whatever they liked.

I lost touch with him. I had my own troubles, because as I had made up my mind never to go back to France I had to get myself an indefinite release from the Naval Health Service. It was far from easy; I will not go into the details.

I came across Willsdorff again in Haiphong at the beginning of 1955, when he was in command of a ship evacuating refugees. It was a few days before the French army abandoned the town for good and our meeting took place amidst a sadness that I can still feel today.

Haiphong is an ugly town, stranded in the mud; but I love it. During the spring-tides, when the north-east monsoon rains are pouring down, all the drains spew black, stinking sludge, mixed with filth, and this flows along the streets. The big merchantmen making their way through the thick soup of the Cua Cam plough the soft bottom with their keels. And in the north-west the Dong Trieu hills fade away in the greyness.

That day the town had been bathed in drizzle since the dawn: you breathed water. On the pavement coolies were nailing up packing-cases, banging away with their hammers – the same sound as the closing of a coffin – and women squatted there, questioning fortune-tellers. The pitiful stream of refugees hoping for still one more boat flowed slowly by with a padding of bare feet; they moved without a word, without a backward look, flooding the quays, the piers, the wharfs like a silent, brown haemorrhage.

In the evening Willsdorff took me to see some friends of his. He had friends everywhere, and these were Nungs whose son, serving under Willsdorff, had disappeared in the Dai engagement. The father had that gravity and that look full of anxiety and question that you see in the old men from the north. The mother, tired and worn, took Willsdorff's hands between her own and squeezed them. Without speaking, Willsdorff raised hers to his lips. The old man invited us to smoke with him, by way of farewell: he was going to stay in Haiphong. He stretched out on a mat with the back of his neck resting on a little Hué-blue brick, and in the yellow light of the lamp his face stood out of the darkness like a Gothic mask. The old woman squatted there, and her wrinkled, work-worn fingers twirled the needle over the flame. Her shadow wavering on the white-washed wall. The jade pipe spluttering. Mimi's purr (the filthy brute loved it when people smoked). The pleasant, sweetish smell of opium dispelling the reek of the town's broken drains. Willsdorff on his mat, like a recumbent figure on a tomb. The dampness; the drizzle on the roof; the ship's sirens far away. Low-voiced talk in Vietnamese. My torpor: my reflections – the next day I was leaving for the south and I knew I should never come back to this town I loved. Never again. Two words heavy with regret and remorse, like old age and the coming of death. Never again: never again. The opium sharpened the meaning; at the same time it blunted the despair a little.

That night remains fixed in my memory. I remember Willsdorff's talking. 'There was an old crab there,' he said. 'They had nabbed him right up on the Chinese frontier, at the back of beyond. Perron, Romain Perron – lieutenant by length of service – forty-five years – from Lanvénégen, Morbihan – nicknamed Mad-Head. An old crab – a thoroughly good sort – rather stupid – didn't talk much, but when he did, it was with a Breton accent you could cut with a knife. He put up with our humiliating round quietly enough – the usual programme; political education, fatigues, self-criticism . . . Mad-Head never said a word. But every day he saved a little of his rice, like an ant: it was heroic, because with our daily ration we were at the limit of survival. That would last two months, three months, and then one day he'd go, just vanish. We were not particularly well guarded. There would have been no point in it, since the camp was in deep jungle, much too far from any French-controlled region. We all, or at least most of us, had tried to escape: once! We were all retaken in no time at all. Result: a thorough beating-up and four nights in the camp pillory, tied to a tree full of leeches with an ignominious card hung round you reading "Enemy of the people" or something in that line. Still, it was better than a bullet in the back of the neck.

'After five days, just as we expected, we would see our old

59

Mad-Head brought back again between two soldiers, rather battered. A moral discourse on his bad behaviour by the chief of the camp, four nights in the pillory, enemy of the people – the usual stuff. But the obstinate old crab was scarcely untied before he started saving his rice again. Then a couple of months later, pffft!' For a while Willsdorff was lost in thought; then he reached out his hand in my direction, the fingers all spread wide. 'Five times . . . and five times he was brought back *manu militari*, a little bloodier and a little more battered every go. The chief of the camp was disgusted and called him *Dien Cai Dau*, Mad-Head. The guards all laughed at him and knocked him about with sticks or rifle-butts. But for all that he would have started again, if we had not been liberated.'

With an authoritative tap the old woman struck the tube of the pipe with the iron needle, to show that the little ball of opium was roasted to a turn and that it was now to be smoked. Willsdorff turned towards her, disturbing Mimi ('Sorry, old Rat'), put the mouthpiece to his lips and drew deeply. In this position his face was fully lit by the little lamp, and it struck me by its gravity. With his eyes closed he let himself fall back, breathing out the smoke; and once again he looked like a figure on a tomb. I thought his anecdote was finished; it was no more than an ordinary prison-camp story, and I could not see why he had told it. But all at once he began again: 'Dien Cai Dau had never intended to escape . . .' Willsdorff's eyes were still shut. He nodded to confirm his words and began to laugh. 'Never! He had found a quiet little clearing with a spring, high up on a ridge a few hours' walk from the base. There he used to camp, and he stayed as long as his rice would last, the rice he had saved grain by grain, day after day. Then he would calmly walk down the mountain until he found a path. He would follow it and of course he was picked up straight away. Picked up and dragged back. Five times! Five beatings, five pillories: enemy of the people.

60

' "I'm sick of listening to all their crap," he said one day, by way of explanation. I asked him what he did up there. "Nothing . . . I watch the ants." There was an ant-hill in his clearing; you find the filthy little beasts everywhere, even on the pillory tree. "I give them a certain amount of hell, making little floods and taking away the food they're bringing in. And I mix two different kinds to see what'll happen: they kill one another." '

After a silence Willsdorff ended in that offhand voice of his, 'A very remarkable man, that Perron. Romain Perron. The last time they must have hit a little too hard. He died in hospital as soon as he came back – his loins. It was when he began to eat something other than rice.'

The hum, the never-ceasing life of Haiphong, had almost died away. The ivory-coloured old man seemed to be dozing. Willsdorff, flat on his back and with his eyes closed, was as still as though he were dead. I thought about the old soldier alone on his ridge. Time flowed by.

Willsdorff sat up and squatted like a Vietnamese. 'I've found our junk,' he said, 'on Cat Ba island. Rather old, maybe, and she's been lying in the mud these last two years; but we can afford her. I'm having her taken south for repairs, and we'll have plenty of time before the north-east monsoon sets in.'

I had been expecting this since the night began, but even so I felt a pang. 'I'm not going with you,' I said.

Silence. I thought Willsdorff had not understood, or that he could not believe it. 'Half-wit!' he growled at last. 'She's teak-built. She's lovely; not too heavy. Come on. Four months at sea; after that things will look better.'

'No, Willsdorff. I'm not going back. I'm staying in the Far East. I shall never go back to Europe; it doesn't interest me any more.'

He looked away and lay back on his mat. His face left the lamp-lit zone, retreating into the shadows; only his eyes,

61

gazing at the darkness of the roof, gleamed faintly. 'Pierre (from the beginning of our friendship he had always called me Pierre, while I called him Willsdorff or sometimes Drummer-Crab), Pierre, you're out of your mind. We've been simpletons, greenhorns . . . and frauds. A couple of boys. We've had fun, true enough. But the holidays are over . . . even that old crab Romain Perron had to come down from his ridge.'

I said nothing.

He closed his eyes, and in a very low voice he said, 'Our Indo-China is finished, Pierre. Finished . . . It fills me with shame and bitterness . . . I knew it would end like this. Come back with me.'

I said nothing.

'So you're ratting on me? What are you going to do?'

'I don't know yet. Wander about the south for a while. Then maybe Cambodia? Burma? Siam? Borneo? I don't know.'

'Why?' he asked, looking at me again.

'You'd like to stay too. You're not sure of being right.'

He sat up, and he paused a little before saying, 'Yes . . . that's true, but . . . So you're quitting?'

Dawn had come, cold, damp, and grey. At eight o'clock I was to go aboard a Dakota at Cat Ba, and the Dakota was to take me southwards. I still had my bag to pack. 'Willsdorff, I have to go.'

'Goodbye. (Once more he was speaking in that offhand tone he used when he was moved or serious.) I'll sail alone. Like my friend Mad-Head. We'll go and see the Thousand Islands, won't we, old Rat?' he added, turning to Mimi.

'Goodbye. We'll meet again in Saigon.'

Outside the drizzle was still falling. It was cold. The refugees clustered under all the eaves and porches were waiting patiently; some were still asleep, wrapped in plastic sacks. The black mud gurgled in the drains and splashed under the wheels of the army's last GMCs.

Haiphong, and I should never see it again, never again, never again. There were all those foolish cocks, too, piled up in baskets in the market-place; they crowed without a stop and I could not help thinking I had betrayed something.

I did not see Willsdorff again in Saigon.

When the north-east monsoon began he set off on his junk, alone. 'After that things will look better.' I do not know what he found out during those four months at sea. Yet it must have been of some consequence.

'That fellow was absolutely off his head,' said an officer of a guard-ship in the Pacific. This was much later, in the 'sixties, and the guard-ship had put into Kota Kinabalu in Borneo: I had met him in a Chinese bar on my return from the upper Sembakung, the Dyak country, and he invited me to the wardroom for a glass of wine, 'of genuine, top-side wine' he said, with emphasis. The wine was good, the wardroom cool, the armchairs comfortable. It was a long while since I had spoken to people from my own country. I mentioned the names of a few old shipmates.

'Willsdorff?' exclaimed my host. 'The guy with the black cat? He's in jug. And lucky not to have been guillotined. Absolutely off his head. You know about his shipwreck? In the first place it was madness to sail alone in a tub of that kind – a junk, for God's sake. It was only the wildest luck that he managed to cross the Indian Ocean in the cyclone season. Some Bedouin prowling about in those parts captured him – fifteen days tied to the tail of a camel, or so I've heard. He had to be ransomed before they would let him go. And to think he might have been a rear-admiral before the age of fifty! There was everything in his favour, and the Navy's not afraid of eccentrics. Yet he had to plunge right up to the neck in the Algerian business. He was in command of a company of native troops, and of course he got himself involved in all that nasty stuff. I was attached to the naval base at Mers el-Kébir at the time of the putsch,

63

and I saw him turn up one day, all alone, a hulking great fellow with a frightful black cat, and he tried to persuade the Admiral to join in their foolishness. He had left the creature in the guard-room and it howled all the time. An hour later he came to fetch it, looking haughty. I can see him still, scratching his head and saying, "Still, the old crab did give me a hearty laugh." The Admiral let them both disappear instead of putting them under arrest. Everyone was mad in Algeria at that time, but the old boy had a head on his shoulders and he wanted to see which way the wind was blowing before committing himself. I thoroughly understand him. Finally your friend did get himself caught – it was because of his cat, by the way. He ended up with twenty years, and he was lucky it was not worse: the guillotine was precious close. He must be in a very bad way now, because . . . well, I'll tell you what I've heard. It seems that in Indo-China he took to – ' With a mysterious look my host leaned forward, raised his fist to his mouth and breathed in noisily. Then he nodded solemnly and said, 'He sucks the bamboo, you follow me? Of course, there are others who do the same: just one more naval tradition.'

The God-damned fool! It was I myself who had persuaded Willsdorff to take opium aboard the junk. There are cases in which it is a splendid medicine, and I can perfectly well see that having been through a cyclone and having reached a sheltered anchorage in the Maldives he should stretch out on his mat and smoke a few pipes. It is the best way of recovering, far better than drink; and I should have done the same. The jars of Phu Quoc *nuoc mam* broken by the cyclone for the greater delight of Mimi, the *nuoc mam* that smelt so strong, the rice, and the dried fish, all that is right up my street too. *Nuoc mam* is a concentrated sauce the Vietnamese make from fermented fish-juice. It differs by region, just like wine, and the Phu Quoc is the best. Admittedly it smells strong, but it is delicious. They put it into every kind of dish, even with meat. In the hospital I used to give my convalescents a large spoonful every morning. I had a sample analysed by a laboratory, and it contains everything the organism needs: salts, calcium, iron, phosphorus and so on. I used to think that with rice and *nuoc mam* and a little opium to dose yourself with you could go right round the world; and I think so still.

CHAPTER 7

Death Lurking

'You were his friend . . .' An exceptionally violent lurch cut the Captain short. The *Eole* lay right over and then recovered herself with such a heave that I was almost flung out of my chair. The books rattled against one another in the shelves. A heavy mass of water could be heard breaking over the bridge-unit. The telephone rang. 'Excuse me,' said the Captain.

The way he crossed the room filled me with admiration: in spite of the stiffness of his movements he tacked through the obstacles on the wildly shifting deck and reached the telephone in his cabin. I heard him answer, 'Right . . . right . . . Eighteen knots is the utmost in this sea. Let me know when you have her in the radar.' He came back and said, 'A yacht in trouble. We are rather far away . . . There's an English trawler close to her already.'

The steel sides trembled. The impact of the waves increased as the *Eole* gathered speed, rolling harder. The Captain returned to his meeting with Willsdorff.

'After my shower I had to use a whole bottle of eau de Cologne . . . In the evening the land-breeze set in, and it brought the reek over to us. The seabirds began their din again, screeching like hell. In the glasses I could see him pumping. That was what drove them wild, as you can imagine, since he was shooting out almost as much *nuoc mam* as water. I sent him the carpenter and his crew to see to the rudder. He lost it again later, on the coast of the Hadramaut, at the entrance to the Red Sea. I went to see him again after dark: there was still a stench, but it was bearable.

66

He lent me a sarong so I shouldn't spoil my fresh uniform, and that night we smoked and talked a great deal.' He paused, and I had the feeling that he was in two minds about going on. 'We'll not go into that. He also spoke about you. He was rather . . . exalted: the loneliness, the wear and tear of the cyclone . . . his own reflections. He said that you could not see – that you didn't wish to see the world as it really was, that the Asia you had dreamed up was no more genuine than the Europe you were running away from . . . He said you were crammed with pride.'

I felt a mounting irritation. The Captain watched me with his dull, expressionless, unreadable eyes: what right had he to speak of my life like this? True enough, for twenty years I had done nothing but chase clouds in vain. But what of it? It was my own life and it concerned nobody but myself. And anyway what about him, the old, dried-up crab? What had he done, apart from chasing shadows with his nose stuck to the window of his bridge?

He must have sensed my irritation, for moving his dead arm slightly, as though to calm me he said, 'No, listen to me. What he told me made me want to know you. He was very fond of you.' He stared at me with his worn yet piercing gaze, and hesitated. 'Doctor . . . I'm sick. I got through the medical, but you are different; I could not take you in for long. I'm . . . very sick. This is my last command, and I want to carry it through to the end. If what Willsdorff told me about you was true, I know you will . . . help me.'

I sat there without speaking, disconcerted: yes; of course he was ill; he was dying. It was not pity I felt, indeed, but extreme interest. He had a poker-player's voice and face and now he had just shown his hand – he had been bluffing all the time. The old crab was obviously going to die; why had I not seen it earlier?

I had the unpleasant feeling that his gaze went right through me, as though it were fixed on something far away. Death was there in that warm, comfortable, brightly-lit dining-cabin: no shouts, no blaze of war, no sounding trumpets; no red blood jetting out, drying and cracking in the sun; only a furtive presence like black water seeping through the ribs of a ship, dirty water making its way into the hold: like cold, inexorable water rising to your neck.

He wanted me to help him to hold on, to hold on physically, by means of injections and medicines. Above all he wanted me not to make a report that would result in his being taken off the ship straight away and sent to hospital. He wanted to stay there with his nose glued to the window of his bridge, watching the flying clouds until the very last moment.

I had no need of a stethoscope to know what was wrong with him, but it would have called for elaborate examinations that could not possibly be carried out on board to give me an approximate notion of how much longer he had to live. Six months? A year? Perhaps a year and a half?

I wondered whether he had told me about his meeting with Willsdorff just because he had been unwilling to take the plunge and because he wanted to gain time, or whether he had been trying to create a bond between us, a complicity. He still had not shifted his gaze, and I had the feeling of being searched, gauged, weighed up. He must have been uneasy, but he showed no more emotion than a block of wood.

I did not beat about the bush: 'Cancer?'

He nodded.

'Lungs?'

He nodded again.

'You know what it means if the spread of metastases is not checked?'

A nod.

'Inability to breathe,' I said, stressing the point. 'Very distressing at the end.'

'I know all that, Doctor. I want to command my ship . . . as long as possible.'

Still that dead-flat poker-player's voice. The words hung

in the air. He said no more. There was nothing more to say, for God's sake; his proud silence conveyed the message with greater force than any amount of argument.

What could he have said? There is never anything that can be said. As far as essentials are concerned we speak and we sing alone. No one listens to us.

Willsdorff used to talk: and what did I know about him? Yet I was his friend. Babourg, poor Babourg, he talked: 'Fucking hell' and so on. Only Romain Perron, Mad-Head, did not talk, if Willsdorff was to be believed; but maybe the old Breton harangued his ants, alone up there on his ridge. Or perhaps he addressed God directly, pointing his nose to the sky. Who can tell? Mad-Head was dead, dead and forgotten, his back broken. In any case he would not have *said* anything, just as the Captain did not *say* anything.

The Captain wanted an answer, yes or no; the rest did not interest him. I shuffled. 'We haven't got medicines of that kind aboard.'

With a motion of the black leather glove like a crustacean's claw he interrupted me. 'I have everything that's needed. My family doctor . . .' Once again the sentence remained unfinished.

I had had enough of this business, this dialogue between deaf-mutes. As far as I was concerned the old crab could die where he chose; so long as he could stand upright, let him stay there behind his window if he liked. Deliberately I changed the subject: 'Tell me more about Willsdorff.'

I thought I could make out a hint of pleasure in those washed-out blue eyes, but I could not be sure. He looked down for the first time.

'The next day,' he said in his flat voice, 'I was to get under way for Diego. My boat came across to fetch me. The cat jumped into it, spitting and howling, his fur on end. There was no getting him out – the coxswain's arms were all covered with blood, and for my part I had no wish to vex a wild beast with claws like that. Your friend had to deal with him. He was furious. He told me that once before the brute had refused to come aboard, and the vessel had been blown to pieces; that was on the Red River, in 1953. And the cat was dead right this time too, because the end of the voyage brought him no luck at all: he died. I think the Bedouin ate him; or perhaps he died of thirst in the desert. The Navy had to pay a ransom to get your friend back: his junk had been found, rudderless, thrown up on the shore, and completely stripped; and on the beach there were the tracks of a raiding party, leading away inland. Three thousand Maria Theresa dollars had to be bought in Aden; it's the only money they accept. An officer who had passed out with me and who was stationed at Djibouti was told off to see to the negotiations. They dragged on and on, and God knows how much undrinkable coffee he had to swallow while he haggled away in obscure corners . . . the first demand had been for fifteen thousand dollars.'

Once again the old crab turned his disturbing, transparent gaze on me. He spoke in the same way as he gave orders, uttering the words deliberately, one by one, so that they lost their life, much as a bird dies when it is smothered. Even in his voice there was death; and this gave his tale a certain unreality.

'After two or three months your friend reappeared, riding on a camel and escorted by a whole mob of ragged bandits firing shots in the air. It seems that they had begun by knocking him about pretty badly: he'd been shown in the villages, shut up in a cage with irons on his legs, and they had stoned him and spat on him; all the usual treatment in cases of that kind. There was a certain amount of tension between France and the Arab countries just then, what with the Algerian war and the Suez business, which was just blowing up. I don't know how he managed to get round them, but he did. At the very best, my friend had hoped to recover a prisoner just a little more alive than dead. He arranged a secret meeting by night, aboard a

70

dhow with no lights, in a lonely creek; and there he was with the bag of dollars, a heavy revolver and some powerful quartermasters dressed up as Bedouin, all volunteers. He was wondering whether he was going to get out of it with a whole skin when to his amazement he came face to face with a very cheerful Willsdorff, his sextant hanging round his neck, sitting in state like Moses among his people, and inviting him to come and eat a sheep. He was forced to mumble an eye, or swallow it whole or get it down somehow so that it did not come up again; it seems that a sheep's eye is considered the best part of the dish, and your friend ate the other with all the relish in the world. The feast went on throughout the night, and those besotted Arabs used up at least enough ammunition for a landing-party a hundred strong out of affection for their prisoner, all bawling in chorus "*El Majnoun, el Majnoun Nazrani*" which I believe means "The Nazarene affected by God". Or "The Christian innocent" if you like. At dawn, after countless salaams and embraces, and after having pocketed the dollars, they finally let him go. They even gave him a sword or a long dagger as a keepsake, and Willsdorff gave them my friend's revolver: back in Djibouti he had to fill out a statement of loss in eight copies for the administration. Three thousand silver dollars, a heavy revolver and six rounds, that was what your friend cost.' The telephone rang. 'Excuse me.' Once again I was surprised by the ease with which the Captain moved his stiff, dried old person, taking advantage of every favourable roll. A real sailor. 'Right . . . right. Double the lookouts. Right.' He came back and sat on the couch opposite me. The *Eole*'s quivering increased. The spray rattled on the plating like small-shot. 'We are pushing it up to twenty-two knots. The yacht has capsized. The Englishmen have rescued two men and a woman. There's another woman still missing.' After a brief silence he carried on with no transition, 'I saw him again in Alsace in '60 . . . it was raining. I was attached to the Rhine flotilla. At

Niederbronn, to be precise, a village near Reichshoffen, for the funeral of his brother, killed in Algeria. An old soldier, a regimental sergeant-major. Did you know him? Two tours of duty in Indo-China. The Germans had called him up in '42 – the retreat from Russia, then from Courland . . . Yes, an old soldier. And he died like a soldier.' A movement of the leather-gloved hand emphasized these last words: was I to take it as a hint of his reasons for wishing to stay on board, or was it involuntary? He went straight on, 'I had seen the news in the local paper. It was raining. The bugle sounded flat. The badly-trained young conscripts presented arms and they did it wretchedly. The ex-servicemen's flag drooped, soaked through and through. There were also two or three unobtrusive Germans from the other side of the Rhine: one of them, a man who had lost his arm, his left arm, and an eye, was weeping. Perhaps it was the rain. The pastor – the Willsdorffs were Protestants – mumbled something about the centurion at Capernaum. You know the piece. *"Lord . . . speak the word only, and my servant shall be healed. For I am a man under authority, having soldiers under me: and I say to this man, Go, and he goeth and to another, Come, and he cometh . . . And Jesus said unto the centurion, Go thy way, and as thou hast believed, so be it done unto thee."* A good prayer for a soldier. "Let it be done to us according to our faith, our faith in the rightness of our choice."' He hesitated for a moment and went on, 'We all went over to the hotel opposite the church for a glass of grog, and your friend said, "My brother would rather have been buried where he fell." That evening I took him back to Strasbourg in my car. He had to catch a train for Brest. He talked about nothing but his brother: his belly had been ripped open, and it took him twelve hours to die . . . he had been in command of a company of harkis in the Djebel Amour. Your friend was very fond of his brother.'

'I know,' I said. 'He told me about him one evening on the roof of the *Magnifique*. When he came back in '45, his brother said to him, "I fought like a devil for those German swine. You do the opposite of what you want: I'd always longed for the defeat of Germany, but every time my company was in action against the Russians I did all I possibly could for us to win. Because our victory meant our survival, survival for me and for the men fighting on my side." Willsdorff thought his brother was wrong: "As for me," he said, "I shall only do what I think right." '

The Captain made an abrupt gesture, his steel claw hitting the table with a crack. 'Nonsense,' he said, with a vehemence that surprised me. 'A man's choice is not between what he believes to be good and what he believes to be evil – that would be plain and clearcut – but between one good and another good. Between two essential values that some grim joke of fate suddenly sets in opposition. You have to choose. And by choosing one good you may deny the other.' He grew calmer and his voice resumed its flat, dead tone. 'Perhaps he doesn't know that yet; perhaps he never will know it. It may be that he is an . . . innocent, as those besotted Arabs called him. His brother, on the other hand, *he* knew it. He foresaw the independence of Algeria, and he dreaded being ordered to abandon his harkis. A little earlier, he had written to Willsdorff, saying, "I am a soldier, but I could not obey an order of that kind." Death prevented him from having to betray his fellow fighting-men on the one hand or his sense of discipline on the other. In the station buffet at Strasbourg we had another drink. Your friend said to me, "I'm going to take his place over there." '

The Captain remained silent and I became aware of the trembling of the steel hull. The hail of spray crackled without a pause. Sometimes a dull blow like gunfire seemed to stop the *Eole* dead; for a few seconds she felt as though she were not moving at all; then she would lie over and a huge mass of sea would break over the deck with the roar of a landslide.

It must have been a splendid sight up there on the bridge: twenty-two knots in seas rising twelve or fifteen feet. Ten

73

thousand horses charging madly.

'She's straining,' murmured the Captain. And after a short pause he added, 'If it were not for that woman . . .'

'What woman?'

'The woman on the yacht. We are going too fast for a sea of this kind. Something is likely to carry away.'

For the moment the fate of the yacht did not concern me much. 'Have you seen him again?' I asked.

The Captain was listening to the working of the hull: he did not appear to have heard my question. I repeated it: 'Have you seen Willsdorff again?'

All at once he seemed impatient to bring our conversation to a close. I thought he was going to say something, but all he uttered was an unpleasant laugh, a laugh whose unexpected echo made him lower his head.

I persisted: 'Have you seen him again?'

His look should have discouraged me. He did not reply, but cocked his ear to the groaning of his ship, the muffled roar of the sea, as though distant drums were furiously beating the charge. He stood up with an effort, saying, 'I'm going on the bridge.'

I still persisted: 'I know he was amnestied four years ago. What happened to him?'

A violent roll threw us both against the table. A sea swept the deck, breaking over the gun-turret with the force of a battering-ram. I clung on with both hands to keep my footing.

'You will see him in the north,' said the Captain. When he had recovered his balance he added, 'He's a trawler-skipper.'

'What?'

'The *Damoclès*, out of Fécamp.'

'Willsdorff a trawler-skipper?'

The Captain grasped the handle of his cabin door; abruptly it opened wide and shot him out. 'He's been on the fishing-grounds this last month,' he cried.

The ship gave a sudden pitch and the door slammed to. I

dropped back into my armchair: Willsdorff a trawler-skipper!

The door opened again. 'Doctor, I was forgetting. On my bridge we only speak when duty requires it.'

The door closed quietly. The old crab! He had guts.

At 15.00 hours we reached the scene of the wreck and the *Eole* circled on the swell until nightfall, rolling like a drunkard and trying to find the woman lost from the yacht. Helicopters from the Cherbourg base were searching too.

There were several false alarms that sent us in short, twenty-two-knot dashes towards refuse that had been tossed into the sea as though it were a dustbin. We spent the night lying to, meaning to start again the next day.

In the morning a radio message gave the news that a little inshore fishing-boat had picked the woman up in the Raz Blanchard current at dawn: she was dead.

The *Eole* resumed her course, heading for the North Sea. The Channel was as green as a Dutch sea-painting, with long white lines in the gusting north-wester. The barometer was rising. At dusk we sighted the Gris-Nez light. The radar showed the echoes of more than thirty vessels within a radius of fifteen miles. The night was clear, and we could see the twinkling of their lights: ferries from Calais, Dover, Boulogne and Ostend, huge tankers from the Persian Gulf, fast American container-ships, calm, rusty tramp-steamers coming from the ends of the earth to be swallowed up by all the greedy estuaries of the great northern European rivers.

That night too I stayed long hours on the wing of the bridge, wrapped in my pilot-jacket. I thought about my friend Willsdorff, the trawler-skipper. I could not make it out.

But I stayed there without speaking, as dumb as our Captain, who was quietly dying over there against his window, watching the clouds go by.

75

CHAPTER 8

———————

Courage

The North Sea.

A little before dawn the wind had started to get up and the thermometer had dropped half a dozen degrees. The look-outs pulled their caps right down over their eyes and turned up the collars of their pea-jackets: they could be heard stamping to keep warm. The old western swell that had been knocking us about ever since we put to sea gave up the struggle. The air became so clear that the first green light of day scarcely dimmed the brilliance of the stars.

It seemed to me that I could make out distant voices coming from outside, as though someone, somewhere, had forgotten to bolt a watertight door. I listened attentively, and I thought I heard the whisper of my name.

The Captain was standing there in his place, motionless behind the screen: and in the red light of the lamp his drawn features made him look like an old clown gazing at himself in a glass, his make-up only half wiped off. He turned at the sound of my footsteps, but he said nothing.

I moved out on to the wing. The incomprehensible call grew more urgent, less clear, and now it was mixed with vague sighs; from time to time it stopped, leaving an emptiness, and then it would start up again, stronger still.

The wind! It was the east wind, dry and grey, in the radar aerial on the tripod mast above me.

It is a wind that smells of the snow, and it is born somewhere in the high-pressure zone far, far away in Siberia, and it whirls about the steppe and the taiga. Then one day the west wind, the king of the Atlantic, grows tired of defending its eastern borders, and, like a Mongol horde, this east wind comes rushing over the Ukrainian plains, over northern Europe as far as the sea, freezing everything that lies in its path.

For a moment I still tried to make out its call and to understand its warning; but I only did so out of curiosity – the charm was broken, and I heard nothing but sound and fury, signifying nothing.

The bugle sounded with a terrible purity in the frigid air.

'There's coffee in the chart-room, Doctor.' A white cloud drifted off to the westward like a great ship under sail.

At noon the Captain changed course, laying the ship's head due north, true north, so that the needle of the gyroscopic compass, which perpetually corrects the variation of the magnetic north, lay plumb on zero, and she steered straight for the Pole and the darkness. The loudspeakers of the interior circuit brought the news to us in the wardroom. We were thoroughly warm down there in our white-painted, steel-walled ghetto. Our duffel-coats hung limp, almost still now that the swell had died away. We ate, we drank (genuine top-side wine), we joked, we laughed. The wind and the sea scarcely concerned us at all.

We listened to the news on the radio: '*Northern Ireland: In the centre of Belfast, so often ravaged by bombs and shooting, young people of both sexes performed a streaking act when the offices closed, running mother-naked before being taken away in a Black Maria ... Lubang (Philippines): The last Japanese soldier hiding in the island's jungle since 1945 has been killed by peasants as he stole a chicken on the outskirts of a village. Caracas: The experts at the conference on the law of the sea state that if industrial waste continues to be dumped at the present rate, the Baltic and the Mediterranean will be dead seas in less than ten years ...*'

We listened to Nicoletta singing '*Tu n'es qu'une larme dans la mer*'. We smoked cigars.

77

I watched my companions: the young sub-lieutenant of the first evening, with his pleasant smile; the second-in-command, still young but already greying; the engineer who was too fond of whisky; the fisheries officer with his charming, high-bred face; the quiet, serious signals officer; the gunnery lieutenant; the purser . . . I looked at them, and I considered them. I still felt that I was on the outside, an impartial observer; but I knew that a few days of the monotonous rhythm of the service would be enough for me to be caught, drawn in. I remembered Babourg, running in the night, his legs wide apart, running between two rows of glum, dismal houses: 'Fucking hell, it's as dreary as death here.'

Another song: *'Ca fait pleurer l'Bon Dieu, la, la; Ca fait pleurer l'Bon Dieu . . .'*

The Chief offered me a glass of brandy. He was a Breton from the parts around Saint-Guénolé, and he loved telling horrible stories. His father had been a fisherman: he had vanished when two trawlers collided in fine weather in the Raz de Sein – the strong tot with the coffee and the fourteen-degree Algerian wine must have had something to do with it. Like many Celts, the Chief drank in order to drown a morbid devil inside himself, a demon his reason could scarcely keep under control – the duality of human nature – but unfortunately when he drowned the one he also drowned the other. I liked him.

I drank, and I watched my companions. The young sub-lieutenant was gazing steadily at a claret bottle; there was a model sailing-ship inside it. (I should have to take a closer look. Ships in bottles made me dream, too.)

'Have another drop of this excellent brandy, Doctor.'

I had drunk too much. The Chief was a cunning seducer, and like all drinkers he loved to convert others. Cowards and weak men are great converters. It is their last, pitiful attempt at saving themselves, for if all men betray, then there is no betrayal – it is human nature to betray.

Still another song: '*Je m'en vais voir les p'tit's femmes de Pigalle...*'

I drank; I was pleasantly fuzzy. The wardroom was bathed in light, warmth, and the smell of cigars. No voices on the wind came below to fill your heart with the unutterable feeling of things to come.

Up there, alone on his bridge, the sad old clown who, through his window, was staring death in the face, had the look of one who will not give in, who will keep true to his choice: like the last Japanese soldier of the war, who was killed for a chicken.

Maybe that's where the secret lies if you want to live honestly and die easy – the making of a choice, the believing in certain things and the rejection of others: a choice, and a hard choice, between the best and the facile. Continually holding out against the gnawing away, against the attrition . . .

That calls for courage. Not the hero's, soldier's or martyr's courage. Not at all: a less dazzling courage perhaps, but one that is more – what can one say? – more human. Willsdorff almost never talked about his time as a prisoner of war, but one night at Hanoi he spoke of that kind of courage. It was in a little red temple by a pond that had been turned into an eating-house. Rats ran about between the tables under the benign gaze of Mimi le Rat – the filthy brute had been so well fed in the kitchens of the naval base that he never troubled with rats.

Willsdorff had said, 'On the Red River, the day before we were liberated, the camp commandant came to say goodbye. Straight and stiff, he stood there in front of us and went through his usual propaganda routine – "You must all be fighters for peace . . . A happy journey to you, and may you reach your homes very soon . . ." In short, all the crap he had been dealing out ever since he knew we were going to be let out; and there was a delegation of well-drilled

79

peasants there to wave little flags and repeat the slogans in chorus.

'I was next to Romain Perron, Dien Cai Dau, propping him up because of his damaged back. I said to myself, "There we are. The heroic times are over and done with. Every man jack of us here in the ranks has only one single idea in his head – to have a decent meal. Tomorrow we'll eat what we've dreamt of eating all these months and months on end. We are being set free and all we think of is our bellies."

'The camp commandant was there in front of us, stiff as a ramrod, expressionless. The Vietnamese don't master their feelings, they repress them. It occurred to me that the heroic times were over and done with for him too. No question of charging a French machine-gun post any more, roaring as you charge; no more sweet smell of powder – conquer or die – all of them things much easier than you think, when you're young and crammed with faith. Or when you've got no hope left. No, the days of death or glory were over for him too. Tomorrow and the day after tomorrow he would have to get up a little earlier every morning to work a little harder in the rice-fields. Tomorrow and the day after tomorrow and every day after that . . . The cold mud waist-deep, the drizzle . . . bending down over the young shoots . . . perpetually starting the whole thing over again. And none of those evenings of victory that so raise your heart: never any more.

'That's what I was thinking while the wicked sod recited his ready-made pieces. "May you reach your homes very soon." Then a strange feeling came over me. For some moments I could not tell which of us was really coming off best. Whether it was us, lined up there, just dreaming of food or our girl-friends or our wives – we who were soon going to head for France and an easy life, with cars, cinemas, cafés . . . oh, you know what I mean . . . leaving all this behind us. Or whether it was that fellow and all the rest of them, who would go back to their forest, their rice-fields, their fierce, severe life, their political education, the whole shooting match. Like monks . . . They'll need courage.'

Willsdorff stopped short, his chopsticks in the air, as though he had just made a shocking discovery. 'My God, it's we who'll need courage . . . Courage not to go under,' he said all at once, in a voice full of conviction.

He prodded his rice thoughtfully with his chopsticks, then he shrugged and went on, 'I'm trying to tell you what went through my mind. Was I out of my wits at that point, an utter fool maybe? A hungry man, a really hungry man, is a fool. Intelligence is a given number of bowls of rice a day, that and nothing more. So is courage. Just how rice turns into intelligence and courage, I've no idea. But it certainly happens.

'Anyway, there he stood, our commandant, while we were lined up facing him. He stumbled along through his foolish catechism and someone behind me said, fairly loud, "Spout away, sweetheart; tomorrow we'll be eating caviar and you'll still be stuck with your fucking bowl of rice." Did he hear? He stood bolt upright, expressionless. He looked at us. I thought I could make out some emotion in his eyes . . . a kind of glistening. But what can you see in black eyes? At the end he added, rather hoarsely, "Goodbye . . . and good luck to you all" – that was certainly not in his hand-book – and then he took two steps forward and held out his hand.'

Willsdorff laid his chopsticks on the bowl and stretched his hand towards me. I looked at it, astonished. I did not know what to do, but in the end, since he kept it there, I took it. Willsdorff pulled me towards him and hugged me.

There was a silence in the temple. The Vietnamese around us gazed open-mouthed at these two Frenchmen embracing over a bowl of rice. Mimi stopped washing and mewed sternly. Willsdorff let me go.

'There,' he said. 'That's just how it happened. He was

standing there in front of me with his hand out. When he began to let it drop I took it . . . And his eyes were in fact swimming; I saw that clearly enough. He hugged me tight, as though he were trying to convey something . . . and I responded in the same way. Then he went on to old battered Dien Cai Dau, who just shook his hand, looking at him hard – the poor old crab, dead in hospital these three days since. Next there was a young parachutist captain, decorated at Dien Bien Phu, a splendid man. He never yielded an inch, standing there rigidly more or less at attention, but he turned very pale. The commandant did not persist; he raised his hand in a sketchy salute to save his face, repeated "Goodbye and good luck to you all" once again, turned his back on us and walked off towards the forest, all alone, in his faded uniform, with his green cloth haversack, pushing his old bicycle.' Willsdorff shivered and passed his hand over his forehead.

'Something wrong?' I asked.

He shook his head. 'For you to be able to understand what I've been saying – or not to understand it at all – you have to know that a whole lot of our comrades had died, had died of hunger, sickness, misery, all because of that commandant. A whole lot of them. No gross cruelty; he never had anybody tortured. But he applied the law – their law. And it was a terrible law . . . He knowingly tried to degrade us, to bring us low, to . . . in his jargon he would have said "to make us find the right path, to go forward on the road of peace and progress", blah, blah, blah. He wanted us to sign his bloody manifestoes condeming "the unjust, criminal war – the evil schemes of the imperialists" and so on. Though mark you, not all his patter was foolish; but that's not the point – the only thing a captured soldier has to do is to keep his trap shut. Just that and no more. I'm no weathercock. I volunteered for Indo-China, I get taken, I pay. Fair enough. I try to escape, I'm recaptured, I'm beaten: fair enough again. If I don't want to be beaten, all I have to do is not to try to escape. They might even have shot me as an example, and that would have been fair too . . . in a way. But to turn your coat, change sides, spit in the soup, even if you can find some good reasons for doing it – no! To rat for a little more rice, for a pill against malaria, for mere survival . . . Pavlov's dogs! The base dribbling of Pavlov's dog! He tried to have us by working on whatever was most – was most doglike in our beings. He didn't succeed; but whether he might have succeeded in time, I don't know: I just don't know. I tell you this, Pierre, because you're my friend: I was frightened of myself. In my own self, just under the surface, I found everything I hate, everything I despise . . . a dog that wanted to live no matter what it cost, there inside me, just under the surface. I don't think I fell, but it was the dreariest fight I've ever fought. In the darkness, nothing under my feet, nothing in my hands, no kind of certainty whatsoever about my cause and still less about the enemy's.

'Your only chance is to hang on. To say no, no, no. You mustn't try to argue: there's nothing to say except NO!

'It's very hard to say no . . . just as hard as refusing an outstretched hand. Poor commandant: he was a victim too. After all, he was a decent fellow . . . He liked Victor Hugo. One evening I recited *Les Soldats de l'an II* for him:

Ils allaient, l'âme sans épouvante et les pieds sans souliers.[1]

'Ha, ha, ha! So did we, at least as far as our feet were concerned; I'm not so sure about our souls. As for him, he used to read us pieces out of *Les Misérables. Les Misérables!* A common misery united us. That's all that's needed to bring a spark of fraternity into being. Aren't I right, you father of the Devil?' he said suddenly, scratching Mimi le Rat between the ears. (Or more precisely, between one ear and what was left of the other: the filthy brute had had an active youth.)

'Turn-coat . . . deserter . . . prophet of misfortune,' murmured Willsdorff lovingly. He turned towards me.

[1] They went, with no dread in their souls and no shoes on their feet.

'When we were shoving off, you know, that night of the Dai, of the ambush, his eyes were terrifying. He leapt about all over the place, fur on end, tail like a bottle-brush. Miow-ow'ow'eee'ee'miow-miow! Horrible. He scratched at the door for me to open it, but he wouldn't go without me. Our mission was pure nonsense. Oh, the bloody fools! It was known there were at least two battalions hidden along the banks, waiting for us. Still, orders are orders. But Mimi was a God-damned bore – I had plenty to worry about with my own problems. I gave him a lift with the toe of my boot. I even told the cook to bring him a bit of fish . . . In the end he cleared out just as we were casting off – Lord, how he jumped! And I felt as though I had been abandoned. Yes, this son of a bitch is my conscience. He's black all over, as you see: and not so pleasant to look at.' The filthy brute mewed his agreement. Willsdorff searched in his bowl for a particularly choice lump of chicken cooked with ginger and offered it to the cat on the end of his chopsticks. Mimi turned his head away. 'But he's also incorruptible, as you see, ha, ha, ha!' Willsdorff scratched his conscience's head again, a haughty, reserved head, and then his voice grew serious again. 'You remember old Huong, our old pirate? The Venerable? He loved telling fables, parables that seemed to him to throw light upon the state of mankind. Well, I'll tell you this: when I was a prisoner I believe I lived through one of his fables – a summing up, a précis of man's life upon this earth. You don't think that so very new, do you? I know there was Dante before me, and then Pascal, with his men in chains, condemned to death, and his executioner[1]; but as far as I am concerned it was not a question of imagination – I lived through it! And then in their tales it's merely a question of death, whereas in mine a

[1] 'Imagine a great number of men in chains, all of them condemned to death and some of them having their throats cut in the sight of the rest every day: those that remain behold their own condition in that of their fellows . . . that is a picture of man's estate.' Pascal, Pensées.

84

man could also destroy himself . . . deny himself without being aware of doing so, without having meant to betray. Deny himself just like that, without any fuss, before having his throat cut like the rest.'

It was the first time Willsdorff had talked to me at such length since he had been set free. I had gone to wait for him on the Red River as soon as I heard the news that he was coming back. He came down the gangway supporting an old fellow who appeared to be in a pretty bad way (I think it was Mad-Head, Romain Perron). They and all their companions — there were about thirty of them that day — looked like grey ghosts in their faded pyjamas, too big for their emaciated bodies. Willsdorff looked at me with that offhand air he liked to assume: 'I kiss you too,' he said, laughing harshly (at the time I did not understand why). Then, suddenly very grave, he added, 'You must never be a prisoner, my dear Pierre: never!'

The old fellow merely said that he was thirsty, and flatly refused to get into one of the ambulances. There was a crowd of journalists hurrying about, taking pictures, asking questions. Willsdorff turned his back on them and helped his twisted companion into the bus that was to take them to the Hanoi hospital.

I must have seen him briefly three or four times after that, and then he asked me to dinner in this red temple by the little lake. It was then that I really found him again.

He felt a need to tell someone about his first thoughts and reflections on what he had been through, and he chose me because I was his friend. I ought to have found the darkness less opaque, but . . . I was not quite certain about what it was that he was trying to tell me. Now, of course, it all seems plain and obvious. Too plain, too obvious: too much like what I think myself . . . And all at once I am no longer completely sure that Willsdorff did in fact tell me all this. I am not certain. It was so long ago: more than twenty years. Have I distorted the meaning of his words?

I do remember – and this I am sure of – that he ended by quoting the *Sapeur Camembert*: 'Bah! Life, alas, is nothing but a network of stabs in the back that you have to learn to drink, drop by drop; and loud and clear I say, for me the guilty man is innocent.'

After that he carried me off to the rue de la Soie to listen to a traditional singer who accompanied herself on a one-stringed instrument. 'As you'll see, she yowls like Mimi le Rat, but the music is terrific.'

And he was right.

CHAPTER 9

The Ship in a Bottle

For three days and three nights the east wind reigned over the North Sea. By the time of the sudden drop of the barometer that foretold the return of the westerlies, daylight was already finished for us: we were in seventy-seven degrees north, in the frigid arctic ocean, alongside the ice-barrier between Hope Island and Spitzbergen, only about 780 miles from the Pole.

At noon the day before, when from below the horizon the sun sent up its last fan of rays into the faint pink sky, the fisheries officer had broadcast on the wavelength reserved for trawlers. '*Eole* calling. *Eole* calling. Good morning, everybody . . .'

A certain amount of information came in. The fishing fleet, about fifteen big two-thousand-ton trawlers, had split into four groups far distant from one another. The largest group – seven ships – was north-north-east of Bear Island on the North Flaket Bank; the others were either on the edge of the ice in the north-east or on the Skolpen Bank. Only two were trawling still farther to the east, in the Barents Sea off Novaya Zemlya: and one of those was Willsdorff's *Damoclès*. There were also a good many Russians and Germans scattered about.

I had made friends with the fisheries officer, a lean young lieutenant-commander whose indefinable, offhand style set him apart from my other shipmates in the wardroom. I liked his casualness and his detached air of being there by the merest chance. I liked the reserve he imposed upon himself and that he required from others. In another time and another place he might have been one of those princes we chose for ourselves. Furthermore, in a way he reminded me of the Willsdorff of twenty years ago; not that he resembled him physically, but they did have something in common: they belonged to the same race.

He had been doing this job for two years now, and he was on friendly terms with most of the skippers. He had met them all in Fécamp, Saint-Malo, or Bordeaux. I asked him whether he knew Willsdorff. This was in the wardroom at about midnight, after the film – an absurd Italian western (though there were some fine horses) – and we were alone together. The Chief, my abettor, had indeed tried to beguile me with Breton legends of death over a glass of whisky, but he had been called away to his engines.

'Yes . . .' said the fisheries officer, hesitating a little. 'I heard you on the bridge the night we put to sea.' (There had certainly been no lack of people to listen to me that first night.) 'On the banks they call him the Alsatian . . . An astonishing character. Last year he was a carrier. And before that a deck-hand, a plain fisherman.'

'A carrier?'

'Yes. A skipper, a skipper fishing the high seas, has to have a master's ticket. Those who've failed their exams and don't possess one, hire a carrying master. The carrier is legally responsible for the ship. Usually he just dozes in his bunk. Not the Alsatian: he was on the bridge all the time. I often talked to him on the radio. Once, and it was a night of heavy weather with everyone lying to, he recited a poem for us: Victor Hugo or God knows who – absolutely mad! And all the rest of them listened. He even succeeded in stopping the endless babble of the Russians. When he had finished we heard a voice coming in over the receiver, a voice with a frightful accent that said, "*Merrci, Monsieur, c'est trrès beau. Vive la Frrance!*" rolling the r's like a Cossack. The officer of the watch aboard a Russian trawler, I dare say, or a merchant ship – we had one on the radar, ten miles to the south, making for Murmansk. Then the Saint-Malo men started singing old Breton songs. Then the Russians took it up. And the Germans. A real party. I was on the bridge: filthy weather, dark and cold, the ship lying to; and it was a genuine party! I wanted to switch over to the interior circuit so that everyone on board could enjoy it, but the captain didn't agree – not this one, the last – which was a pity. At 22 hours, because the trawler's radio-watch pipes down at 22 hours, I had Lights Out sounded; our bugler was magnificent, ending up with variations. You should have heard the silence that followed. Then all at once every single one of them started up with their fog-horns – I don't know which thought of it first – thirty or thirty-five fog-horns and sirens howling in the storm!'

'And before that he was a deck-hand?'

'Yes, aboard the *Marie de Grâce*. He had a black cat – he has it still. With a Chinese name. The fishermen didn't care for it, because a black cat brings . . .'

I interrupted: 'You've heard he was court-martialled and broke, and sentenced to twenty years?'

The fisheries officer nodded. 'He's still a great figure in the Navy, you know. His sailing back in a junk, his company of harkis – I believe he was the only sailor who ever commanded an army unit in Algeria – his behaviour at the trial . . . I was in the 1964–66 class at the naval college, and they were still talking about him there: one of our instructors had known him. He said he was a great hand at athletics, and every month he somehow managed to break one of the college's records, running or swimming, because every record broken meant a forty-eight-hour leave. He used to spend it on a little boat he'd bought and repaired. The really cunning thing about it was that he would only beat these records by a few tenths of a second each time. It would never have done to smash them altogether, because then it would have been the devil's own job to break them again the next month. You talked about the cat – Monsieur

Dégouzzi, that was the name. Well, he already had a black cat then. When he was not busy with his boat, it seems that he used to take this cat aboard his motorbike and tear about all the Saturday-night dances and weddings in the neighbourhood, after the girls. They say he was very keen on them. One of his girls made him a kind of knapsack that hung across his belly, like a kangaroo's pouch, and he stuffed his cat into it. His ploy with the records lasted for his two years at the college. Every month he did it, for two years on end. Since then the rules have been changed ... I wanted to ask you, Doctor, why do you call him the Drummer-Crab? You used the name the other night.'

'Oh, that's quite simple. In the days when I knew him he had a habit – a habit that I caught from him, by the way – of calling people crabs. Instead of saying a guy or a fellow or a type or a character he would say a crab. Everybody was a crab: there were good and bad crabs, old crabs, poor crabs – crabs throughout. He had it from his father. On the river one night, when we were sitting on the roof of the *Magnifique*, he told me how his father had nicknamed his brother and him *crabele*. It's the Alsatian for little crab. As a child Willsdorff had a fine round belly, and when he'd eaten well he used to thump on it with both hands, going boom boom boom. So that's why his father called him drummer-crab. At breakfast every morning, before kissing him, his father would ask, "What noise does a drummer-crab make when it's trodden on?" And he had to answer, "Crrrack," with a ghastly imitation of the sound of a shell being crushed, and then "crack, crack" for the two claws. It was a ceremony. That night on the roof it still made him laugh, remembering it ... I can't make it out, how he came to be a deck-hand, an ordinary deck-hand on a trawler. Why?'

'I don't know. He amazed them aboard the *Marie de Grâce*. At the end of the fishing season he invited them all, the whole crew, to a prodigious dinner at the best hotel in Saint-Malo. The party lasted all night, with the brandy flowing like water: some people thought he was flinging his hard-earned money out of the window. They knew he'd just come out of prison, but nobody liked to talk to him about it. I think he impressed them.'

'What's he like? Does he . . . does he drink?'

'No. He's a tall, lean guy. A pirate's face with a great hooked nose and reddish-yellow hair, rather curly. No, he doesn't drink: at any rate, he hasn't the face of a drinker . . . I had lunch with him, the owner, and another captain before he put to sea. Never for one moment did he give me to understand that he was senior to me. But every time he looked at me, his eyes – they're blue, with crow's feet at the corners – seemed privately amused. You know what I mean? The kind of look that . . .'

'Yes, he already had it in my time. You say to yourself, is he making a fool of me?'

'That's it . . . He had no difficulty finding a crew, although they had only given him an old tub, the *Damoclès*, an antique that still goes in for salted cod – he had an eye painted on her bows, as if she were a junk – and although this was his first fishing command. Plenty of men who had sailed in the *Marie de Grâce*, in spite of the black cat. He – the cat, I mean – lunched with us, very well mannered. "Give him a plate, but no knife or fork," said Willsdorff to the waitress. All through the meal he kept passing the cat the best pieces on his plate. And the devilish creature ate them very neatly. The only thing was, it disliked cigars, and it vanished when we lit our havanas – the ship's owner was our host. Willsdorff called it Monsieur ma Conscience and sometimes Minh hao or something like that: a Chinese name.'

'I should be surprised if he gave it a Chinese name,' I said. 'Vietnamese, more likely. He spoke Vietnamese in the old days. Con Meo, maybe: it means cat.'

'No. Minh Dao – Dinh Dao – I don't remember.'

'Dien Cai Dau?'

91

'Yes, that's it. Dien Cai Dau.'

I burst out laughing. 'Dien Cai Dau, the Mad-Head, the Natural. It was the nickname of a friend of his, a Breton from Lanvénégen,' and I told him the story of Romain Perron.

The fisheries officer listened to me, smiling, and I found out what it was in him that reminded me of Willsdorff – his smile and his crow's feet. His eyes were brown, but they expressed the same rather casual, offhand reserve.

'It was he who gave me this,' he said, reaching me the bottle from where it lay wedged among the books on the shelf. The claret bottle that I had seen in the young sub-lieutenant's hands: inside it was a barque with all its rigging, all its sails and even a little French flag at the mizzen-peak. The hull was grey with the ports painted black and the waterline red, like all the ocean-going ships belonging to the Bordes Line that I used to see rotting in the Erdre Canal at Nantes before the war, when I was a boy. There were also marks of white foam at the cutwater and along her wake. '. . . He made it in prison. And after our lunch together he gave it to me. I'd gone aboard his ship because the Captain had asked me to have a word with him about the case of our man from Gaboon.'

'Bongo Ba, the big cheerful black man who swears so well?'

'I see you know him already.'

'He came to have himself sewn up. He'd split his forehead during the blow in the Channel. I put three stitches into him. Rarely have I seen such a jovial crab. The sickbay attendant gave him a little pick-me-up and he went off to finish his watch.'

'Well, it's not so long since Bongo Ba was sad. "I'm a child of misfortune," in his deep bass voice – it would have made you laugh. He wanted to sign on again, but the Navy wouldn't have him. The Owner had just taken over command – by the way, between you and me, don't you think he looks ill? The Captain, I mean.' I gave a vague assenting grunt. 'It's his first sea-command for twelve years – the first since the putsch.'

'Did he take part in it too?' I cried, astonished.

'Oh no, not him. He was entirely against it. I'm not really sure what happened exactly. A murky business: at Mers el-Kébir. They say it was him, and not the admiral, who gave the order to the fleet to put to sea – to be out of the way of temptation. At that time it seems he had some very rough things to say about the Alsatian. And afterwards he gave evidence at the court-martial.' ('Oh, indeed,' I said to myself. 'The old crab took care not to tell me all that.') 'There was a very disagreeable incident during the trial . . .' The fisheries officer came to a halt, and for a moment he seemed to regret what he had said. But then, raising his head, he went on in rather a curt voice, 'Listen, Doctor, it's not for me to talk about it. In any case, as far as that business is concerned, the last word has not yet been said. And I've no doubt it never will be said. But to go back to Bongo Ba: it was the Captain who suggested that I should go and see the Alsatian. He even insisted upon it. Bongo Ba was due to finish his service in January, and since he couldn't sign on again, he wanted to find a place in a trawler. That's settled: your friend takes him on for the Newfoundland trip. That's why he's so cheerful – he won't have to go back to Citroën.'

He made as though to get up, but I kept him. 'How did he come to give it to you?' I asked, nodding towards the bottle.

I felt him relax. 'There were half a dozen of them in his cabin,' he began, still somewhat reserved, 'ships, four-masters, and a little Napoleonic corvette with all her guns, in a whisky bottle. I looked at her, just as you're doing now; and I think that pleased him. "Built for privateering," he told me. "The English used to envy us those ships; in those days, when they spoke of a pretty woman, they'd say she

93

was as lovely as a French corvette. I made her in the Santé prison; a screw gave me the bottle, empty." That was the only time he ever mentioned his past while I was there; he spoke in that offhand voice and his eyes were amused, but I felt that he meant it seriously.'

The fisheries officer took the bottle from my hands and held it to the light; the faint shadow of the sails barred his face. 'I took this one off its stand,' he went on, without raising his eyes, 'so as to look at it closer. And then Willsdorff said, "It's dream symbolized, dream squared, dream to the power of two – escape – devil take the hindmost! A bottle full of wine is dream in itself; but with a ship in it, all sail set . . ." He laughed, none too pleasantly. "An illusion, of course. We sailors know what the sea is really like – our daily bread – right? Yet still and all. You keep on searching – you still keep on searching. You hope for something . . . Like your black man. Keep her. She's a present." And then he added, "Tell your captain I'll take his black man. And tell him too – " Just at this point someone knocked on his cabin door. "No . . . nothing," he said, and then he called out, "Come in." That was how he gave it me,' ended the fisheries officer, standing up. He handed me back the bottle. 'Good night, Doctor.' And he went out, leaving me alone in the wardroom.

CHAPTER 10

Luck

I held the bottle in my hands. Really beautiful workmanship: the full set of lifts and braces; the bowsprit and jib-boom with their bobstays; the set and flying topsails . . .

What a strange notion, to put a ship into a bottle . . . bottled dream . . .

I did not feel like going to bed. I had a drink. The *Eole* was quiet; all that could be heard was the distant throbbing of the turbines. I forgot Willsdorff, the old Captain slowly dying, and their different ideas of the soldier's duty. I gazed at the little barque and I dreamed, sinking down into old, old memories that I thought I had forgotten.

Black water. The Erdre Canal . . . Before the war you could see perhaps thirty great sailing-ships laid up there; some, with their painted ports faded and weatherbeaten, that had belonged to the Bordes Line. Everything that could be sold had been taken out of them, the sails, the brass and mahogany rudder, the running rigging, the bronze bell for marking the watches, the boats; and they lay there motionless, quiet, slowly rotting in the stagnant water of the canal; yet even so they had been chained to stone bollards, as though their show of resignation was not to be trusted.

In the winter smoke from a stove used to rise from one of them: she was the *Shamrock* of Le Havre, I recall. My friend Verne and I would take a boat and go aboard her, carrying tobacco and some bottles of muscadet that Verne swiped from his father's cellar. The old caretaker, a retired man-of-war's man installed in the forecastle, used to tell us tales.

95

He said he had been through the Magellan Strait three times and seven times round the Horn.

He was a testy old crab, and by the end of the second bottle of muscadet or the first third of the next he would fly into a passion, quite unprovoked. He would chase us with his stick, and we had to look alive to get back into our boat. Leaning on the rail he would bawl curses after us – 'Little bastards! You try to make me talk, but I shan't tell you anything any more . . . Sods! Sods!' He waved his arms, the crazy old man – once he threw his stick at us – and Verne and I laughed like maniacs.

Verne was shot at the Liberation together with three other young fellows of the same age. As I knew him, he would certainly never have done anything dishonourable; but God knows what confused, wrong-headed ideas his over-excited mind might have seized upon. God knows what wild, dogmatic statements he may have made. In those days a firing-squad was ready at the drop of a hat. I never tried to find out . . . Still, I was told that after the summary trial, during which Verne had behaved very arrogantly, one of the judges was supposed to have said, 'Don't you worry about that little shit: we'll take him down a peg or two.' They took their belts to him before he was shot.

On Sundays in springtime before the war, my father used to take me down the Loire to Trentmoult, to see an old friend of his, a master-mariner who had commanded ships of the Bordes Line. (It was he who taught me to recognize the old firm's black ports.) We would take the little motor-boat at the Quai de la Fosse, pass under the transporter-bridge, and run along the shipbuilding yards. There would be merchantmen going up to Nantes, and I read their names and their home ports – Antwerpen, Saint-Pierre, London, København, Fort-de-France . . .

The old captain lived in a little house on the bank. He had an incurable disease, and he spent his days in an armchair behind a window, his feet on a stool, watching the movements of the ships. He had thick white hair and he looked like the photograph of Victor Hugo in my book of selected extracts. He was prepared to leave 'all this': he was not sad about it.

With him there was an ageless, austere woman I did not like who was for ever knitting things in dull-coloured wool. When he could still walk, I remember how the old captain would sometimes let my father persuade him to come for a little stroll in the sun, a stroll that always finished up at the café by the landing-stage, where there were other Cape Horn captains drinking muscadet, eating little cheeses, and telling stories: before leaving the house he used to turn towards the woman with a meaningful gesture. She would rummage in her bag and slip him some coins; and every time she whispered, 'Above all, don't you spend it.'

The surprising thing was to see the glance they exchanged at this point. The ridiculous words must have been a kind of rite, a secret communication; and the captain would set off quite brisk and lively.

He had gone to sea as a cabin-boy in 1871, just after the Franco-Prussian war, in a ship-rigged vessel ('built on the Clyde, all Malabar teak except for the decks') bound for New Caledonia with a cargo of convicts and Communards. When she reached her destination the ship stayed there for three months and more, loading nickel ore. ('The Kanakas would still eat a man every now and then.') It was there, during his spare time, that he made his first ship in a bottle: it was broken on the homeward run, west of the Horn, in a furious blow that lasted seven days and carried two seamen overboard.

'On the seventh night, Wood-Head, our old captain, looked up at the sky. The great Kériadec from Morlaix – we used to call him Wood-Head. He'd made us ship a jury foremast so we could run before the wind; and once it was up we all took shelter under the poop, shivering in the cold and looking like men condemned to death who knew their hour had come. Kériadec, the great Kériadec – his eyes were red with the salt and sleepless nights – the great Kériadec looked up at the sky and shouted, "I've done all I can for my ship: now it's up to You to show what it is You want." '

The old blue-water captain who looked like Victor Hugo (and rather like Pasteur too) often used to tell us this adventure of his young days; the details might vary, but every time it ended with Wood-Head, the great Kériadec, calling out to the Almighty.

'Luck,' he finished once, 'luck: that's what it is. You do all you can for the ship. The rest is out of your hands.'

'For the ship, or for the men?' asked my father.

'Oh, for the ship! As for the men, do you see . . . their happiness is not in themselves but in the acknowledgement of a duty. Without a ship we don't amount to much, eh? Just look at me,' he added, smiling.

The ageless grey woman was knitting. I watched for her look. She seemed to be saying 'Carry on, carry on; I'm interested' or perhaps 'Don't talk nonsense': the interpretation of glances is by no means certain.

There was a ship in a bottle on their chimney-piece. A four-master ('rigged like the American clippers; running down the China Sea with a brisk monsoon she could make her sixteen knots'): the *Pamir*. The old captain had commanded her for three years.

One fine spring Sunday long ago, when I could not have been more than eight or nine, he said to me, 'Every time you come here, you must look at that ship for a long time, never saying a word. Then one day, if you're lucky, you will find out the Great Secret.' Perhaps he only wanted to get rid of me, to prevent me being a nuisance when he was talking to my father.

The old captain died in the winter of the phoney war. There were still a few old Cape Horners to take him to the graveyard. It was very cold, and the ground was frozen. My father had been called up, so he asked me to represent him; Verne went with me. The grey woman, dressed all in black, behaved with great dignity. Even so, when we went to warm ourselves at the little café by the landing-stage, she drank three stiff grogs one after another (the first in her life, I believe). She brought the *Pamir* in the bottle out of her bag and handed it to me. 'I saw you looking at it every time you came, just as he told you . . .'

The *Pamir* and her Great Secret vanished when Nantes was bombed.

I put the little barque in the bottle back on the shelf, wedging it firmly between the detective-stories so that it should not break when the ship rolled.

I climbed up on to the bridge. It was eighteen degrees below zero. The pack-ice gleamed faintly. In the west a vast shadow darker than the night was slowly blotting out the lower stars, one after another.

Immediately overhead, right above us, the Pole star was still shining, as though through a veil of mist; then it too disappeared. Devoid of all reflection, the sea appeared to have grown solid. 'Something is brewing,' muttered the officer of the watch, 'something very special.' In the dead-calm, freezing air his voice carried as far as the wings. Even as far as the end of the night, maybe.

A few southerly gusts swirled over the deck, like skir-mishers probing the enemy's defences. There was the groaning and the rumble of a nascent wind: vague howls that came from nowhere. There was a distant roar that brought an army to mind, an army setting itself in motion. There was a strange, disturbing silence; and the throb of the turbines.

Then all at once, without the least warning, the invisible gale from the south-west flung itself on us with the raging fury of a cavalry-charge.

99

CHAPTER 11

The Buoy

The south-westerly gale struck us astern. The unseen black waves raced up, broke, and fled forward. The *Eole* bucked, rode them, quivered furiously, scarcely moving at all; and then with a muffled roar she plunged her lee-quarter deep. The luminous figures of the gyro-compass skipped to and fro across the index-line with a frantic clatter, and the man at the wheel had all his work cut out to keep her on her course.

The voice of the wind grew deeper, still more urgent. The lookouts were relieved every half-hour.

With the Captain's consent, the fisheries officer had decided to begin the tour of assistance with the group of trawlers farthest north (in latitude 77°), those fishing just off the ice-bank east of Spitzbergen, because one of them, the *Belle Normande* of Fécamp, was having trouble with her depth-finder, and we had the necessary spare parts aboard.

At the beginning of the afternoon, in total, inky darkness, our radar picked up half a dozen echoes at the limit of its range, echoes confused and distorted by the snow-squalls and the ice. Among them were those of the *Belle Normande* and the two other French trawlers we were looking for.

The dirty weather grew dirtier yet; the wind blew at close on sixty-five miles an hour; the seas were even deeper, and the glass was still dropping; but the temperature rose to minus four or five.

At about 15.00 hours we were no more than a few miles from the three Frenchmen. Between two squalls it was possible to make out a hint of pallid light in the north-east –

the reflection of their lights against the cloud. The radar showed them very clearly, and beyond them the wavering line of the ice-bank. The Captain, hunched behind his screen, decided to send the mail and the spare parts for the depth-finder across by postal buoy.[1] The swell and the wind made it quite impossible to carry out the operation by launching a boat. The skippers grumbled a little over the radio, because they would be deprived of their fresh victuals; but in the end they agreed that there could be no question of risking the boat's crew just for the sake of a few cabbages and lettuces. They had been making good catches so far; but fishermen – and these were Normans into the bargain – are like peasants: they will never admit that things are going well. It is a kind of superstition: never tempt the Devil. They also know that everything has to be paid for and that the fat kine will be followed by the lean; and the weather-charts contain nothing to make them change their minds.

Up there on the bridge I gave a few consultations over the VHF radio-telephone. Nothing very serious: one case of 'flu, some sprains and bruises, a whitlow; nothing apart from a leg with an ulcer several inches long that I should very much have liked to see closer to. At the last moment I joined the party of seamen who were preparing the buoy, working on a deck covered with slush-ice. I wanted to add some antibiotics and some further instructions for the treatment of that ulcer: it worried me.

[1] A postal buoy is an unsinkable container attached to a phoscar (a little marker that lights up the moment it touches the water). The principle of using it is quite simple. A ship, with all its top-hamper, has a greater wind-resistance than a buoy that is almost entirely under the surface; it therefore goes to leeward very much faster. This being so, the delivering ship lies a little to the leeward of the receiving ship and rather ahead of her. The wind does the rest, or almost all the rest. As soon as the buoy is in the water the delivering ship drifts away down the wind, while the receiver, on the other hand, comes gently towards it, and all that is needed is for the receiving ship to make a little headway and seize the buoy with boathooks.

There was neither sky nor sea, only a total darkness. The *Belle Normande* had just hauled in her trawl, and we were now rolling so heavily that her lights swept up to a dizzy height and then plunged into the depths; they grew dim when a squall bore down on us, shrieking with the savage voice of the storm. We turned our backs, and the hard frozen snow rattled on our jackets. Bongo Ba, clinging to the rail with one hand, swore heartily in French and Gabonese; his other hand grappled with the lid of the buoy held tight between his knees. The white of his eyes and his teeth was all that could be seen of his face, muffled in a balaclava.

'Look out!' bawled a voice, and the *Eole* pitched so hard that we all let go – it was as though someone had rapped our fingers – wrenched away from the deckhouse rail in a body. We all of us slid across the deck together, fetching up with a painful grunt against the bulwarks. An evil black sea reached up for us, gurgling as it came. The *Eole* righted herself abruptly, and we began sliding in the other direction. First one, then another, then the whole party broke away, sprawling heavily against the side of the deckhouse. Someone got hold of the rail and all the rest of us clung to him.

'God above, can't you hail when . . .' The quartermaster's rage was cut short by another lurch, a lee-lurch that left him speechless, wholly taken up with clinging on. The upright side of the deckhouse might almost have been the deck. The man hanging on to the rail kept his grip, growling and kicking like a wild beast; but nobody let go. Another black wave soaked us through and through.

'You give a hail when you change course, God above! Do you hear me, up there?' roared the scandalized quartermaster, towards the wing.

Again the *Eole* righted herself, bringing floods of icy water across the deck.

'Hell,' cried the quartermaster. 'The buoy!'

'I've got the bugger, Chief. I've got her under my belly.' It was the deep voice of Bongo Ba. He had not let it go:

kneeling there in the water he had his arms round it, while at the same time he clung to a leg in front of him with both hands.

Once more the *Eole* lay over, but this time we were ready for it – all of us except the poor black man on his knees, who splashed and gasped without losing his hold. 'Yais, yais, what a bloody life, yais, yais,' he bawled, and his voice seemed so ludicrous that we all burst out laughing.

I returned to the bridge. The young sub-lieutenant was officer of the watch. The Captain was not standing behind his screen but sitting in the armchair reserved for him. The fisheries officer was talking on the VHF.

The wind and the frozen snow came swirling in through the doors with such force that we might have been in an open shed. Once again I was surrounded by that atmosphere of mingled confidence and tension which I had noticed at Lorient, when we put to sea: the same series of short, clear, unmistakable orders.

'Ahead one: helm five a-port.'

'Ahead one signalled, sir.'

'Five a-port it is, sir.'

'Right.'

With the wind on her beam the *Eole* was heeling thirty degrees, but the night was so dark that I did not realize it until we ran under the lee of the *Belle Normande*, a few cable's lengths away and lit up like a liner. With the bridge as my only guiding-mark, it seemed to me that she appeared above the rail, rose majestically into the void, reached the lintel of the door, mounted still higher, with a slight hesitation, and then, some moments later, sank down with the same magnificent deliberation. Out on the wing, the illusion no longer held: it was we who were rolling.

She passed by on a parallel course with the easy, gliding movements that one sees in a slow-motion film. She was truly beautiful: high, fine bows like those of a cruiser, her superstructure a dazzling white. A face was gazing at us from one of the windows of the entirely shut-in bridge. Sodium lights threw a pitiless glare on to her deck, where shapeless men in orange oilskins were mending her trawl, all staggering together with the ludicrous movement of drunkards. The smell of diesel fumes and fish came across on the wind.

'Helm amidships. Steady.'

'Helm amidships it is, sir. Course 315.'

A furious gust of snow veiled her beauty, as though she had suddenly moved behind a screen of frosted glass. Our eyes stung and watered; we turned our heads away. The squall passed, and there she was again, a little astern of us, white and immaculate, rising effortlessly on the swell with a catlike swing.

'Zero astern.'

'Zero astern signalled, sir.'

'Right.'

The sub-lieutenant went out on to the wing to check his position.

'Zero astern carried out, sir.'

'Right . . . Let go the buoy.'

The order was passed on. It could be heard going farther away, blurred in the howling of the wind. 'Let go the buoy . . . buoy . . . oy . . .'

The answer came back like an echo, clearer and clearer: 'oy . . . buoy . . . buoy let go.'

'Right. Zero ahead.'

On the VHF the fisheries officer told the captain of the *Belle Normande*. 'There you have her.'

'Thank you, thank you,' said the crackling voice in the receiver. 'Can't see anything yet . . . your bloody phoscar must have missed fire.'

Leaning over the rail, the lookouts stared into the impenetrable darkness. All at once a very small flame lit up, went out, lit again, seemed to leap into the sky, and vanished under a breaking wave. 'There she is!' cried the lookouts.

'Ha, I've picked her up,' spluttered the receiver.

'Ahead,' ordered the sub-lieutenant, coming back to the bridge.

The Captain had not stirred from his armchair. His eyes were shut and as far as one could see in the watch-lights he seemed to be asleep. Abruptly he said, 'Don't stay too close: you never know how these trawlers are going to manœuvre.'

'Yes, sir.'

The little yellow flame moved farther off; it winked, disappeared, obstinately bobbed up again, wavering: farther and farther off. It made me think of the souls of the Vietnamese legend wandering in the everlasting night.

While the *Eole* was lying head-on to the sea, waiting for the *Belle Normande* to send back the buoy with her crew's letters, the wind shifted; a shift heralded by the increasing fury of the snow-squalls.

Suddenly the darkness lightened; stars could be seen where the wind tore the clouds apart; and the icy blast of the north-easter swept the sooty sky.

The moon came from behind a cloud. The effect was dazzling. The ice-bank, very close at hand, glittered like a sheet of steel. Everything became luminous; everything was bathed in a ghostly milk, the lookouts on the wing, the frosted radar aerials, the bridge, the gun, the ice-covered stem, the Captain's face – a face that seemed hollowed-out, like those of the ancient figures in some calvaries. Only the swell was still black, the shining black of coal.

The temperature dropped by at least twenty degrees centigrade: the ice could be heard cracking above the shrieking of the wind. And now the sea was covered by a rising fog.

'It's steaming like a stew-pot,' muttered the starboard lookout in a Burgundian accent.

The water must have been a few degrees above freezing –

the last traces of the Gulf Stream – and the cold seemed to make it boil. The black waves were no longer to be seen: the *Eole*, the *Belle Normande* some way from her, and farther still the lights of the other trawlers, floated above a layer of pale fog; and low beneath the moon this fog was racing by at sixty-five miles an hour.

'We'll never pick up their fucking buoy.'

The fisheries officer suggested to the Captain that he should take over the operation.

'No. He's managing very well.'

The sub-lieutenant's face spread in one of his fine smiles.

The *Belle Normande* moved slowly to the windward of us to take up her position. In spite of the howling of the wind, in spite of the cracking of the ice (it was like distant shelling), and in spite of fierce buffeting of the rollers, invisible under the thin racing layer of fog, everything seemed calm, strangely set and petrified.

'Lieutenant.'

'Sir?'

'You won't see the buoy until the last moment. Don't be afraid of pushing the ship. Warn the engine-room.'

'Yes, sir. I've sent a party out on to the wing.'

The Captain did no more than nod and close his eyes. The metallic voice from the *Belle Normande* crackled in the receiver. 'I'm casting off . . . Don't you miss our mail, for God's sake. There she goes – the phoscar's lit up. Christ, already you can't see a thing. Do your best not to miss it. My old woman would not be pleased.'

'Right,' said the fisheries officer. 'Stay where you are: we'll use you as a sea-mark.'

Out on the wing the sub-lieutenant and four or five lookouts stared into the pallid fog, their eyes stretched wide. The wind howled in the perpetually-turning radar-aerials . . . A feeling of the most appalling cold . . .

The *Belle Normande*, all ablaze; and behind one of her bridge windows a vague outline gazing at us.

Nothing: we could see nothing. Only the infernal steam that blotted out the sea. Our eyes watered, our breath froze on the wool of our balaclavas, the steel rail burnt our hands right through their gloves.

A ghostly yellow wavering gleam that instantly vanished. 'There! One to port.'

'Ahead two. Starboard fifteen.' The sub-lieutenant reacted like a horse to the spur. His orders echoed along the repeating choir. 'Ahead two signalled, sir.' 'Starboard fifteen it is.'

Still the same cold, the same wind, the same exhausting roll; but we took no notice: the buoy was there, somewhere ahead of us, on our bow.

Nothing. Pale fog beneath the moon . . . the tears froze on our cheeks. The lookout must have got it wrong . . .

'There she is! There, there!'

An orange glow, a wavering halo gliding like a shark in murky water: it dived and disappeared. It was going to cross our stem.

'Hard a-starboard.'

We were hypnotized. Our eyes stung. The glow vanished under our bow-wave.

'Astern three. Helm amidships.'

The sub-lieutenant's voice was perfect: just enough tension for the orders to snap out sharp and clear.

'Helm amidships it is, sir.'

'Astern three signalled, sir.'

'Right.'

In the fierce lurch that followed the change of course the ghostly gleam seemed to leap up into the sky. It was racing by, very close, on the opposite tack, quivering with violent life.

'Steady.'

'Astern three carried out, sir.'

The *Eole* trembled from stem to stern, the way taken off her by the sudden reversal of her screw. The light gave a few more leaps in every direction and then glided smoothly towards us.

'Zero ahead. Helm fifteen a-port.'

A cloud veiled the moon and instantly the sea of fog grew dark. From the deck incomprehensible cries arose, snatched straight away by the wind. For a moment a huge orange flame lit up a tight-packed group of seamen leaning over the rail – I had the absurd impression that they were fighting among themselves – and then went out like an extinguished match.

'. . . oy . . . fast . . . buoy made fast.'

'Fifteen a-starboard. Ahead three.'

The *Belle Normande*, white and splendid, was very close, dangerously close: she had gone to leeward slower than the *Eole*. The man behind the bridge-screens was watching us still. He lit his pipe. It seemed to me that he had a beard. He waved and turned his back.

The fisheries officer on the radio: 'There you are: we've picked up all your love-letters.'

The anonymous voice from the *Belle Normande* in the receiver: 'Love-letters, love-letters . . . don't come it. Still, thank you kindly, sir; though you were rather closer than I liked. Hope to see you again soon. I'm going to start fishing again – just one run of the trawl, and then head south. With this wind the pack-ice will be coming down.'

The *Belle Normande* moved off. On her clear afterdeck men in oilskins were breaking the ice with sledge-hammers.

We had the north-easter on the beam, and the wind tore into the bridge: twenty-one degrees centigrade below zero.

The Captain seemed to have died; his breathing was only just perceptible. What astonished me was that he was capable of sleeping like this, in spite of the wind and the cold and in such a comfortless position, sitting straight up, completely still. I ought to wake him, help him below, to his cabin. His face was grey and stern, as though petrified; it really did look like a wax mask. The fisheries officer turned towards him, struck by his trance-like immobility. For some moments he stayed there, leaning over him and holding his breath.

Suddenly, without opening his eyes, the Captain said, 'What's the matter with you?' His voice could scarcely be made out over the deafening roar of the storm, but I was close and I heard: the tone was far from friendly.

The fisheries officer started back, as though he had been detected in some wrongdoing. 'Nothing, sir, nothing. I . . . no, nothing.'

'Then what are you waiting for? Why haven't you set course for the North Flaket? There's nothing more for us to do here. Twelve knots: no point in covering ourselves with ice in this heavy sea.'

'Yes, sir.'

For several minutes the Captain remained in the same torpid state: no muscle in his face that stirred, no movement in his body. He took no notice of the orders.

'Deck-party go below. Ahead both engines: a hundred and forty . . . Course 223.'

Then he stood up and leant against the screen in the attitude he liked best, his elbows on the brass rail.

The *Eole* headed into a choppy sea – a 'moderate' sea, as the sub-lieutenant wrote in the log-book – under the glitter of a hundred thousand stars and the deep shadow of the clouds. Wafts of spray, instantly frozen, swept aft from the bows, rattling like small-shot against the plating. The hull quivered; the entire ship was seized with a sympathetic vibration. The *Eole* rolled sharply, like a tripping horse, righted herself, and then gradually returned to her long, easy gallop over the limitless moving plain, black, white, and cold. The strange, the very sad complaints that were to be heard through the howling wind from time to time might have persuaded one that the world possessed a soul.

I too moved forward to the screen; I stood right against it, filled with wonder. I could feel the silent, perfectly motionless presence of the Captain beside me. I had the feeling that his eyes were still closed; but I no longer presumed to look at him too directly.

He came out of his numbness, turning slowly from the glass. 'Eh, Doctor?' he said, jerking his chin towards the sea.

Before leaving the bridge he spoke again, this time to the young sub-lieutenant: 'All right: but take care not to come too close.'

'She answers very well to starboard helm, sir, and I knew I could . . .' The sub-lieutenant's voice hung in the air. The Captain had gone without paying attention to him.

I left the bridge myself. It was too cold.

The Chief had already come up from the engine-room. He was waiting for me with a glass of whisky in front of him. 'Come and have a drop with me, Doctor.'

My jaws were completely numbed and I could barely pronounce the words: 'A grog.'

'That sod of a sub-lieutenant,' went on the Chief, 'he handles the ship worse than an infantry subaltern. Shame on him! He might at least tell people when he's going to lay her broadsides-on to the sea: I very nearly smashed my skull against a compressor. And the steward's broken a whole pile of plates; when I came in he was still crawling around on all fours picking up the pieces, swearing almost as hearty as Bongo Ba. I'm sorry the Navy has seen fit to give up the cat – for sub-lieutenants, I mean – a real pity . . .'

His prattle irritated me; I could not manage to get warm and I felt utterly emptied. I broke in rather sharply, 'Stuff. He behaved very well. Even the Captain said . . .'

'Hey, hey, Doctor, anyone would say the sea had got on your nerves,' replied the Chief, cackling. He held his glass up to the light, rattled the ice-cubes, and took a sip. 'What is there to be seen up there?' he went on after a silence. 'What is there to stir the heart of man to this high pitch?' Another sip. 'Why, nothing at all. Ha, ha, ha! Much less than there is in this glass.' I shrugged. He settled himself comfortably in an armchair. 'Doctor, if you bring me another whisky, I'll tell you a story. A story from my part of the world – the story of a drunkard who saw what he wanted to see. Ha, ha, ha!'

CHAPTER 12

The Sign

'One of your stories about death?'

'No . . . a funny story; a joke; something in the style of those about your one-eared Chinese philosopher.'

'Not Chinese: half Vietnamese and half Cambodian. The Venerable Huong.' .

'That's right.' The engineer held his glass high, gazing at the lamplight through the amber-coloured drink. He looked like a Mongol, a fair-haired Mongol with grey eyes.

The *Eole* ran on through the frozen night of a dead planet, but all that was to be heard was a distant growl on the far side of the plating, a kind of muffled boom. I called for another glass of grog, stretched out my legs, lit a cigarette, and listened.

'A couple of miles from my place, in the Bigouden . . . the Bigouden is the chin of France. Look at the map: you see that eagle's head jutting into the Atlantic? My part is the chin. And what a chin! Cassius Clay – Muhammed Ali – and all his prophets might batter away at it. All the Atlantic storms batter away at it. Nothing happens. It never yields. The Bigoudens don't yield either. Heads like iron . . . One day a fellow who loved his joke, a wine-salesman from Quimper-Corentin, told my father for some reason that the Sicilians or maybe the Turks who emigrated to Australia were so stupid that the only thing they knew how to do over there was to butt the trees with their heads to bring the fruit down. "They must have harder heads than Christians," says this fool of a traveller, slapping his thigh. "Sicilians, Turks: bah! That's nothing," says my father, and he darts out into the kitchen-garden – I think he must have tasted the traveller's samples a little too often. Bong against the apple-tree. Bong, bong! Three times, and at least a hundred-weight of cider-apples come tumbling down – this was in autumn. He comes back and sits down without a word. He was a real Bigouden, my father! When it was blowing a gale, he'd stand there on the quay in his cap and his sabots, his hands in his pockets, leaning on the parapet with his back to the sea, smoking and spitting with his friends over against the bar, never saying a word. An iron-headed man, my father . . . But that's not what my story's about. A couple of miles from our place, on the moors beyond the Pointe de la Torche, behind a beach that stretches out grey as far as the horizon – you ought to see it in the winter when the wind's blowing from the west: huge breakers that send the salt spray five or six miles inland, so you'd think all the air had turned into water . . . Then farther out, black boulders everywhere, like schools of whales. You ought to see that under the rain! At night! It would make you believe in the darkness of Hell and all its hairy devils with claws and hooks, shrieking birds with death's heads. Or maybe you'd say they were only gulls, you man of little faith. Well, a couple of miles from our place there's a half-deserted hamlet – who'd want to live there, dear Lord above? – thatched granite houses, a chapel, a calvary. It's called Guenn-an-Avel, which means "the wind strikes". That's where our old Rector retired to. They used to say his wits were not quite in order – the *gwin ru* and holiness. He did drink a good deal, particularly in the evening, when a man's heart is softened by the coming of the night. I know, because once upon a time I was one of his choirboys. Well, one night, and it must be at least fifteen years ago, the holy man woke up and rushed out to the chapel in his shirt and sabots to toll the bell. His flock came running with hurricane-lamps – he was not a parish priest any more, but he still had influence in those parts – and they amounted to half a dozen old women, some children, and the completely harmless village idiot who lived with his mother. No men: they were all away fishing in the Guilvinec or the Saint-Guénolé trawlers. "Behold, an angel of the Lord has appeared to me in a dream," cried the exalted old man. "He said to me: Presently a sign will cross the sky. Do not fear to take thy flock with thee and follow the sign; it will lead thee to the new Land of Canaan . . . etc., amen."

'And everybody, the old women, the children, the village idiot and his mother, they all believed in his vision. Everybody! Iron-headed Bigoudens! Don't laugh. Man of little faith, we Bigoudens believe in the *Ankou*, the angel of death . . . For instance, if you suddenly shiver, just like that, without any reason, the old people say it's Death passing by. It passes by, it passes by; and then one day it stops. And why not? Take me, for example: the day my father disappeared in the Raz de Sein I was aboard a store-ship off Martinique; it was night-time and I was sleeping after my watch. Then suddenly I was cold; I shivered. My porthole opened and the green sea came in and there was my father swirling about in it, his arms held in a cross; he was wearing his old mended oilskins, his lifebuoy and his seaboots. It was perfectly clear that he wanted to speak to me. What could he have said, eh? What can you say? And yet he did want to speak to me: I could see that . . . but then I woke.

'I checked up, and everything was just so, the seaboots, the oilskin and the time: it was daylight at that point in France. God above, the way you disbelieve makes me speak about very private things . . . Well, as I was saying, they all believed in his vision because he was a holy man, and that's all there is about it.'

At this point the Chief's story was interrupted by the young sub-lieutenant, who came below, blowing into his hands and rubbing his fingers. 'A boiling cup of tea, please,' he called out to the steward and then dropped into an armchair. He looked hard at me and added, smiling, 'Doctor,

I've a feeling that the Chief has got you pinned.'

Sipping away at his whisky, the Chief watched us with narrowed eyes – mere slits. 'As for you, my infantry subaltern,' he said quietly, 'it would be better if you were to learn to handle the ship properly, rather than talk such balls. You've smashed a heap of plates – they'll be put down to your account – and you very nearly killed me.' The sub-lieutenant's face took on a look of extreme delight. 'Verily I say unto you, all will be put down to your account,' concluded the Chief, with unction.

'Amen,' said the brazen sub-lieutenant. 'I'll bet you're telling him one of your stories about the mad Rector tearing about the moors in the night.' Turning to me he said, 'Don't you listen to him, Doctor: he's a blasphemer.'

'He was not mad, my holy man,' protested the Chief, 'only a little cracked. And anyhow, what do you know about the Bigoudens, young soldier? Iron heads they may have, but their hearts are those of little children . . . Yes, they all believed in his vision. But the wonders did not stop there, ye men of little faith, because in fact a sign did appear in the sky a few days later. Yes! And it happened just as I am telling you. Our old Rector was walking along the beach – he loved talking to the wind and the sea. Once when I was a choirboy, I was hiding behind a rock and I heard him. Beating his chest, he called out "Lord, cast out the devil that is in me; fling him into the gulf, as Thou hast done for others" and so on. "*Mea culpa* . . ." And there I was behind my rock, terrified. And the bloody tide coming in and wetting my breeches. Maybe his devil was the *gwin ru*, the red wine. What do you think, Doctor? No creeping, sliding, wriggling devils, eh? I don't know anything about it, ha, ha, ha! Well, anyhow . . .

'So there he was one morning, walking along the beach, and a huge arrow, a white cloud, ran across the sky: the finger of the Lord stretching towards the east. The old man fell on his knees, weeping with joy. He gathered his flock in front of the chapel and said to them, "Behold, a sign to us is given."

'They could all see the sign. And they all followed it, singing hymns. In front there were two choirboys carrying the cross and St Ninnoc'h's banner, and then came the old women wearing their coifs, the other children, two cows, some chickens, a cat with no known owner, and closing the march, the village idiot with his mother: all gazing up at the slowly-dissolving sign and singing

O Chanaan, divin séjour, ô cé-é-leste patri-i-e . . .'

'You're out of tune, Chief,' said the young sub-lieutenant coarsely, 'and this time you're coming it a trifle too strong. A sign in the sky! And in full daylight too! I prefer your tales of grave-diggers, hanged men on calvaries, or dead souls howling on stormy nights. They are far more amusing.'

The Chief took no notice of the interruption. 'And they all followed, singing. Not a single bagpipe to go with them, I'm sorry to say: it would have been much prettier, but the fact of the matter is that there was never a one. When there was nothing left in the sky, they stopped, ate pancakes and drank the Algerian wine the old women had taken care to bring with them. Another sign appeared in the afternoon, but this time it pointed to the west. The old Rector interpreted it: "The Lord means to try us," he said. And they all set off back again across the country, rather tired.

'That night they took shelter in a barn, and the good Rector exhorted his sleeping flock . . . No, I wasn't there, but I know very well what he might have said to them: don't forget that I was one of his choirboys. He was a man who never minced his words, and he was often very enthusiastic. He would certainly have quoted his favourite text: "*These things saith he that holdeth the seven stars in his right hand . . . I know thy works, that thou art neither cold nor hot . . . so then because thou art lukewarm and neither hot nor cold, I will spew thee out of my mouth.*" Or else something very much of the same kind.

'But it is possible that he gave way to discouragement for a moment – he was a very old man, after all, and he had walked a long way – because at one point in the night he suddenly set about his flock so fiercely that they heard him in the neighbouring farm. The dogs began to bark and the farm people could not understand a thing he said.

'The next day it rained and there was no sign, but they thought they heard the Lord's voice rumbling deep. The rain went on for three days on end, and the farmers began to have had enough of feeding the troop of pilgrims and listening to the old maniac's sermons. Then on the fourth day the sky was clear. And there was the sign. Pointing east. They all set off eastwards, singing their hymns. A Portuguese farm-hand followed them for a long while, bringing up the tail, far behind the cat, the village idiot and his mother.

'They saw the sign every unclouded day, but the Lord certainly meant to try them, because although He might point out the east in the morning, in the afternoon it was the west, and the holy man's sheep, thick and heavy with their pancakes and the Algerian wine, moaned and ground their teeth as they retraced their steps. Still, they covered less distance in the afternoon than they had in the morning, and so, slowly but surely, they moved farther east. They walked, walked, walked – march and countermarch – singing hymns and drinking red wine. Never did a single farm refuse them bread and wine . . .

'There's nothing like telling stories to dry your throat,' said the Chief abruptly, getting up to pour himself out a drink.

The faster-moving sub-lieutenant seized the bottle. 'Doctor,' he said, passing it to me, 'be so kind as to hold on to this whisky. Don't give it to him until he's finished his story.'

The Chief sat down again, laughed inwardly, and remained mute.

'Well, what about it?' said the sub-lieutenant. 'You won't

get a drink before . . . Just you finish your tale of the old madman who saw signs in the sky, if you can.'

'Not mad, only a little cracked,' growled the Chief. He lifted his empty glass and gazed at it in the lamplight for a moment: his eyes were no more than slits. And suddenly, without the least warning, he flung the glass at the sub-lieutenant, who caught it in full flight. (Tricky, because of the roll.) 'Well held. Good reflexes,' he said. 'So you don't believe in signs, eh? Poor simpleton. It's a pity your mum's not with you to stop you talking nonsense. What do you think you're doing here yourself, anyway? You're just following an old – what did you call him, Doctor? – an old crab stuffed with pride who spends his time behind a window watching the sea. And on your radar you watch out for an echo, a sign, that will give your helmsman his course and some meaning to your whole concern. And what about our worthy Doctor here present, who goes and freezes himself up there without any sort of reason – what is he hoping for?'

'No, Chief,' broke in the sub-lieutenant, 'you won't get out of it with your usual bar philosophy this time. I believe you've got right out on a limb with this story of yours, and you just don't know how to end it.'

The Chief turned towards me with a wink: 'In the end they all arrived, all of them, the cat with no known owner, the village idiot and his mother, the old ladies in coifs, the Portuguese and the others, all of them: they all arrived at Orly. Alleluia!'

'Absolute stuff,' growled the sub-lieutenant. 'How do you account for this sign of yours, Chief?'

'That was the year they put the first Boeing 707's into service between New York and Paris. Every morning a jet came in from America, leaving a long streak of condensation in the sky, and every evening it set off again. Stick your nose up into the air and you'll see it, young man of little faith. Now give me a drink, Doctor; I've earned it!'

*

'That coped with him,' said the Chief when the sub-lieutenant had gone. 'If you don't watch out, these young fellows will treat you like dirt.' His Mongol face was all wrinkled with delight. I laughed with him. 'No, Doctor,' he said, grave all at once, 'it wasn't a funny story. Of course they never reached Orly, but their search for the New Canaan did last seven days. Every morning there were desertions. The last to stay with the old Rector were the cat, the village idiot and his mother; then they too left him. The morning of the seventh day the holy man was found curled up in a little lane. He was still holding his breviary on his lap, and he looked happy . . . They buried him at Guenn-an-Avel.'

'I don't believe you, Chief. You're telling me wild, imaginary tales.'

'Man of little faith! Ha, ha, ha!'

CHAPTER 13

Don Quixote

Darkness. The wind. The cold. Time slipped past.

The lookouts swayed heavily, bulging in their watch-coats, pallid under the Northern Lights. The helm ticked like a clock, a clock that sometimes lost its head. The fluorescent figures of the navigational instruments shed a starlike light. The turning radar-beam, revolving like the second-hand of a chronometer, tirelessly scanned the empty screen.

The swell swept in, swept on, shining and growling. The cold: the night starred with frozen jewels.

The bugle sounded. Come, it's seven o'clock.

The wardroom.

The smell of coffee, hot bread, jam: the smell of eau de Cologne and toothpaste, too.

'Pass the butter.'

'Thank you.'

The Chief, well shaved, pink and fresh: 'Well, Doctor, still up there on the bridge?'

The news: *Chou En-lai, prime minister of the People's Republic of China, says, 'Nuclear war is inevitable, and all the nations of the world must prepare for it.' Valparaiso: A giant tanker has gone aground in the Strait of Magellan. Tens of thousands of tons of crude oil have entirely wiped out the flora and fauna over more than forty miles of the coast.*

'The Captain wishes to see you, sir,' murmured the steward in my ear.

Neatly dressed in his uniform, the Captain was lying on

his bunk, reading. He had shaved, and in the light of his bedside lamp his skin showed as grey as dust. A small clot of blood was drying on his chin.

It called for no effort of the imagination to see him dead: all he had to do was to close his eyes and cross his two hands on a crucifix.

When I knocked on the cabin-door and walked in, he laid the open book on the blanket. He noticed my attempt at making out the title. 'The parable of the talents,' he said, tapping the Bible with his leather-covered artificial hand. 'You know it? The last parable before Judas's kiss, Peter's denial, and the crucifixion. A terrible parable. The most terrible of them all. What hast thou done with thy talent? Doctor, will you give me an injection, an intravenous injection?' He handed me a little chemist's package with an ampoule in it: a commonplace stimulant based on vitamin B 12 – the kind of thing that would set him up for a few hours. 'We'll be on the North Flaket at noon,' he added, by way of explanation.

I shrugged. 'This is merely trifling with the matter, sir. You are killing yourself. I ought to . . .'

'I am only asking you to give me an injection, Doctor: no more.' His tone was brusque, disagreeable.

'There is a sick-berth attendant on board for that kind of thing, sir,' I said coldly.

He sank back on his bunk. His tight-shut lips were thin. His long straight nose cast a shadow on the ring under his left eye.

I have often observed that the ravages of disease seem to bring out a character's basic nature; they remove the merely adventitious features, setting the essence free. In some cases you are astonished to find a hitherto unknown strength; in others an unsuspected baseness and vulgarity; still others show a childlike innocence. In the Captain, that morning, the dominant impression was that of nobility. The hard light of the bedside lamp emphasized the underlying bone-formation of his lean face, and suddenly I was reminded of Gustave Doré's illustration of Don Quixote on his death-bed.

He closed his eyes. His body relaxed. 'Doctor, none of this has the least importance. Not the least ... The second-in-command will take over ... or the fisheries officer ... until they find someone to fill my place.'

A silence. Once again the strange din of the storm outside, beyond the armour-plating, was with me: the regular series of impacts and jarring blows remote and deadened; unmeaning cries. And nearer to, the grinding, the working of the hull: and the muffled panting of the turbines.

'Death is not so terrible,' went on the toneless poker-player's voice. 'There's still something ... still something, still something ... And then suddenly nothing left at all. I know, because I've already died once: very nearly, that is to say. A few spasms; isn't that right? You must have seen it often, Doctor. A quivering ... the beast within still alive. It struggles frantically, and then ... You can't prevent yourself from going to sleep ... sleep!'

Another silence. And the far-away noise of the sea.

'Well, don't just stand there, Doctor. Do whatever you've made up your mind to do. Do it quick. And let me go to sleep.'

'Roll up your sleeve, sir.'

The old crab had got the better of me again. He irritated me, and yet every time he filled me with respect. I looked at him hard, watching for the gleam of joy that I thought I had seen in his eyes some days before. Nothing.

A good strong pulse; the veins quite sound. A slight smell of sweat mingling with his eau de Cologne: he must have a touch of fever. Ether, cotton-wool, rubber tourniquet, syringe. He had everything ready in the drawer of his bedside table.

'If you want me to go on looking after you, you'll have to let me examine you. Your family doctor is no doubt very competent, but ...' I wiped away the drop of blood oozing in the crook of his arm. The more human smell of the disease was drowned by the ether, a hospital odour so familiar to me. He lay back in his bunk and closed his eyes. '. . . but you'll have to let me examine you.'

'Very well, Doctor, very well. After North Flaket. But no preaching, eh? You can do whatever you like, but no preaching. It would do no good . . . and it would put me into a bad temper.'

'Why did you wait so long before taking another sea-going command? I'm afraid it may be too late.'

'I no longer intended to go to sea. But then . . .' A long silence. '. . . there was one thing I wanted to do before leaving.' He opened his eyes and with something like a snarl he said, 'What's the matter with you, staring at me like that?'

I was staring at him, to be sure; but in fact I was thinking about old Huong, about the Venerable. He too had looked like Don Quixote on his death-bed as he lay there, lit by three candles, under an army blanket that showed the outline of his body (he even had Don Quixote's little beard). Willsdorff had taken me there one evening at the beginning of the south-west monsoon: it must have been in April or May. He was in a pretty bad way and he had a roaring fever. I suspected an attack of pernicious malaria and put him under perfusion. In the course of the night his temperature climbed still higher. The nurse on duty called my colleague, Dr Cao Giao, and me.

The old prophet seemed to be utterly exhausted: only his deep-sunk black eyes looked at me, like those of an animal hiding far back in a cave. Three candles were burning on the bedside table, and the fan was no longer working (our generator was having one of its usual breakdowns). There was a buzzing of flies. Near the bed, two bodyguards, armed with swords, squatted over a spirit-lamp, making soup. Another, with his forehead wrapped in a pink towel, lay curled up on the ground, sleeping with his mouth wide open. An ancient witch-like figure, her head shaved, chewed betel, sending an accurate jet of red saliva into the copper spittoon from time to time. (It was a great while since I had stopped protesting against these ways: when a Vietnamese goes to hospital, his whole family turns up at once and camps by his bedside. Hygiene suffers, of course; but the patient, above all if he is going to die, has all his own people around him. It was only in cases of contagious disease that I was ever really firm.)

On the far side of the french window opening on to the verandah, the darkness seemed to rise up like a wall. Huge clouds had silently invaded the sky, putting out the stars one by one with the disturbing quietness of natural forces. I felt deeply uneasy, rather like a dog that senses the coming of death. There was nothing I could do in that room, and yet I could not make up my mind to leave.

A little later the old inventor of a faith grew restless; his shadow, thrown on the wall by the candlelight, seemed jerkingly alive. Then he began to talk in a high-pitched delirium. Cao Giao listened attentively; I was struck by the gravity of his expression. The two bodyguards kept perfectly still, holding their breath. Even the witch forgot to chew and spit into her pot.

I could make nothing of his gibberish, but there was something in the old man's tone, something like panic or a most intense and catching anxiety, that disturbed me even more. 'What is he saying?' I asked.

Cao Giao made a sign for me to be quiet. Then a sudden gust wrenched at the mosquito-netting. The three candles went out all at once, plunging the room into darkness. Doors slammed, and somewhere windows were shattered. The storm was breaking at last. I went out on to the verandah and stayed there for a long while, watching the rain. I felt an indefinable relief.

The fury of the storm passed away. When I returned to the room, the Venerable was resting peacefully, his temperature almost normal. The two guards were eating their soup; the third still slept on, unmoved; the ancient witch chewed and spat; the flies buzzed steadily.

'I've given him a sedative, a shot of phenergan,' said Cao Giao.

'What was he saying just now?'

'Oh, all sorts of things . . . He said he'd been taken in by the . . . by the French. "I have deceived my people and I must pay." And then again, "Dying is not such a terrible thing." He said his time was come: "When the ox-herd sounds his flute, the old buffalo must go back to the byre." He is a poet, you know.'

When I made my rounds the next morning, our one-eared Don Quixote was as lively as a grig. He gulped down the bowl of soup his ruffians had made him. The old witch was chewing and spitting as before.

'They are waiting for me over there,' he said, gravely.

I believe we managed to keep him in another twenty-four hours, but I am not sure. He was cured, extraordinarily enough, and our analyses could not discover the least trace of malaria in his blood.

Willsdorff took advantage of a patrol going upstream and had him set down in his own piece of the country . . . There were a great many wild tales about his disappearance going about – stories of tigers, dragons, and *mah-quoui*.

When he came back from the patrol, Babourg put into the rach by the temple for the night because of trouble with his outboard. ('Fucking hell, it was impossible to put the bloody thing to rights in the rain.') He arrived in the darkness, silently poling. Later on he was perfectly happy to talk about his night, particularly if he was given a drink. At midnight he had heard an appalling scream. ('Hell, you would have said it was a pig having its throat cut . . . only it wasn't a pig. I know what I'm talking about.') He came out of the cuddy on his sampan to see what was happening. 'My sentry was snoring; I kicked him up the arse and shouted,

"What's going on? What is it? Who's there?" Fucking hell! They were absolutely amazed, all those sods swarming about there on shore! You should have heard them – all screeching blue murder. One of them showed up on the bank like a ghost, holding a lamp. "You fuck off," he bawled, and disappeared. They were always bawling in those days . . .' Babourg got his sampan ready for action, but he did not like to risk himself in among the reeds. 'You couldn't see a bleeding thing – niggers fighting in a coal-cellar. In any case, as far as the pig was concerned, the two-legged pig, it was all over. No more screaming: *het roi*!' The rain was still falling steadily. The night was pitch-dark. 'Suddenly plop, plop, splash, splash . . . fucking hell, they were cutting him up with a jungle-knife! Carving him, the poor sod. Plop, plop, splash . . . stewing-meat, mince. Meat – I know what I'm talking about when it comes to meat. I ought to: two years apprentice to a butcher at Picpus. My little buggers behind their sandbags, their ears were drooping, believe you me. They knew what was going on too. Plop, plop – splash! Hell, now they were chucking in the offal! Splash, splash. I fired a shot in the air, just to see. The sod with the lamp popped up straight away. "No shoot, no shoot, *du me may*." Ah, the bastard . . . and ill-mannered into the bargain. Plop and plop again. Fucking hell, plop for hours and bleeding hours on end. It would be worth while going back to fish just there.' And the horrible loose-mouthed loquacious Babourg prattled on and on, drinking the eating-house's lukewarm beer.

At first light he went ashore with two of his Vietnamese sailors to see what had happened. Some way upstream of the rach the reeds on the bank had been trampled and the rain-puddles there were pinkish. ('Fucking hell, there was something fishy there: too much raspberry jam in the juice. But we never found anything. A well-scraped butcher's stall.')

He went as far as the temple, and there he woke the old

witch with the shaved head and a few dazed, sleepy body-guards. '"What was all that hullaballoo last night?" I asked. "No know, Chief, no know." No know my arse. They were all of them still soaking, dripping. And there was the lamp in the corner. And puddles everywhere. "Where's your boss?" I asked. "Him sleep, him sleep." "Him sleep where?" "No know, Chief, no know." I searched everywhere, I rummaged . . . nothing. The sods.'

The Venerable Huong, the one-eared prophet, the discoverer of a new faith, had vanished.

Willsdorff had been very fond of his old crab, and the news affected him. He set an inquiry on foot: it came to nothing. 'No know, no know . . .'

CHAPTER 14

The Innocent

'What's the matter with you, staring at me like that?' said the Captain again, his expressionless eyes fixed upon me.

'I am watching the effect of your family doctor's prescription . . . nothing extraordinary.' I should have liked to say something that would bring us closer together. I had a feeling that if I stood up and left at this point, I should lose an opportunity.

Once again the Captain was the better man. He laughed harshly and relaxed. 'You get on my nerves, Doctor.'

It was not the commonplace words, it was the tone in which he said them: I seemed to detect a little warmth; a delicate hand reaching out timidly, as it were. In the cabin everything was silent: I heard nothing but the distant throbbing of the turbines and the muffled sea-borne voices from outside.

'You get on my nerves, Doctor; you get on my nerves . . . let me go to sleep.'

It was all over; he had returned to his habitual brusque, colourless voice. He looked at me as though he were looking at a stranger; his eyes repelled me. The opportunity had gone by.

'So you already know what it is to die?' I said, risking everything.

He nodded: he raised his gloved iron hand slowly and then laid it on the open Bible. I remained silent. So did he. For a long while. The remote roaring of the sea and his ravaged face were in harmony. The opportunity had gone by . . .

Suddenly he cried, 'With this everlasting darkness you never know what time it is . . . Let's say it's the hour when criminals confess, or when vicious men repent, shall we? I like you, Doctor, but don't look at me like that. I've nothing to tell you. Nothing. Though perhaps I have: it's absurd!' A silence: I did not move. 'Three steps to my door. Four steps in the alleyway, if there's not too much roll. Eleven rungs – I've counted them. Two or three steps on the bridge . . .'

Another silence. The sea a great way off. Once again he raised his black, leather-covered claw. 'A mine. In 'forty-four. During the Provence landing. The barge heeled over. The carriage of a forty-millimetre gun caught my arm. Impossible to get it free, and the barge was sinking. I held my breath. I don't know why. The beast within? A hell of a din under the water – explosions, the propellers . . . My ear-drums hurt appallingly – the pressure of the water – and I heard a kind of drumming: blood, heart, life. Impossible to haul free. I did not feel any pain. Blood flowed from my arm like a cloud of brown smoke. The water growing darker and darker. What a time it was taking! I thought no, no, no. And at the same time I was curious to know what was going to happen . . . Yes, very curious. As though I expected some kind of a revelation. The barge touched the bottom and righted itself. The gun-carriage shifted: I was free. I saw light above me. And huge bubbles – jelly-fish? Or the air escaping from my lungs? And I knew that was the last thing I should ever see because I could no longer hold my breath. Pain, physical pain – life still! The last feeling of life – like the first, perhaps? It's absurd, I thought. And . . . and I died.'

Silence again. And the steady roar of the tearing, foaming sea.

'There you are . . . it's absurd! My last thought was, it's absurd! Absurd . . . And what could I add to that today? It's absurd, ha, ha! Absurd. There's nothing else to be said. There's your revelation for you: everything's absurd!'He spoke in a low voice, not looking at me. He brought his left hand over to his claw, which was already lying on his chest; the attitude of the dead. 'I suppose my Mae West must have carried me up to the surface as fast as a cannon-ball . . . And the people who were floundering about up there brought me back to life.'

The Captain sat up. For a moment there was a flicker of uncertainty in his eyes, a kind of uneasiness. But it vanished, and once more he fixed me with his expressionless gaze. 'You get on my nerves, Doctor. I don't like talking about myself . . . is it this goddam drug you have injected?'

I made a vague denying movement, and he shrugged. 'Yes,' he said, 'I do deeply believe that it is absurd . . . All my life I've stood on guard. A sentry on the battlements, all my life long. Ten paces to the left, ten to the right: at dawn, when everybody else is still asleep. I've done what I knew to be right . . . I think I've been useful. Only . . . once I . . . You can take one thing for dead certain, Doctor, and that is there's no discharge, no release, no lifeline. The danger is always there. You can slip right up to the very last moment – slip and fall. Even Him, you remember: *Eloi, Eloi, lama sabachthani?* My God, my God, why hast thou forsaken me? It's a very, very unpleasant thing to find out. But you must know that as well as I do.'

I had the impression that I was seeing our enigmatic Captain coming out of the fog, like a ghost-ship or like the great trees of my forest in the early morning during the rains, when the monkeys fall silent and the mists that rise from the soaking ground slowly melt in the sun. It was an uncertain impression and I was by no means sure of what I thought I had seen . . . or understood. I had the feeling of having missed some shades that were too delicate, too fugitive.

And then the fog-bank closed; the veil came down. He looked at me with a mocking air. 'Archimedes was drawing geometrical figures on the sand. When the soldier came to kill him, all he said was, "Do not spoil my circles." One day you'll come to give me up, Doctor. Don't deny it: I know. Harsh reaper . . .

> *Le dur faucheur avec la large lame avance,*
> *Pensif et pas à pas, vers un reste de blé . . .*[1]

That settles your hash, Doctor!' He gave a grim laugh. 'Oh, you're only His messenger . . . But in the meantime let me go to sleep. And don't spoil my circles.'

The North Flaket. Noon.

The sea had gone down. It was more than an hour since the wind had shifted into the north-east, and now it was even colder. The Captain was standing there, his forehead against the glass. It was the most beautiful night in the world.

The southern sky seemed to be very faintly touched with dawn. The air was as hard, as transparent as the purest crystal. All around us the sodium lights of the trawlers blazed as they fished; there were about a score of ships, almost motionless beneath the stars, scattered over this smooth white and black immensity, filled with the wandering moan of the winter wind.

Whole sections of the bank-ice had drifted free. Vaguely they rose and fell in a sea as thick as black blood. Sometimes we ran through them with a tearing, grinding, grating noise, and the masses of ice clashed together, rising over one another and sinking, striking heavily against the *Eole*'s sides. The swell, stirred up by the propellers, streamed away in phosphorescent spirals that ran aft to lose themselves in the blinding reflection of the full moon.

Sparse flat voices echoed the orders. In the twilight of the bridge the faces seemed on edge with tension; but strangely enough all the eyes were like liquid mirrors filled with moonlight.

[1] The grim reaper comes forward with his broad blade/Thoughtfully, step by step, towards a remaining stand of corn.

'Are you there, Doctor?' It was the fisheries officer speaking.

'Yes.'

'There are some patients for you. Fifteen or so. One an appendicitis perhaps; we'll start with that. Aboard the *Colonel Mevel*.'

The *Colonel Mevel*, a big stern-gate trawler from Saint-Malo, lay wallowing heavily a few hundred yards to windward. She was covered with a layer of ice, and her crew were doing their best to break it with hammers. A pilot's ladder hung over her side.

'Launch the dinghy.'

Cries rose from the deck just below the wing: the seamen busy at the tackle. The rubber dinghy hit the surface with a great splash, throwing up the water. Two men in skin-diver's suits jumped down at once to start the outboard before it had time to freeze. On the heavy swell with its coal-black gleam the dinghy rose now to the height of the rail and now sank as low as the bilge-keel; and all the while the crew loaded it with boxes of spare parts and crates of fresh vegetables.

'All aboard, sir.'

'Shove off.'

Sheltered by the mass of the *Eole*, the dinghy roared away. As soon as it had crossed our stem the gusts of wind covered it with spray, forcing it to slow down: in the bows one of the frogmen switched a torch on and off so that we could follow it. The *Colonel Mevel* lay outlined against the moon, and once the dinghy had run into her huge shadow nothing more was to be seen of it, nothing but the little light, pulsing like a heartbeat.

'Your appendicitis will be here in quarter of an hour, Doctor.'

Before going down to the sick-bay I stepped into the wardroom for a cup of coffee to warm me. The radio was playing the tail-end of a song, *Cent loups sont entrés dans Paris*,

132

and the steward was clearing away the remains of lunch. 'There's a film tonight, sir: *The Death of a Captain*. It won't be much fun, I suppose.'

It was good coffee. The steward had added a little drop of brandy. The turbines throbbed faintly, with the sudden stopping and starting of a night-train. I was still numb with cold; my mind was empty.

The news:

Lorient: The collapse of fish prices. The fishermen are holding demonstrations to draw the government's attention. All fishing-ports from Boulogne to Saint-Jean-de-Luz are blocked by groups of trawlers . . .

Phnom Penh: The river-convoy that left South Vietnam loaded with food and military supplies has been unable to break the Red Khmers' blockade of the Mekong. The Cambodian capital has only enough rice for a few weeks . . .

The river!

Fucking hell, as Babourg would have said . . . I knew very well just where the Red Khmers waited for the convoys. The water is comparatively low in November, and they can dig in along the dyke.

The river! The empty river, matte, quivering under the sun right overhead!

One morning Cao Giao came to pick me up at the hospital. 'The new officer commanding the flotilla has just arrived. Let's go and have a look.'

We did not like the former commander, a fool, an evil-minded, mischievous fool who hated the country and the river, a fool who bored us to tears with his erotic memories of the time when he was a gunner aboard one of the big, unmoving cruisers moored at Toulon – 'They respect the sailor there.' He pulled strings to get back, but before returning he very much wanted to get his hands on 'one of those gold Buddhas they have in their temples, you know; yellow, twenty-four-carat gold!' It was quite simple: he dreamed of stealing one during an operation. (He did indeed dream, the fool! Asia stirs up all kinds of dreams – there never was a gold Buddha anywhere in that whole region.) He behaved like a vulgar clod, and he called all Vietnamians *nha que*, which is not only in the poorest taste but also a proof of the deepest ignorance. Whenever the civilian authorities complained of his excesses, he would reply, 'This is war. You can't make an omelet without breaking eggs,' with other nonsense of the same kind. The flotilla was in very poor order and the crews did exactly what they liked; every night there were drunken battles with the Cochin-Chinese auxiliaries. One idiot had painted a crossed-out head with a conical hat for every rebel killed on patrol, and he had done this on the deckhouse of an LCVP, 'like the conning-tower of the German submarines' (another dreaming half-wit). And Babourg had nailed a black death's-head flag to the mast of his sampan.

Although the sun was already high, the day was still pleasant enough by the time we reached the little eating-house. Blue smoke was wafting through the ill-fitting pieces of canvas, as usual; chickens pecked at the grains of rice that had fallen to the ground, and the melancholy dog slunk furtively between the tables, ready to flee with its tail between its legs at the least threat of a kick. But the coolies in black pyjamas, perched on their stools like crows – silent for once – seemed interested; and Cuc had raised a piece of canvas to see better.

'That must be him.'

Far along the jetty, by the pierhead, stood a very young sub-lieutenant, all in white, very straight, clean-lined, perfectly motionless; he was looking at the river, his back turned to the flotilla. That was my first sight of Willsdorff.

He was looking at the river, perfectly motionless under the sun, quite straight. You would have said a good, thoroughly clean young man, just like those that are to be seen in such numbers at every passing-out at the Naval

College or Saint-Cyr, and who die in such numbers on the battlefields. Below the landing-stage, Babourg and his crew were busy with his sampan's outboard; he had a red scarf round his head, no shirt, and he was smeared with oil. From time to time he cast suspicious glances at the motionless white figure.

At last Willsdorff turned round; he seemed very pleased and his eyes were amused. 'Good morning. Who's in charge here?' he asked.

'I am,' said Babourg, casually.

'What did you say?'

Babourg stood up in a rather more proper attitude. 'Well, I mean . . . Beg pardon, sir. Babourg, quartermaster.' (Dubourg? Anyway, he gave his name, whatever it was.)

'Right.' Still Willsdorff did not stir; he gazed down on the four pitiful tubs, looking pleased. 'I shall take over command of the flotilla at noon . . . In the meantime you'd better – ' With a careless gesture he pointed out the black flag. 'We aren't Death's Head Hussars, are we? And scrub those – ' Another wave towards the deckhouse of the LCVP. 'We aren't head-hunters, either.'

Babourg's mouth dropped open. 'Yes . . . sir,' he said at last.

'Very well, very well; thank you. I'll be seeing you presently.' For a few moments longer Willsdorff stayed looking down at his fleet, his eyes filled with joy; then he strode off, long-legged, to the headquarters office.

Babourg leapt on to the jetty. 'You heard him?' he said to us. 'Cuc, give me a beer, *mau len.*'

When he had taken a pull he wiped his forehead and dropped on to a stool. 'Fucking hell! He's an innocent . . . This is going to be a real party for us,' he said, looking dismayed.

I was not there when the command was handed over, but that same evening I found Willsdorff listening to Cao Giao over a glass of the eating-house's sickening tepid beer. At their feet was a black cat (Monsieur Dégouzzi, but I did not yet know his name), and he was taking a malignant delight in terrorizing the melancholy dog by glaring at it. The day had been very hot, and the landing-stage was covered with exhausted men asleep, lying there like so many shrouded corpses. The night gave a false impression of coolness; the damp air weighed down like a woollen blanket; the full moon blazed. Willsdorff was still in spotless white; he looked as though he had just had a shower, and his eyes were laughing. As he smoked his cigar he had something of the air of a spoilt, spirited boy. On the other side of the table, Cao Giao was carrying on with his monologue.

Poor Cao Giao paid much attention to all French new-comers. He invited them to dine with him, to smoke (or to visit Madame Nam's establishment); and he listened to them as though every time he hoped they might provide an answer to his uncertainties, his torments and his contra-dictions. But this particular night it was he who was talking, and my arrival cut him short. (Oh, I have a very good idea of what he was talking about: the ambiguous nature of the war, his love and hatred for France, and all the other problems that obsessed him; the whole interspersed with quotations from French writers.)

The melancholy dog crept furtively away and from a distance it barked a few insults, but without conviction. (It was never seen again.) Monsieur Dégouzzi, now the master of the landing-stage, began a voluptuous smoothing of his coat.

'Babourg thinks you're an innocent,' said Cao Giao suddenly, after a long silence.

'Who?' asked Willsdorff. 'Oh, the quartermaster. Babourg! You saw how he was dressed up? A pirate; a pantomime pirate. All of them dressed up as buccaneers . . . Treasure Island! A half-wit, you say? Ha, ha, ha!' He drank a sup of beer and made a wry face. 'Filthy stuff, this . . . Dressed up,

136

all of them in fancy dress. So what do they do? They play at being pirates, like boys. They're stuffed with frightful stories and they can't see what's there right under their noses. We'll change all that. We'll open their eyes. This isn't the Dry Tortugas; this is Indo-China. I don't know exactly what's happening here, but God above, it's worth while keeping one's eyes open!'

'Your patients are in the alleyway already, Doctor.'

On my way I passed the three men: huge, covered with ice, armoured and helmeted in shining yellow oilskins, as awkward and clumsy as astronauts. We peeled them like onions: first the oilskins, pulled over their heads, then four or five pullovers, then leggings, trousers, long woollen drawers, vests – the smell of *nuoc mam* spread about the sick-bay. Three lean men, their hands and faces red, their skin very white, who smelt of fish and the sea. And who were in pain . . .

It took twelve hours, twelve hours of going to and fro in the freezing darkness, for the rubber dinghy to board the seven French trawlers, carrying them their mail, spare parts, fresh victuals, and to take off their sick. Twelve hours in which I was very busy. I had seventeen patients, Normans, Bretons, Basques and one young fellow from Paris who had never seen the sea before setting off on a far-north trawler. He was feverish and he had a large boil that was turning nasty; I had to carry out a little operation with a local anaesthetic. I suggested that he should stay aboard for a while to get over it: eight or ten days, until we came back to see his ship again.

'Oh no! What would my mates think? Besides, it would mean cutting my share by a week.'

I talked to him – I talked to them all – but talked to him more than the rest because he interested me. (The others moaned about the drop in the price of fish, their daily bread.)

He was eighteen. When he had finished school, he hesitated about going on to the university. 'What would be the point? . . . There I was, getting nowhere in Paris; so I said to myself, I'll get out of it for a while, just to see. I don't want to be like my father. Oh, I'm very fond of him; he's a decent fellow; but . . . No, I don't want to be like him.'

A good-looking, muscular, athletic young fellow, with a grave, almost a scornful look except on those rare occasions when he smiled: then everything changed and you saw he was still a child.

'It's not so easy to get taken on, but I managed to pull strings – an uncle in Bordeaux. To begin with the others were stand-offish, but it's all right now. It's tough, but it's all right. The skipper's straight, and the other guys are a decent lot . . . The sea? You don't see it all that much. It's like a factory – everything goes on inside – you have to bone the fish, freeze it . . . a factory. The deck is just for shooting the trawl, hauling it in, mending it if it's torn . . . and smashing the ice. That's what the stern-gaters are like. I ought to have gone aboard one of the old kind – there's still one left, the *Damoclès*, from Fécamp. That's really tough, with everything on deck; but even so . . . The skipper of the *Damoclès*? The Alsatian? I heard him once over the radio. God, he was so funny! Some people say he's mad – he had two eyes painted on the bows, like a Chinese ship. Then there are some Chinese among his crew; Arabs too – ex-soldiers, from what I hear. Things seem to be doing pretty well with him; he's had some good weeks, just with the cod – he only does salted cod. In January I'd like to go with him for the Newfoundland season. After that? After fishing, you mean? I don't know . . . I really don't know . . . I'd rather like a job in television – journalist, cameraman . . . I'd like to get away. Travel. A long way off.'

At two in the morning I climbed up to the bridge again. The

138

Captain was there, motionless against his screen, his eyes brimming with moonlight. He did not seem to have stirred these last twelve hours. The wind had dropped: there was a deeply moving silence. The glaucous sea, lit by the projectors, had the consistency of melted fat in the act of setting. Here and there round, silver-blue sheets of ice with raised edges, the kind that the English fishermen call pancakes and the French water-lilies, rocked on the surface like jelly-fish. The pack-ice was farther off, but you could hear the roar and crackle of the floes as they ground together in the remaining swell. The moon overhead brought to mind the cold glare of a naked electric bulb on the marble slab of a morgue.

'Doctor, the Norwegians have given us the green light,' said the fisheries officer.

I had telephoned him to say that I should be keeping my appendicitis; an operation was necessary, but it was not urgent, and there would be time to take him to the hospital at Hammerfest, even to send him home by the regular plane.

'Things are brewing up,' went on the fisheries officer. 'There's a very deep depression coming for us. Look at the barometer.'

The dinghy was making its last round-trip. The little light winked away. A voice could be heard over the whine of the outboard. The dinghy came nearer. Someone was singing. Now I could recognize the voice. It was Bongo Ba's:

When Therese makes love
Oh Lord above,
It's like you dipped into glowing embers.

CHAPTER 15

―――◆―――

The Great Secret

'Have you got a Bible, Chief?'

We were sitting alone in the wardroom, clinging to our glasses. The *Eole* was rolling in a south-west gale: still the same vast muffled noise outside, the same huge voice. With every heave you felt crushed, compressed, lifted up; then the chair seemed to slip away from under you and for some moments you floated as though you were weightless. Then, stiffening in spite of yourself, you plunged down. And everything began all over again.

My words almost made the Chief drop his glass. 'What? God almighty, what's wrong with you, Doctor? Have you killed one of your patients?'

'I wanted to read the parable of the talents again. The Captain spoke to me about it and I no longer have it clear in my mind.'

The Chief let out a whistle. 'The parable of the talents, eh? Yes: *For unto every one that hath shall be given, and he shall have abundance: but from him that hath not shall be taken away, even that which he hath.* Our old Rector, the holy man, drove that into our heads with a sledge-hammer, when I was a choirboy. "What are you doing with your talents?" he would roar like the angel of doom up there in his pulpit – I'm talking about the days when churches still had pulpits and when they chanted in Latin – and the women in their coifs would all bow their heads at the same moment.' The engineer broke off for a moment to take a sip and then he went on in an ironic voice, 'What have you done with your talents, Doctor, do you know? But you don't know the story,

140

to be sure. I'll give you a rough idea. There was a lord, and he set off on a journey. He gave his slaves money. Five talents to one, two to another, and just one to the last. Mark you, he was no fool, this lord: to every man according to his several ability. The two first made shift to do business and make money. As for the last, he just hid his share – buried in some corner, I believe. Right: so the lord comes home again. The first two slaves turn up right away, very pleased with themselves, bringing their profits – I had five talents, I give you back ten: I had two talents, I bring you back four. Fine! Fine! You are good and faithful servants: splendid, enter into the joy of your lord . . . so be it.

'The last slave wasn't in such a hurry. Still, he does show up in the end, and he says – and our Rector made us get this by heart – he says . . . just a minute now. He says, *Lord . . . thou art an hard man, reaping where thou hast not sown . . . I was afraid* – bringing the coin he has dug up out of his pocket – . . . *lo there thou hast that is thine.* The lord's furious: bad servant, he says. Stupid! Useless! *Thou knewest that I reap where I sowed not . . . Thou oughtest therefore to have put my money to the exchangers, and then at my coming I should have received mine own with usury.* In short, he gives him a hell of a telling-off; then he takes his money away from him and gives it to the one who already has ten talents. There's the story for you. And finally the lord adds this piece: *And cast ye the unprofitable servant into outer darkness, there shall be weeping and gnashing of teeth.*' The Chief finished his drink in one gulp. 'As you see, a story about a Jew . . . or a Scotchman.' He gave me a quick look. 'What did the Captain say to you?'

'Nothing . . . He was reading: I just asked him what it was.'

Our eyes met. He turned his aside and gazed attentively at his glass. 'Of course. He's not a talker, the Captain. I'm only a clown . . . What hast thou done with thy talent: do you suppose he asks himself that question?'

'Everyone asks it . . . sooner or later.'

'Yes: no doubt . . . His business with your friend the Drummer-Crab lies heavy on his chest.'

'What happened, Chief?'

'Everyone knows the story. Although it was tried in camera, being a special case, everything came out in the end. Your friend, wearing mufti and sitting there in the dock between a couple of gendarmes, risked the death-penalty: plotting against the state, armed rebellion and God knows what. The Captain, in full-dress and wearing his decorations, wanted to give evidence in his favour: I think he was very fond of him. When he'd come to the end of his eulogy, your friend got up and said, "At the time of the putsch, sir, in Mers el-Kébir, you gave me . . ." '

An unusually violent roll obliged us to cling on so as not to be flung out of our chairs. The Chief swore in an undertone. When the motion had grown more even, he went on, 'Even over there, among your Indo-Chinese, you must surely have heard of the generals' putsch and what happened afterwards?'

I nodded.

'Good,' he said. 'Well, your friend was in it right up to the neck. The admiral in command at Mers el-Kébir was hesitating which side to commit himself to. Our Old Man was his chief of staff. No question, as far as he was concerned. Discipline! The Navy is and will be loyal to the Republic, full stop. He sent the squadron to sea immediately. He saw your friend in his office and I imagine your friend must have shaken his convictions a little . . . They stayed shut in there together for more than an hour. Nobody knows what they said to one another. And when they came out the Old Man looked much disturbed. He shook Willsdorff's hand and let him go instead of arresting him as he had meant to do.'

'When was Willsdorff arrested?'

'A year later; at a little road-block in the Oranais. At that time he was one of the chiefs of the Secret Army. It was his cat that made a policeman think: the wanted-list described him as "often accompanied by a black cat".'

After a period of comparative calm, the *Eole* once more began to caper wildly. The Chief let out an oath. 'I'll swear,' he cried furiously, 'that that young soldier is officer of the watch. He still doesn't know how to steer so as to favour the ship.'

I did not let him go on pouring out his ill-humour on the sub-lieutenant. 'What happened at the trial?'

The engineer seemed to hesitate; then with a shrug he said, 'It was held in camera, but . . . in the end everything always comes out. It was one of the two gendarmes – a Breton; he keeps a bar in Saint-Pierre now, the *Morue Joyeuse*. You'll meet him when we go over to the Banks. He was in court, in the dock "to the right of the accused party". It was the first time he had ever been on court-duty. He was impressed by "majestic words of the indictment: Honour, Discipline . . . Officer's Duty", but rather disappointed because "it wasn't as good as on the telly". I'm giving you his own words. At that time they were having a very successful series of programmes on well-known trials. "At the end of the crippled old captain's evidence in his favour," he said, "the accused stood up. I put my hand on his shoulder to make him sit down again but he shoved me off and said, 'At Mers el-Kébir, sir, you gave me your word that whatever the outcome of the . . . of the revolt (I forget the exact word he used) you would resign from the Navy when it was all over.' The captain turned ghastly white. 'Did you give me your word as an officer?' repeated the accused party. At that the Old Man stood up very straight. He was as pale as death. After a silence he said Yes. It had a queer kind of an effect . . . queer, Lord above! If he'd fired a revolver through the ceiling it wouldn't have shaken up the court so much: all the service judges poked their noses down into their books, looking grim. Even my colleague Fougou Ernest, the other gendarme, opened his eyes wide and looked flabbergasted. The old captain stood there bolt upright in his uniform with his medals hanging on it: no expression at all, but there wasn't a single drop of blood left in his face. You would have said he was dead on his feet." That was the gendarme's report, more or less.'

The engineer paused for a while. 'The Captain added nothing . . . and it seems your friend didn't turn the knife in the wound either. Maybe he understood that he'd just killed the Old Man. He never said, "Where's the honour of a naval officer now?" or anything of that kind: no fine, noble phrases. Nothing. According to my gendarme he looked as if he were smiling: but you've already told me he always looked amused, so that proves nothing much. They stood there, both of them, face to face, in "an icy silence", the young man and the old, looking straight into one another's eyes. Your friend said nothing. He sat down. And ten minutes later he got his twenty years.'

The Chief fell silent. His grey eyes were watching me as though I were his quarry. Suddenly, and with a feeling of extreme awkwardness, I remembered my first night on the bridge, my story of the bugle-charge, and the way I pressed the point – 'Willsdorff, you must surely have heard of him? Willsdorff!' And the old crab unseen, standing straight against his screen, listening without a word.

But then again, why did he not resign? I asked the Chief. His eyes moved away and he laughed bitterly, 'Ha, ha, ha! A farce, an odious farce! Ha, ha! He *did* resign. I know it for a fact. But the Navy would not accept his resignation. They all came down on him, admirals, officers who had been in the Free French Navy, the minister, and even . . . God the Father away up there, the General: "Withdraw your resignation: that is an order." '

'But why?'

'State policy . . . *You* can't know; you have to have lived through those times to understand. The army had come out of it broken to pieces, all torn apart. But the Navy had to be protected, because the Navy was the future – the means of exercising the force of dissuasion. The Navy had remained loyal; that was a dogma. There'd only been one black sheep. There could be no question of officers beginning to resign for reasons of . . . for states of mind, for moods. And above all not our Captain, who was an example for many others: above all not him.' The engineer looked at me intently, with something like strong ill-temper in his eyes. 'Don't you judge him, Doctor, don't you judge him. Who are you to judge?' he added aggressively.

I did not reply, but he must have seen the reflection of my feelings in my face, and I saw that he was gradually calming down. 'I beg your pardon,' he said at last.

He struck a match – it cast a yellow light over his Mongolian features – lit a cigarette and drew on it long and hard. 'That was how the old crab had his talent . . . stolen. Pfuitt!' He blew out the match: it had very nearly burnt his fingers.

We remained silent. The *Eole* rolled in the frozen night and we had to grip the arms of our chairs not to be torn out of them. The lamp swung in its gimbals – it was our only light – and our two shadows rose and fell on the wardroom bulkhead. The Chief smoked. I wondered whether the Captain was up there, standing at his window, as mute as ever: *Sentry on the battlements* . . .

The Chief let out a sigh. 'A farce,' he growled, 'a God-damned farce, cooked up by the Devil.' Suddenly it occurred to me that perhaps he was somewhat drunk. 'Do you . . . do you believe in God, Doctor?'

His question disturbed my train of thought, and this time it was I who darted an ill-tempered look. 'No . . . that is to say . . . I don't know. I don't think so. Oh, shut up! Ask a damnfool question and you get a damnfool answer.'

'Ha, ha, ha!' His laugh rang false. 'Man of little faith! I don't know either – my poor old Rector must be turning in his grave – I don't know whether we have a Lord or not, a

God who will require us to give an account at our last hour. I don't know. But I do know that I was given a talent, and a bigger one than my father's. I know that at my last hour I shall certainly be required to give an account ... to myself. I know it.' He glanced at me furtively. 'At least I hope to be able to give it back – whole – before I'm cast into the outer darkness. Like the useless servant. I hope so, but ... maybe it's rusted in the hole where I buried it? Maybe I've lost it? Frittered it away for a few glasses of cognac? Perhaps it's been stolen: stolen from me too ... I'm thirsty.'

The Chief stood up and almost fell with the roll. A sudden thrust flung him over to the little table where the spirits were kept. He pulled out a bottle of brandy, uncorked it and poured himself a drink. 'Yerc'h mad,' he said, raising his glass. He drove the cork home with the flat of his hand: his face had a look of weariness. 'I'm going to tell you something,' he said, taking advantage of the roll to get back to his chair. 'I'm forty. I've lived forty years! And it's taken me all that time ... But I've discovered the Secret: I know. In the end everybody discovers it. It's very simple: obvious. Long ago my grandmother said to me, "Life's hard." Ha, ha! That was her way of telling it. She knew. Now I know ... and the poor holy man walking on the beach and beating his bosom, he knew it too. He used to say, "We aren't here to enjoy ourselves." That was his way of putting it. So there you are: I've discovered the Secret, I know ...' He hesitated; he was finding it hard to express his meaning. Once again I wondered whether he were drunk. 'I know the Great Secret ... There are quite a few of us aboard who know it: you, the Captain of course ... not the soldier. He doesn't know it: too young. But still, it's strange, it's very strange – one is not happy. I know one is not happy. Not at any time. That's the secret: there has never been a happy man. Never since there have been men on this earth; never, from the very beginning. You knew it, didn't you? It's written in all the books. Do you believe your drummer-crab friend is happy?' After a pause he added, 'God I'm so thirsty. Let's have some cognac, Doctor.'

From the time she ran into Hammerfest fjord, the *Eole* rolled no longer; but the south-wester was still roaring and the long, stinging lashes of the snow-squalls still streaked the grey darkness.

Far away through a gap in the storm the star-like lights of the town dotted the sides of a dark ring of mountains; and upon these mountains clung fragments of singularly and even astonishingly black cloud.

The officer of the watch was manœuvring to make it easier for the Norwegian pilot to come aboard. The red and green glow of the boat's lights: the rumble of the diesel through the enormous howling of the wind. The searchlight came on: the blinding arrows of snow blurred the black silhouettes on the deck. Shouts. Taking advantage of a yaw, a heavy form leapt aboard; the accelerating diesel drowned the cries; the searchlight went out like a dropping curtain: an even blacker darkness.

The pilot was a huge, taciturn creature. 'Good day, Captain,' he mumbled, reaching the bridge.

'Good night,' replied the Captain, in English.

'No good ... Too much wind ... you'll have to anchorage here.' The pilot's English was harsh and heavily accented.

'He says we'll have to moor outside,' interpreted the fisheries officer.

'I understood. Reply ... we have a sick man aboard, and we must pick up stores. Tell him I am going to take her in. It will be all right. Give him some coffee.'

The pilot muttered something incomprehensible: oaths, perhaps. The Captain turned towards the officer of the watch, whose face was invisible to me. 'I take over.'

Then he stepped to the interphone: 'Captain to engine-room: we have a tricky piece of manœuvring ... watch out. Captain to forecastle and afterdeck: stand by the hawsers and line-throwers. You'll have to look alive.' He hung up. 'Bosun.'

'Sir?' (It was the old gnome-faced warrant-officer.)

'I don't want to have to shout. Stand by me and repeat my orders. Forward two; starboard fifteen.'

'FORWARD TWO; STARBOARD FIFTEEN.'

Roughly speaking, the port of Hammerfest, seen from the sea, looks like a semi-circle whose eastern aspect is half-closed by a mole. To the right, the town, the canning-factory and the inshore-fisherman's quay. To the left, a small shipyard, a few villas, and a pier that runs out a little way. On this pier stands a coal-store called the Bunker Depot, and it was there that the *Eole* was to moor.

The snow was covering the glass, and the windscreen-wipers laboured as they swept it off. Very close at hand the lights of a road shone bright, but the Bunker Depot's beacon-buoys could scarcely be seen at all; their vague, uncertain glow loomed from the darkness and then plunged back into it again.

'You'll have an ambulance for your appendicitis,' murmured the fisheries officer in my ear. He took me by the arm. 'Come into the chart-room; I'll tell you something.'

He closed the door and lit one of the red lamps. 'The Owner doesn't like people talking on his bridge. I went to see him in his cabin this morning – just routine questions – and I found him studying the charts of the port and the Sailing Directions. He said, "Unless the wind drops, we'll anchor in the roadstead." I told him that last year the Alsatian – he was a carrier then – had managed to bring his trawler in with the weather just like this: brought her right in because one of the crew had had his leg broken by a trawl-rope and it would have been dangerous to take him across by boat. The Old Man seemed to be far away; you would have said he wasn't listening. "He's the best seaman of his generation," was all he said. The toughest part is

148

coming alongside – you'll see – because with a south-wester blowing the Bunker Depot is very awkwardly placed. Your Drummer-Crab literally had to graze the shore. His boss was out of his mind, bawling "I'm not responsible!" – it was the pilot who told me. The bows passed at a few . . . at less than a yard from the pierhead. And the rest followed. Four astern, the helm hard over, and it was done: for a few moments the trawler was right alongside the quay, just long enough to pass the hawsers before the wind shoved her off. It was magnificent, they say.' The plating vibrated beneath our feet – the turbines exerting their full thrust. 'Let's go back; we'll see how he handles it.'

The moment the door was open we were deafened by the howling wind – you would have said a pack of wolves beneath the moon – but the tension on the bridge was so great that strangely enough one had an illusion of silence. The snow came swirling in by the open starboard door.

'FORWARD TWO,' the voice of the gnome.

'Forward two signalled.'

Out on the wing the wind cut off your breath. To the right, wind-tossed yellow lamps, the headlights of cars, the red advertisement of a shop – a camel and a palm-tree: Tobakoniste. Ahead, something vague, blacker than the darkness; and we were racing towards it.

I felt a pressure against my shoulder: the young sub-lieutenant, his eyes fixed on the Captain and nothing else.

Excited shouts rose from the forecastle, where shadowy figures were in active movement. A lantern right ahead, waving madly. More shouts, incomprehensible, frightening.

'Astern four.'

'ASTERN FOUR.'

The pierhead loomed up alongside, glided into contact: the man with the lantern leapt out of the way. The bows grazed the pier and seemed to hesitate. The *Eole* was quivering from stem to stern. White snakes pierced through the darkness and I heard the muffled report of the line-throwers.

'FORWARD TWO. HARD A-PORT.'

Through the cold fury of the wind a kind of shrill lament could be heard: two headlights, a blue revolving beam, and the ambulance arrived, skidding among the snowdrifts, its sirens howling full blast.

The trembling *Eole* hung there poised like a rearing horse: this was the very climax of the manœuvre. Her bows were touching the quay. Her stern was still far from it and the wind was about to thrust it still farther off. Everything seemed static, suspended. I was intensely aware of the power in the column of water that the propeller was throwing against the rudder-cheek – I could feel it in my being.

'Zero forward.'

'ZERO FORWARD.'

The Captain was giving up . . . he had failed.

And then slowly, oh so slowly, the *Eole* came alive and the stern swung in towards the quay. The force of her remaining way! As in chess, our master had been playing two moves ahead.

'I don't think the other one did any better,' murmured the fisheries officer.

'Take her,' said the Captain to the officer of the watch; and for a long time he stood out there on the wing, leaning over the rail and keeping an eye on the mooring. In the full blast of the wind. But you would have said that he felt neither the wind nor the snow: he stood motionless, leaning forward. When he came back to the shelter of the bridge his face had not even reddened.

'Do you like to have a drink while I'll sign the papers?' he asked the pilot, again in English.

'*Ya tak*,' said the pilot, adding in a kind of French, 'I . . . I need one,' and he muttered something else that must surely have been a Norwegian oath.

As he left the bridge, the Captain brushed against the

sub-lieutenant. 'Never do what I have just done,' he said to him. 'It is not justified. It would have been better to anchor in the roadstead.'

The *Eole* stayed at Hammerfest for twenty-four hours. The hospital stood on the side of a hill, not far from Bunker Depot. I spent almost all my time in it. There was a delightful sunburned nurse, Gunilla, who had just come back from a fortnight's holiday at Djerba, in Tunisia.

At seven o'clock I heard a bugle-call. A very faint bugle-call swept away by the wind; down there in the harbour the *Eole* was waking up.

At noon the turbulent chaos of the clouds reddened in the south – it might have been a whole world ablaze – and the snow on the ring of mountains grew pink. It was almost daylight. Happy sailors with red pompons hurried off to ski with the schoolchildren, their broad collars blown by the wind.

At eighteen hours the starboard watch were given liberty; I watched them running along under the street-lights towards the town, as clean as new pins. It seems that Bongo Ba was seen dancing lovingly in the Grand Hotel discotheque with a pretty blonde from the canning-factory.

The fisheries officer arranged a cocktail-party on board for the French consul, the superintendent of the hospital, the ship-chandler (who was also the French trawlers' agent), some other personalities and a few young women (I brought Gunilla). The Captain only made a brief appearance.

It was a very cheerful evening, and our guests all grew a little drunk.

Was it her sunburned skin, her breasts free under the light dress, the curve of her rump, her lips, her eyes, the scent of woman? I do not know. Or was it rather that 'alcohol had unkennelled the dogs dozing in some corner of my mind' as the engineer put it? Anyhow, at one point I felt a simple-minded urge to show Gunilla Willsdorff's ship in a bottle and to tell her what the old blue-water captain who looked like Victor Hugo had said to me.

'If you look at it long enough, perhaps you will discover the Great Secret.'

'Your secrets! I'm going to find out all your secrets!' Laughing, she snatched the bottle, missed her hold and let it drop. The bottle fell to the deck and broke.

CHAPTER 16

The Devil

The wind howled. Howls that one was always just on the edge of understanding . . . And that one never understood at all.

I went up on to the bridge less often. What point was there in perpetually watching the black swell, the black clouds, the black lookouts stamping their feet, the vast black emptiness, the moon and all the stars – the black infinity that broke and ground and writhed beneath a wind from another world?

I had examined the Captain. He submitted to everything without a word. No error in the diagnosis.

'No preaching, Doctor, no preaching . . .'

The wind veered north-west and then north-east. The cold came back, the cold that numbs with a dreadful torpid well-being, the cold of the retreat from Moscow: in just such a cold the soldiers of the Old Guard ripped up their wounded horses and huddled into their steaming bodies to keep alive. Our woollen balaclavas hardened and froze over mouth and nostrils. The cornea of men's eyes grew all red. 'As far as we are concerned, Doctor, let's stay in the warm and drink brandy.'

The Skolpen Bank: seven hours of lying-to: the dinghy going aboard three trawlers: five patients crackling in their icy armour. The warmth of the sick-bay went to their heads. The skin of their cheeks stung; they rubbed their black, curly beards with both hands. Their eyes, half-closed under the flickering lids, remained set, withdrawn, atonic. They were reminiscent of peasants of former times, their day's labour done, ruminating on a bench.

All the ills peculiar to deep-sea fishermen: bruises caused by rough weather, deep cuts caused by the work on the fish, abrasions, deep infected chaps, whitlows, boils, carbuncles . . . Gradually they began to talk: the fishing was not bad – 'not as who should say *bad*' – but the slump in prices was worrying. 'And then the cod are going off on to hard bottoms, under the ice . . . the sods.'

They stayed for a few hours, visited the lower-deck canteen and sometimes the kitchens, where they drank a little tea laced with rum with the second crew of the dinghy, climbed back into their half-dried clothes, their stiff oilskins, their long boots, and vanished again into the frozen night from which they had come.

The stars were astonishingly brilliant. All the shades of darkness seemed to be touched by unearthly lights. The sky was so pure that it evoked a planet that had died.

'Let's stay in the warm and drink brandy . . .'

The Sole Banken, north of Vardö. Two trawlers; three patients. I kept one of them, the only man who never spoke a word. Scorning explanations, he flung himself on to a bunk, shivering with fever from head to foot, and went straight to sleep. It took two days for the sick-berth attendants to tame him. 'You grow more unsociable than a wild beast.'

East Bank . . . The skipper of the *Mara* tersely announced the loss of a man: 'He slipped on the ramp . . .'

The wind had dropped: it was not even absolutely dark any more. The Northern Lights sparkled like a fine spray of emeralds; they took on the appearance of a huge rolled-up theatre-curtain, rising over a black and empty stage. The lookouts were worried; they turned their heads away. Why was everything blazing so? Why? What was up? That is what seemed to be going on in their heads.

The *Mara*'s winch screeched; the trawl-boards clashed

against the derrick; the trawl slid up the after-ramp. Men were heaving on the frozen deck – we could hear their shouts. The cod-end rose up, swaying with the roll, and opened. The fish slithered down the open hatchway. One has to earn one's daily bread.

Imperceptibly the wind got up, coming by wafts and gentle gusts.

'Let's have some brandy.'

The fisheries officer took off his pea-jacket and dropped on to the wardroom's sofa. 'The barometer's falling,' he said with a disgusted look, and glancing at me, he added, 'I had the Drummer-Crab over the long-wave – the Northern Lights are jamming the VHF. We'll reach him in about twelve hours or so. And if the blow hasn't reached us by then, we'll be able to go aboard.'

Deep in his armchair, the Mongol was watching me with his cat-like eyes. He began to laugh. 'Poor Doctor!'

'What's the matter, Chief?'

'Nothing. I'm just looking at you ... I can see you jibbing, as though all at once you were rather frightened of your friend. True enough: here you were in the warm, at your ease, quiet and sheltered, and now suddenly here's this pro-digious type with his black cat ... Ha, ha, ha! A sword hanging over your head, eh? What have you done with your talents?'

I was extremely angry; there was some truth in his nonsense and I loathed the feeling that he had been able to look into me so deeply. 'You drink too much, Chief,' I said with deliberate grossness. 'You are beginning to wander in your mind. I shall have to take a look at your liver.'

'Ha, ha! Don't be upset, Doctor ... you're not the only one to be frightened in this mortal world here below. No, I'm not talking about our ...' He pointed upwards. '... I don't know about Him. Doctor,' (he was very grave now) 'what you're afraid of is yourself ... You're afraid of your

155

own shadow. Like poor old Gwen. Ha, ha, ha!'

The reserved fisheries officer, who had disliked all this, seized the opportunity of changing the subject. 'I really don't understand,' he said. 'Who is this Gwen, Chief? Is it another of your horrible stories?'

'Gwenaël was his real name,' said the Chief, without waiting to be asked again. 'A countryman of mine. The most besotted drunkard in creation . . . but he had good cause for it; he believed in what was going on inside his head more than in what existed . . .' The Chief's narrowed eyes gleamed wickedly. 'When I was a choirboy, we used to run after him – though we kept our distance – and we threw filth and dog-turds and even stones, shouting "You're frightened of your shadow . . . of your shadow!" Then he'd stop and stare at us, reeling as he stood. He'd kneel down, with his arms out in a cross . . . or sometimes he'd roll into the ditch. The Germans shot him during the war: he'd knocked out a Kriegsmarine officer with a bottle. I bet he insulted them right up until the very last moment. Iron-headed Bigouden! But, do you see, this Gwen of mine was a . . . an imaginative man, like our worthy Doctor.'

The Chief paused. 'He'd been the strongest, toughest young fellow anywhere along the coast from Saint-Guénolé to Guilvinec, and as was right and proper he'd married the prettiest – and the most virtuous – girl: Annick, from Kerity, near Penmarc'h. He went briskly to work, and by the time he had to join the *Primauguet* at Brest the girl was – what shall I say? There was a bun in the oven, ha, ha! In those days – I'm talking about before the war – a cruise lasted three years. Three years is a long time . . . However . . . At the end of the three years, Gwen got out of the Brest bus one fine morning: quartermaster, with elegant red stripes on his arm. Annick, his wife, was working at the canning-factory by the harbour; so Gwen, all dolled up, went to Guenn-an-Avel – the Wind Strikes – to fetch the little boy, who was being looked after by an old woman. To pass the time he started playing with him: "You get on my back; Papa will be a horse." The kind of nonsense you expect from a father. "You aren't my Papa," says the little boy. "What?" "No: my Papa never plays with me. He comes in every evening when Mama gets back from work. He sits down when she sits down, and he says nothing. And he goes to bed when she goes to bed . . ." '

The Chief lit a cigarette and laughed silently. 'The old, old story, eh? Poor Gwen! He gave the child back to the old woman and made straight for the harbour. He was too early, so he sat down in a bar with a grim face and treated himself to *gwin ru*, big glasses of it; and maybe something stronger too, because he had plenty of money – a three years cruise!

'Twelve o'clock. The hooter. Annick, smiling all over her face, comes out of the factory with her friends. And Gwen stands there in front of her, fists clenched, very drunk . . . and with everybody watching, in the open street, at noon, he loads her with all the filthiest sailor's insults. "You have fun when I'm away, you bitch . . . and in front of the kid, you whore . . ." And a good deal more of the same kind, enough to turn Bongo Ba as white as a sheet. He hits her hard, knocks her into the gutter. And he goes for the crowd, too. An uproar! Horrible, I tell you. And nobody dared do anything because he was very strong and very drunk, which breeds both respect and dread . . . Then he went off and walked on the beach, by way of brightening his wits – you could see him there all by himself, waving his arms. Things were better by the evening: his eyes were red, but things were better. He went to fetch his little boy from the old woman and took him home. Annick had not come back. When it grew dark he lit the lamp – there was no electricity in those days – and all at once the little boy piped up: "Why, there's Papa." "Where?" "There!" said the child, pointing at Gwen's shadow on the wall. Ha, ha, ha!'

The Chief looked at us, very pleased with himself. 'Every

157

evening, when the little boy cried for his father, Annick had
shown him her shadow, saying, "There he is, you see; he's
watching over us . . ." That's all. As for Annick, it was too
late . . . she'd thrown herself off the Rocher de la Torche.
It was the village idiot who brought the news, laughing and
drooling.'

An anonymous voice on the interior-circuit loudspeaker:
'The fisheries officer and the surgeon to report to the radio-
room.'

The Captain was there. 'Doctor, you won't be meeting
your friend again this trip: we're going back to the North
Flaket. There's a badly injured man aboard one of the
Mevels. See if you can do something for him over the radio.
A stab in the region of the liver.'

'If it's his liver . . .! How long will it take us to get there?'

'Twenty, twenty-two hours. It will depend on the sea.'

Over the long-wave I talked to the radio-operator of the
Mevel (the *Sénateur Mevel*) while the *Eole*'s ten thousand
horses charged the night at twenty-two knots. A man had
gone mad – a crisis of delirium tremens, perhaps? – had
knocked out one of his mates, his only friend, and had burnt
his face. Later he had stabbed another man with his cod-
knife. He had threatened the skipper and now he was hiding
somewhere in the ship, still carrying his knife.

I tried to make a long-distance diagnosis: the man who
had been knocked out almost certainly had a fracture; the
burnt face was less worrying. What about the one with
the stab-wound? The liver was probably affected; the
stomach certainly. I gave some directions.

The expected gale started its furious assault. The *Eole*
reduced speed to fifteen knots, pitching heavily in the swell
from the south-west. Tons of water swept the forecastle;
spray leapt as high as the radar aerial, and there it froze. The
lookouts came in for shelter. For the first time the Captain
had the windward door closed.

The stabbed man's pulse was weakening. 'Have you any camphor solution aboard? Give him an injection.' The madman had still not been found.

Ice. Growlers, huge drifting ice-sheets, could be heard but not seen as they roared among the breaking seas. The *Eole* reduced speed still further, to avoid running into them.

The *Sénateur Mevel* had moved north for the shelter of the pack-ice; for the pack-ice, calming the swell, would allow the dinghy to be launched.

The stabbed man had died. No news of the maniac.

The wind was blowing at more than seventy miles an hour. The swell was no longer breaking, and one could just make out the ice-pack by that indeterminate paleness which is always perceptible, even on the darkest nights. Though paleness is too strong a word; it was in fact little more than a faint alteration in the depth of the blackness – it might even be the effect of eye-fatigue . . .

The *Mevel*'s lights: their reflection glanced on some of the long black waves, leaving others in total darkness. The dinghy was ready. The Captain handed the *Eole* over to the second-in-command; he was coming with the fisheries officer and me. Article thirteen of the disciplinary code lays down that '*The captain of any naval vessel present in the waters is entitled to take cognizance of serious offences against discipline*'.

I cannot tell how he managed to get into the boat with his artificial hand. The dinghy was rising and falling prodigiously: you had to take advantage of the rise to jump, and then the frogmen would catch hold of you. There you were crouching in the bottom with icy water swilling about, and as soon as you had managed to get up someone else landed on you.

'Let go the painter.'

The coxswain, his hand on the throttle, ran cleverly through the waves, taking them on the slant; and at the top

159

of every rise the wind snatched our breath away. Whenever he was not quite quick enough, a mass of water like a liquid battering-ram overwhelmed us: we coped with it as well as we could, rounding our backs and hanging on to the rubber gunwale. It occurred to me that a man shipwrecked in water as cold as this could not survive more than a few minutes.

From time to time the *Mevel*'s lights would show blinding bright; then we dropped down into a black emptiness. In the bows Bongo Ba waved his torch and bawled furiously 'Big lump! Big lump!' The coxswain would heave on the tiller and avoid the grey-green shattered wildly-heaving roaring and spouting growler, its sharp edges perfectly suited for ripping the pneumatic craft or breaking its propeller.

The *Mevel*'s side. High, streaming with water. The pilot's ladder: sometimes the roll swung it away, and then it would fall back with a clash like jaws snapping to.

A huge wave came out of the darkness. It rose straight up, black and gleaming. The dinghy soared, poised high, and plunged down once more. The bilge-keel passed before us, foaming, covered with slimy weed. The Captain had hooked on to the ladder. Hanging there, high above our heads, he looked like a clumsy beetle caught in a spider's web. The *Mevel* gave a lurch as though she meant to crush us.

Another sudden wave heaved us up. The ladder clashed. The Captain was still there, flattened against the side. He climbed three rungs. A shout: 'Carry on!' Now the fisheries officer caught hold: he vanished suddenly, wafted upwards. The bilge-keel once more. And the mass of the hull, like a streaming hillside. With the next wave it would be my turn.

The *Sénateur*'s deck, rigging and superstructure were coated with ice. A trawler-hand helped me over the rail and led me below.

The man who had been knocked out was lying flat in his bunk, still in his working clothes (I had forbidden them to move him). He had a diminishing hemiplegia – certainly a fracture of the cervical vertebrae or the otic bone. He did not complain; he waited. There was a little clotted blood on the mattress near the back of his neck, but the gash was merely superficial. He did not move; only his black, expressive eyes followed me continually, sometimes squinting in order not to lose sight of me. The other man, my guide, explained what had happened: 'The deck was all covered with ice, and he fetched him a crack. Sometimes he was what you might call not quite right in the head ... it was the trawl-board coming in twisted – no way of hooking the chain on. He was singing out, but what with the wind and all, you might as well stuff it up. So then he jumped on him and stretched him out: he lay there like he was dead. It was his mate; always together ...'

Somewhere an iron door was slamming – bang, bang, bang – a kind of dreary passing-bell. The sea roared, and the wind; but the sound was unlike that which we heard aboard the *Eole*: more muffled. There was a strange and unpleasant atmosphere. I had the feeling that I was picking up the inner tensions in this ship, as a Geiger counter picks up radioactivity.

The whole of the right-hand side of the patient's face was deeply burnt: I had not noticed it when I first came in because of the darkness.

'He came back down here and gave him the fakir's trick right in the face.' The patient darted out his arm and seized my shoulder firmly. 'Just for the laugh,' he said, without moving his head. His voice was thick and it was hard for him to pronounce his words. 'It was to make me laugh ... Wanted to make me laugh; wanted me to show I wasn't put out. He was my mate.'

'I dare say,' went on the other. 'But she was rolling, and then he was still full up to the brim ...'

The door slammed. Bang, bang.

At last I got to the bottom of the story. The men had

been working too hard for too long in heavy seas, wearing themselves out fishing a bank that yielded well. As they were heaving in the last trawl, the gale blowing hard, a certain Yorick flew into a sudden rage and knocked out his friend over some trivial matter of a badly-hooked trawl-board. ('He must have been looking too hard at the bottles of rum he hid under his mattress.') Even so, he finished his work, 'bawling out worse than the Devil', shook his fist at the skipper working the winch up on the bridge, and disappeared for a while. ('Must have been sucking at his bottle again, in my opinion.') Then he came to look for his mate, who in the meantime had been laid on his bunk. In order to be forgiven ('just for the laugh') he performed his fakir's trick, a trick he had learned at Hamburg when he was serving in the Navy: he drew in the petrol from his lighter and spat it out again in an enormous flame. ('Used to do it for us on deck sometimes: in the wind it came out like a red sun farting off in the darkness. The fakir's trick, he called it. A red sun, lovely to look at!') But the *Sénateur* was rolling in the storm and Yorick was rolling with tiredness and the drink; he tripped right in the middle of his act and his mate got the flame full in his face.

This did poor Yorick's state of mind no good. I believe he went for a last suck at his bottle, and then he hurried off to abuse the skipper. He roared out something incoherent about hell and Satan. Meanwhile the hands were working furiously in the factory below. ('Fifteen ton in the pounds and almost nothing but first-rate stuff: just imagine that!') The fish had to be sorted, prepared, filleted, deep-frozen . . . The whole crew was mobilized. Yorick took up his station muttering to himself in a tone that disturbed his companions; he was still inclined to make trouble. ('I'm no bleeding idler. I can earn my living and my mate's living too.') It was from that moment on that things turned really ugly.

Did his neighbour get in his way? Did he make fun of him?

Weariness, the storm roaring outside, the sickening reek of fish guts, the exhausting roll! Yorick took his knife, all sticky with cod-blood, and stuck it into his neighbour's belly – into his liver, most unfortunately.

The stabbed man stood there clinging to his bench with both hands, saying never a word, looking amazed. Yorick burst out laughing. ('I shouldn't like to hear another like that. You couldn't tell whether he was laughing or crying.') Then he darted out, still carrying his knife. That was the long and the short of it. This had happened more than twenty-four hours ago. Nobody knew where he was hidden. ('Maybe he went overboard?') At all events he had not been near his bottles again.

Bang! Bang! The ear-splitting door ehoced as though it were in a crypt.

I arranged for the patient to be taken away: a metal stretcher would answer, but the job was not going to be easy. Then I joined the Captain and the fisheries officer, who were carrying out their inquiry in the skipper's cabin. The Captain's face was deadly pale. He was sitting behind a table, stiff in his uniform – a uniform that was scarcely made any less severe by the colour of his medal-ribbons. He was listening to a big, nervous seaman who kept kneading his cap in his hands.

'He had no friends, apart from the other guy. A loner . . . kept himself to himself. He used to spit his fire when it was blowing hard. He said he was the Devil . . . I'm the Devil! And we'd laugh and laugh.'

The sound of feet racing along the alleyway. An excited voice: 'Captain, Captain! We've got him . . . he's almost done for. In the chain-locker.'

The chain-locker was right forward: narrow, cold, dark, stinking, dripping with wet, grimly lit by a bulb behind a steel grid: the anchor-chains grated and rattled as they shifted with the roll; every now and then freezing water gushed in through the hawse-pipes; more water splashed about at the bottom; soft slimy things gleamed down there, smelling like the filth of a port at low tide. The guts of despair itself. Yorick was hanging from a link, his eyes starting from his head, his tongue lolling out, his legs kicking. No one had dared to cut him down. The sight was so fantastic that I was torn between horror and almost hysterical laughter.

I had him laid down in the alleyway. He had failed; his larynx was not crushed and his vertebrae had stood the strain. A convulsive trembling shook him from head to foot. His mates cut the rope and shared out the pieces.

'Bring him a glass of rum.'

'He mustn't drink; he'd go off his head again.'

'Do what I tell you.'

Yorick choked on his drink, spat out a little of the rum and recovered his breath. He gave me a long stare. I thought he had a fine face; it was lean, covered with grey bristles – the face of an old soldier worn by toil, hardship, and debauchery, and by too many doubtful battles.

His lips began to quiver. Tears came into his eyes. He hid them with his hand. He said nothing. You could feel the effort he was making to keep back his sobs.

CHAPTER 17

'Save This Man!'

The storm soon died out. Once again the weather was fine and cold. In the darkness the *Eole* left a white wake that faded slowly beneath the stars.

The bugle sounded when we were at the mouth of Hammerfest fjord. We had to wait for a pilot . . . Towards noon the sky at the rim of the horizon flushed a delicate pink like the inside of a shell, and far away the lights of the town grew pale. The sub-lieutenant supervised the mooring at Bunker Depot. As he gave the fateful order 'Engines off' he smiled one of his elegant smiles. The Captain remained sitting in his armchair. Grey and motionless. The trips in the dinghy and the inquiry on board the *Sénateur* had exhausted him, and his family doctor's injections could no longer do anything. The time when I should have to give him up was close . . .

Death ought not to be this slow decline, this torpidity; it ought not to be this prospect of a drugged apathy in hospital, this . . . accident in one's sleep at the very end. Death ought to shout and bleed . . .

I found my appendicitis in very good shape. He complained about the lack of wine (the 'sailor's milk'), so I brought him a few bottles from the ship and arranged with Gunilla that he should be given a glass with every meal. The stunned man's hemiplegia was slowly growing less. The medical superintendent put him into the same ward as the appendicitis so that he should feel less lonely; but he did not speak to his neighbour. He lay motionless, staring at the ceiling and revolving obscure thoughts in his mind.

Yorick, the sun-maker, did not talk either. He had been shut up in the *Eole*'s cells with neither belt nor bootlaces, and he had started off by sleeping twelve hours at a stretch under the light of the electric bulb, sometimes uttering short sighs that made one think of an old man gasping under a burden. After he had woken up I went to see him several times; he was always sitting there, bent, pulling at his short black pipe (the Captain had not wanted his tobacco to be cut off and he was also entitled to two half-pints of wine a day, like the rest of the crew). A massive trunk, a bull-like neck – and one that had held firm against the rope – a fine, tormented face, seamed with wrinkles. He did not speak in reply to questions: he nodded or shook his head in agreement or denial, his eyes obstinately set on the ground. Once or twice he sent me an astonishing glance – I was by no means sure I understood it – a deep, ironic look as though he no longer had either doubt or hope, as if he had already carried out his own silent inquiry into the case and had accepted his own private verdict.

'He's got a cat, a black cat.' I think these were the only words I ever heard him utter. I had mentioned Willsdorff, the Alsatian, I hardly know why. Somebody had to do the talking, after all. I sensed his interest. He stopped pulling on his pipe and it was then that he looked at me. 'That type,' he added, 'he's what you call a real captain.' Then he bowed his head and relapsed into silence. It was over: the contact was cut off.

The purser arranged for him to be flown back to France. He wired the consul in Oslo so that the man should be under guard until he was put on the plane for Paris, where the gendarmes would be waiting for him.

Before he left I took him to the hospital to see his friend. I left them alone together. Later my appendicitis case told me they had remained silent almost all the time. ('Looked at one another like two friends, without talking. He left him

166

his pipe and tobacco; but you aren't allowed to smoke in this hospital.')

The stabbed man's body travelled in the same plane as Yorick . . . When the time came for loading it, sewn up in canvas, into the dinghy, the Captain asked the skipper of the *Sénateur* to call all hands and say a prayer. 'Why, as for that, I don't know any,' said the other in a temper. He was sprawling on a sofa in his slippers and he grumbled about 'all this time being lost'.

It was our Captain who spoke. His voice loud and high in the gale: *Man that is born of a woman is of a few days, and full of trouble. He cometh forth like a flower, and is cut down: he fleeth also as a shadow, and continueth not.*

The rest was less orthodox. He turned his face to the wind and added, 'Lord, you said you did not come into this world to judge us but to save us. So save this man!'

The body hung at the end of a tackle, swaying with the roll. Someone shouted 'Lower away', and Bongo Ba, standing in the dinghy, received it in his arms.

I met Gunilla again, the breaker of bottled dreams: the smooth, warm, sunburned Gunilla, so full of laughter . . .

At six o'clock it was the turn of the starboard watch to wander happily about under the street-lights of Hammerfest. Bongo Ba switched with one of his companions, and it seems that he was again seen at the Grand Hotel discotheque, affectionately entwined in the arms of the pretty blonde from the canning-factory.

The fisheries officer gave his cocktail-party. He invited the local chief of police by way of thanking him for his co-operation 'throughout this unpleasant business'. (He had helped the purser in his dealings with the authorities, and two stalwart policemen had led Yorick to the foot of the embarkation-ladder, supervising him with an air of disapproval.)

Once again the Captain put in no more than a brief

appearance. As soon as he had returned to his cabin our guests grew very cheerful and the steward brought on fresh drinks. My friend the engineer talked nonsense, as usual. In a barbarous English that the other was luckily in no state to understand, he tried to tell the chief of police that there was an infallible way of telling whether a man had really hanged himself or whether he had been hung up after he was dead to make people believe in a suicide. 'You have to look in his trousers: it was the gendarmes back at home who told me – it's in their handbook. You have to look in his trousers, because . . . well, hanging has a certain effect . . . ha, ha!' He winked horribly at Gunilla, who giggled. 'An aphrodisiac effect, it seems – it's in the gendarmes' handbook. If . . . if there's nothing, then the whole thing's suspicious: it might be a hidden crime.'

The exquisite Gunilla was delighted. 'As far as I am concerned, there's no doubt at all,' she cried. 'This evening, I assure you, you're all genuine suicides, ha, ha, ha!'

The little trollop.

The Skolpen Bank . . . the Norden Bank . . . Bear Island, whose ragged coast now showed on the radar-screen.

I found a schoolboy's exercise-book among a pile of papers. It belonged to the dead man, the one who was stabbed. I had taken it away and had forgotten to send it on with the rest of his belongings.

I leafed through it. Plumb in the middle of the first page THE SEA, written in capitals with a ball-point pen. This had been firmly crossed through. Beneath it, still in capitals, though smaller, THE GREAT, followed by a word that could not be read because of a blot. Right at the bottom a date: 17 November.

The next page was completely filled. The writing was clear, straight, and careful. All the sentences had been crossed out except for one, but it was still possible to read:

'*Among the black hills of water, the ship . . . The waves, like*

black hills . . . The stout ship sailed over the black watery hills . . .
Lost amidst the black h . . . the black mountains . . . In the night the
young sailor was watching the black . . . the steep black hills of
angry water . . . The stars shone on the . . . The moon was reflected
in . . . The black sea, as rough as . . . One cold November night the
stout ship was rearing like a high-bred steed over the black mount . . .
It was night-time . . . Cast away on the bl . . .' and so on.

At the foot of the page there was a revealing observation
that had nothing to do with fruitless gropings that had
gone before and it was underlined: *'I wish the* Sénateur *were*
already homeward-bound.'

I turned the pages. There was an unfinished, abortive
sketch of a tale or novel, no doubt abandoned by its author.
A whole page was taken up with a search for rhymes: *'After*
the winter I shall not be so cold . . . bold . . . you will be my prey . . .
and to you I say . . . look out for yourself by night and day . . .
Suzon, Suzon . . . Hell on earth but heaven instead . . . your bed . . .
I dread . . .'

And on the opposite page, the poem, with many words
crossed out:

> *Little Suzon look out, take care,*
> *When the cold winter's gone you'll see me there.*
> *Little Suzon, you'll be so gay,*
> *I'll be your king once the fishing's away.*
> *Little Suzon, let me into your bed,*
> *I'll show you heaven, all gold and red.*
> *Little Suzon, life can be fine,*
> *When you've cash and to spare for the food and the wine.*

I turned more pages. Here and there I came across
strange little pieces, some of them naive; odd sentences
jotted down in no sort of order: some were underlined.

'My father used to say . . .' (He never wrote what his
father had told him.)

'Sometimes we see waves, clouds and stars; and now and
then birds.'

'You are alone and yet you can't get away from the others.'

'A tongue of flame came out of his mouth and the wind carried it away and the night was all lit up.'

'You can make fun of him up to a certain point. Up to what point?'

'He knew all the names of the Devil: Satan, Lucifer, Beelzebub, the Prince of the Morning, the Demon, the Tempter, the Evil One, Behemoth, Azrael . . .'

'He said, perhaps God doesn't exist, but the Devil certainly does.'

The barometer fell.

The Sole Banken. I restored my patient, the one who said 'You grow more unsociable than the wild beasts', to his ship; and the skipper having invited him to dinner, the fisheries officer suggested that I should go too. 'He's a friend, you'll see. Nothing remotely like that brute in the *Sénateur*.'

He was a young man of about thirty, friendly, talkative, full of generous ideas. Something about his look gave the impression that he had outgrown the enthusiasms of unthinking youth and that he had reached the more aware, more deeply-felt stage of maturity. He spoke about the slump in the price of deep-frozen fish, of course; but most of his talk was about the sea. 'The free, open sea is over and done with . . . You followed the Caracas Conference? The Norwegians want to push their territorial waters out to two hundred miles, and the Canadians will follow them. Still, we do have Saint-Pierre and Miquelon in those parts, so they won't be able to shove us out . . . not like the Germans, Portuguese and Japanese. It'll be pretty quaint when there are frontiers on the sea like those on dry land! But then again, things are in a hopeless mess at present – they will have to be set in order.'

He talked about his calling, and his first command. 'A ship of my own! Much more mine than the owner's. It was old Mevel who gave her to me, the old colonel, the senator's brother.' (We were aboard the *Marie-Louise-Mevel*.)

'Captain! That's one of the real powers still left in the world, you know, a kingly power. We are the last kings: on the cargo-ships that's all over; the computer and the telex are king. But not in deep-sea fishing, not yet, not with us. Still sole master under God! . . . When I got my ticket I signed on as a plain deck-hand for one last trip; my father said I was a fool – I was wasting my time. But he had never been a skipper, only a deck-hand . . . Because, do you see, in a ship you also have to deal with men.' He uttered this truism so calmly that for a moment I doubted whether he really had any sense. He went on, just as calmly, 'Commanding men does not mean asking them to do the impossible but insisting on their doing what can be done. But it also means going as far as ever you can, as near as ever you can to the impossible . . . You have to know.'

The fisheries officer glanced at me knowingly, as though to say, 'Not bad, eh?'

Willsdorff had shipped as a plain deck-hand too . . . That could not have been for the same reasons: he was much older and he knew life and he knew men. Why? In Haiphong he had said to me one day, 'I'm like a cat; I've got seven lives. I've already used up some of them.' Was he now in his seventh and last reincarnation? Had he wanted to go in by the strait gate, to compel himself to labour like a convict on the cruel sea alongside humble men who earned their daily bread the hard way before he became king, as the skipper of the *Marie-Louise-Mevel* put it – sole master under God? Or had seven years of prison secretly broken him – 'You must never be a prisoner; never!' – so that when he came out, cynical and disillusioned, he had, like his friend Mad-Head, preferred to escape, to go back to his spring, carrying his store of rice? And to the certainty of being beaten when he came back?

'Have you met the skipper of the *Damoclès*?'

'The Alsatian? He's sharper than Old Nick, that fellow, for all his cheerful look. He's gone in for salted cod: no slump there – the market stays firm. How does an Alsatian come to be a sailor? He told me it was because he used to watch the Rhine flowing by . . . the flow of the Rhine! We were in London together, once, in the East End: he took me to Tower Hill – he said they used to hang pirates there in the old days – and to Greenwich, to see the *Cutty Sark*. We wandered about the docks and had lunch in a pub built on piles, overhanging lighters grounded in the mud. He was very fond of their beer; I'd rather have had wine. He told me stories about his cat: every two or three months, it seems, the cat ran off. Then it came back, thin as a rail and very pleased with itself. He'd given it an odd kind of a name . . .'

'Dien Cai Dau.' (At last I understood why he called it that.)

'Maybe . . . We were there for an international meeting organized by the Fisheries Institute. The Alsatian gave a talk – very odd – on the fish that live in schools – cod and herring. In what he called loveless societies . . . the cod recognize one another as belonging to the same species, but they cannot tell each other apart; every cod is anonymous for every other cod. His theory was that each cod acts as one cell in a single brain. A school of cod is a huge brain, and a sweep of the trawl amounts to a lobotomy – much as you can do to a human brain without seeming to diminish its intelligence. He carried his idea very far; he said that if you cut off more than two-thirds of the school the brain can no longer function and the surviving cod turn mad or witless, wandering without any defence. But an untouched school reasons and protects itself against attack. By way of proof he said that at present, during the legal fishing-season, the cod take shelter far under the ice or on rocky bottoms that trawls cannot work. Or even in territorial waters! And it's true, it's perfectly true: you realize that every year . . . A most unusual fellow, eh? So of course a good many people thought he was cracked. He ended up by saying that fishing was rather like hunting German submarines in the war – "and the submarine-commander is no sort of a fool," he said, marking the point. Cod already react to sonar and depth-finders; nowadays the school scatters, whereas only a few years ago you would see them clear on the screen. The Russians and the Japanese have had the idea of recording the emissions put out by a terrified squid when it's attacked by a cod – squid's their favourite food – so that their trawlers could reproduce them under the surface. It worked: the cod rushed in to the kill. But it only lasted for a while. The brain discovered the trick. I'm only giving you my potted version. How he can talk! While he was speaking everything he said seemed to me obviously true . . . Very strange fellow. His conclusion was not so cheerful. He said, "It's war! Total war: if we win, as I believe we shall, our victory will be our defeat; we shall die with the disappearance of our opponents. Creation will survive – it will even survive pollution: it's seen a good deal of it throughout the geological ages – creation will survive; but as for mankind, I'm not so sure." But in the meantime we've got to go on fishing: one has to live.'

CHAPTER 18

Ecce Homo

The wind was rising.

The East Bank . . . the North Flaket once more . . . the *Eole* was carrying out her postman's round 'over the black watery hills'.

The *Damoclès* was too far to the east, and she was alone; we should not be seeing her this trip.

'Still one more reprieve, Doctor, before you have to look at yourself in the glass, ha, ha, ha! So have a drop of brandy with me.'

The news: *Tokyo: A Japanese shipbuilding yard has just finished a giant tanker of five hundred thousand tons; it is completely automatized and will require a crew of no more than nine, including the captain.*

Phnom Penh: About thirty rockets fell on the suburbs last night, killing forty-two people, seventeen of them children.

Belfast: A bomb in a Catholic public-house – three dead, seven wounded.

Hammerfest.

We anchored in the roadstead. A big German trawler was lying in our berth at the Bunker Depot. She had been stopped by a Norwegian patrol-vessel while she was fishing inside the twelve-mile limit – an offence that carried heavy penalties: the whole catch and all the fishing-gear confiscated.

Hammerfest. Street-lights tossing in the wind, swirling snow, candles and a star shining behind the windows – *Jul!* (In less than a month it would be Christmas.) Gunilla, so sure of her power, so innocent: her scent of flowers and of woman mixed, the heavy swag of her hair. Gunilla who so loved laughter . . .

The port watch in the town: the pretty blonde from the canning-factory. A Norwegian boat brought Bongo Ba back at five in the morning, drunk and happy. He was singing the song of the moment: '*J'suis content, j'suis content; j'suis cocu mais content* . . .' The master-at-arms instantly clapped him into the punishment-cell.

The idle crew of the German trawler, almost all Portuguese or Turks. 'Only the decent jobs are held by Germans,' said the fisheries officer. 'Deck, engine-room, bridge. You can't get Germans to work with the fish any more. It's hard and it's filthy, so they take on immigrants. They never see the sea at all! Oh, they're comfortable enough – two to a cabin. And they're paid overtime. If they're seasick they're given a Nautamine suppository. It's all very well organized, in the German fashion . . . soft music coming out of loudspeakers all the time, like in a Volkswagen factory. There you are – that's the sea nowadays. And it'll be the same in France presently, when we've used up our good supply of Bretons, Normans, and Basques . . .' His voice was curiously bitter. 'We've still got genuine seamen. They grumble, but they work hard. They never, never whine about their lot. They don't talk much – iron-headed Bretons, as the Chief says . . . there are still some of them about. How long will they last? Your friend the Drummer-Crab had no difficulty in finding a crew for his *Damoclès*. Yet she's an old-timer, an ancient tub; all the work's done on deck, in all weathers . . . They are real men! You'll see – one of these days we'll come up with him at last, somewhere at the far end of the Barents Sea.'

He brooded for a while, a hard line on his forehead. 'The sea's changing. Everything changes, of course, but . . . I'm not so sure that it's for the better. The day when the sea . . . I mean when what the sea has always stood for . . . that illusion of an immense freedom.' (He laughed shortly, by way of excusing himself for his big words.) 'The day when all that is considered as just something you can deal with by stuffing suppositories up your arse . . . oh, it's too hard to explain. We'd better go and have a drink with the Chief. He'll tell us one of his horrible stories. It will cheer us up.'

The Chief's story was as horrible as anyone could have wished: the bar at Guenn-an-Avel (the Wind Strikes) one stormy, drunken night, the kind of night when men go mad. The beslobbered idiot, laughing and capering for another glass of red wine. The terrible anger of the old Rector coming to look for a choirboy, his black cassock soaked with rain and mud. He beat every man there with his stick and broke the bottles. ('Yet he loved wine, *the fruit of the vine and work of human hands.*') And finally all the drunkards went down on their knees in the wreckage, sniffed their tears away and, between two fits of vomiting, sang a hymn to Our Lady: 'Have pity on us . . .'

My appendicitis was playing cards with the hemiplegic. An eager Turk in pink pyjamas watched the game; he spoke no known language, but at every trick he uttered a flood of excited comments, interspersed with motions towards the heavens. A greyish Lapp slept open-mouthed on a bed, his pixy hat and his knife laid by him on his bedside table.

'Your girl-friend won't let him have any of my milk,' said the appendicitis, pointing his chin at the hemiplegic. 'Try and fix it for us. And him too, our mate here, he'd like a drop. I got him to taste it.' A wink at the beaming Turk. 'Eh, Mémette? Wino, wino, good, good.'

A flood of incomprehensible words from Mémette (the name on his temperature-chart was Méhémeth) in which I thought I caught the word wino several times repeated. Mémette was in favour of the scheme.

The appendicitis drew me towards him and added in a confidential tone, 'He's a curious article, you know. He was a road-sweeper in Hamburg. Then he went on the stage at

Sankt-Pauli: every evening he had to stuff two tarts – every evening. And in front of everybody, too. That's what the show was all about: one at ten 'o'clock, the other at midnight.'

'Disgusting,' growled the hemiplegic.

'Well, anyhow, it's true: two every evening. And three on Saturdays and Sundays. Pretty tarts – he showed me their photos – but even so, he didn't really care for it. He's got a wife in Turkey, and five kids. He was earning good money, but . . . in front of everybody! One evening a French warship came in on a visit, and the sailors turned up for the fun: they laughed all the time and made jokes and kicked up a din. Well, it checked his . . . he couldn't do a thing. That made him fed up with it. And that was how he came to sign on in a German trawler, because he was fed up with sweeping the streets, too.'

'How did you come to learn all that, without his talking a word of French?'

'Oh, we understand one another. Don't we, Mémette?'

Beams from the Turk. It was quite true: they certainly did seem to understand one another.

I had to go right up to the medical superintendent to deal with the problem of the 'sailor's milk', since Gunilla would not take the responsibility. The ward was granted one bottle with each meal.

The purser was seeing to the question of sending the two Frenchmen home, but they would still have to wait some time longer: the Germans had booked all the available seats in the plane for the immigrants. When they did leave the hospital at last, the aged greyish Lapp burst into tears. Three days later he died.

This time the Captain did not attend the fisheries officer's cocktail-party. The launch went to fetch our guests at the fishermen's quay. The wind had fallen, and the night had that unbelievable clarity which is only to be seen in the

177

high latitudes. Faint wafts of vapour wandered over the surface of the black water, as evanescent as a sigh. The lament of a blues reached us from the Grand Hotel's discotheque, travelling through the frozen air.

'. . . to let my people go . . .'

All sails set, Gunilla, 'as beautiful as a French corvette', laughed loud, and the ring of white cliffs sent back her laughter, echoing on and on.

North Cape. The East Bank.

The ice-barrier had come down as low as Bear Island. The cold. The frozen sea, crackling under the cutwater – the sound of steel chilled in water. The starry night, enough to catch your heart. The *Eole*'s warm, fragrant, comforting bowels.

'Brandy, Doctor?'

Time passed by. The radar-beam swept the screen. As life goes on so it grows harder, colder, more exigent.

The Skolpen Bank. The *Belle Normande* had lost a man overboard. I went across with the fisheries officer: expressionless faces, set looks, silences. 'He went over without a word . . . We could still see him; he wasn't moving any more . . . He looked at me; I saw his eyes wide open and he looked at me . . . No relatives that I know of . . . from the Public Assistance . . . I think he had worked on a farm before . . .'

The lost man remained an enigma, a man with an almost empty past; a shadow, and everything about him had been fleeting. He was already forgotten and it did not matter. He had laid out his modest possessions with the utmost tidiness, as if he had arranged them before setting off on a long journey.

The slump in fish: a vague anxiety in the hearts of these forgetful men. 'What will become of us?'

The grinding of the winch. The fishermen staggered on the

icy deck. The heavy net swung and shot its gleaming fish down the hatchway.

Time passed by. We sailed on, guided by an echo continually jammed by atmospherics. The North Bank, and a falling glass. I amputated a finger crushed by the heavy shackle of a trawl.

The Captain asked me to give him an injection of morphine.

He was lying on his bunk. His cheeks and lips were the same ashen grey and his nostrils were drawn towards the corners of his mouth. He had cut himself three times while shaving and the clotted blood was black. It seemed to me that his features had an even greater nobility; that terrible beauty which comes from suffering alone.

'Don't look at me like that.'

In spite of his calm – the calm assumed by a man in the grip of a violent convulsion who nevertheless means to keep his dignity – I could follow the sequence of the spasms by his eyes: and by the sweat that oozed from his pores. As soon as the drug began to act I said firmly, 'It's all over, sir.'

He did not misunderstand the meaning of my words. He looked at something far away beyond me and the ghost of a smile quivered on his grey lips. 'Don't put me ashore at Hammerfest.'

'I ought to . . . I should have done so . . . long ago.'

I looked at him. I knew he was going to talk me over and gain more time, because I was very fond of the old skeleton, the old crab three-quarters dead. And then once again, as usual, he took me by surprise. 'In fifteen days – in fourteen, more precisely – we shall be heading south. We'll have the sun again . . .' He waved his claw vaguely, a gesture that might have meant 'We'll see. Insh' Allah.'

The waves of pain that had been so evident in his eyes only some moments before had almost disappeared, and my gaze no longer irritated him. Suddenly, in a brusque voice, he added, 'Don't look so glum, Doctor . . . you're only the messenger.'

As I left I paid him back in his own coin. 'It will be a very great inconvenience to me, if you die on board.'

I heard him laugh as I closed the door.

The wind was getting up.

The wind's piercing lamentation, like the cry of the mourners at an Asian funeral.

The swell was getting up, gleaming under the light of distant worlds.

The deck ghastly in the moonlight. I felt some knot come free inside me. I was carried away by one of those emotions that sometimes come after a battle when death has been very close: the feeling that my two brains were wholly in tune and that they were dreaming of great things together, side by side. And at the same time, very deep down, like an unmoving pool, this certainty: I was alive.

Life!

And it rose up in me. It was dazzling: I was alive, I was living! Everything was clear, everything was obvious. It was a hymn to the joys of the flesh and the spirit. It was a glowing truth that soared high above the gloomy reality of the human state, harsher than this frozen sea with the gale blowing over it. That soared . . .

and that burst like a bubble, suddenly, for no reason.

I was living! So what?

At this the cosmic sadness that is man's lot gripped my heart again; I felt that I must have a drink, smoke a cigarette, take shelter in the warm bowels.

The Mongol was there, deep in his armchair. 'Don't look at me like that,' I said.

He chuckled and said in a pompous, moralizing tone, 'Life is sweet for those who know nothing of the terror of height, either because they are free from care or because they lack imagination . . . Let's have a drink, Doctor:

alcohol will restore a clearer view of things.'

'Yes, Chief, a clearer view . . . and filthy dreams.'

The *Damoclès* was sailing west at ten knots. We were heading east. In eight hours' time we should meet somewhere on the longitude of Archangel. The barometer was still dropping. *Wind force 9, snow-squalls. Sea rough becoming very rough.* Beyond the glass screens nothing could be seen at all – pure black violence, absolutely invisible. The lookouts had taken shelter.

Twenty-five miles away, the echo of the *Damoclès* on the radar-screen, distorted by the snow-squalls and the ice. Another smaller echo some way off.

'The Russian patrol,' said the fisheries officer. 'They don't trust foreign trawlers. Some of theirs are spy-ships stuffed with electronic gear, so they think others do the same.'

The Russian patrol-ship had several very powerful radars. In the radio-room you could almost feel them listening to us, probing and searching, trying to get a clear idea of our strength and our purpose. Sinusoidal curves appeared and vanished on the fluorescent indicators. Shrill crackling and whistles could be heard whenever a burst of waves struck us.

'A Rostov-class corvette,' said the radio-officer, taking off his earphones. 'She must have made us out already. They've improved their gadgets since last year.' And he added some technical remarks that were right over my head.

The lights of the *Damoclès* in the distance, lights that sometimes vanished in the snow-squalls and that seemed to wink, signalling like Bongo Ba's little torch in the dinghy. (The Russian could be seen only on the radar-screen.) The fisheries officer was talking on the VHF. I recognized Willsdorff's voice. He was discussing the movements to be carried out for the launching of the postal buoy. Willsdorff then asked if the *Eole*'s canteen could let him have four hundred and fifty litres of wine: 'I'd like to stay here till Christmas and I'm rather short. The crew won't function unless they have their wine. A litre and a half a day a man – it's in the signing-on contract.'

The fisheries officer glanced at the Captain sitting there in his armchair: the Captain nodded. (I had given him an injection two hours earlier.) 'All right; I'll fix it. I'm going to pass you someone who wants to speak to you.'

He handed me the microphone. 'Hallo . . . hallo . . .' I wanted to say How are things, Drummer-Crab? but I did not like to; it would have sounded absurd, and in any case my own voice in the loudspeaker embarrassed me. 'It's Pierre . . .'

'Who? Pierre . . . Pierre?'

He had not recognized me. Of course not: how could he have recognized me? Twenty years!

It was seven o'clock. The bugler wiped his mouthpiece for the last time before sounding the reveille. 'Hold on, hold on a second; don't cut off,' I said. And I held out the microphone towards the bugler . . .

I heard Willsdorff's laugh. 'Pierre, dear old Pierre. What are you doing in these parts?'

'I'm the *Eole*'s surgeon . . . how are things?' I no longer knew what to say. I loathe speaking into a telephone or a mike; I have to see the person I am talking to. And what could I say? What can one say?

'So in the end you came back. I feel you're rather neglecting our little Vietnamians, eh? It's now they need a doctor, if the news is to be believed.'

'Yes. I was expelled . . . at the beginning of the year.'

'And what about Maï Li. You brought her back? How . . .'

I interrupted him. 'She's dead.'

'Oh . . . my poor old Pierre . . . We'll be seeing one another soon, Pierre, I must . . . Give me the fisheries officer.'

The *Damoclès* was close at hand. She switched on her powerful working lights and all at once the storm became visible. Sometimes she put her stern down and the whole forward part of the trawler seemed to rise from the sea – close on a third of her keel could be seen – and then she came slowly over and dived into the gleaming abyss, like a whale sounding. As her bows struck, the waves burst in a prodigious spray – a spray swept aft by the wind, veiling her entirely . . . She reappeared, streaming with water, all her lights ablaze. She was beautiful: a high forecastle, a low deck very near the waterline, set off from the little poop, with a derrick and the trawl-gallows, the superstructure right aft, with the funnel, a deckhouse and the other gallows – rather the shape of a tanker. She was beautiful: less stocky than a stern-gater, but with finer lines.

She reduced speed. Men in yellow oilskins came hurrying out on deck. We manœuvred to lie on her leeward bow so as to let go the buoy – the quartermaster had had a dozen plastic drums of wine made fast to it.

We worked closer. I could see someone out on her wing: he was waving his arms at us. Through the shrieking of the gale I heard a cry, 'Pierre ahoy!' The man vanished and immediately afterwards three blasts from the *Damoclès*'s siren overcame the fury of the wind.

We worked closer still; I could see the eye on her bows. The waves covered it from time to time and it seemed to me to be winking in a friendly manner.

'Let go the buoy . . . go . . . uoy . . . uoy . . .'

Willsdorff's cheerful voice on the radio. 'There you are; we've picked it up. Thank you, gentlemen, and a happy voyage to you . . . Pierre, hallo Pierre. I'm so glad to know you're here.'

The Captain rose from his chair. He took the microphone from the fisheries officer: I could not make out his face in the darkness, only a vague red reflection in his eyes. He turned his back to us and leant against the screen.

'Goodbye, Captain.'

He switched over and we could hear the loudspeaker

crackling: Willsdorff took a long while to reply. 'It's you, sir.' (I thought his voice sounded muffled, like that of another man.) 'I rather expected you . . . I was wondering whether you . . .' He did not finish his sentence.

The Captain switched over again. 'I just wanted to say goodbye before leaving . . . for good. That's all. I have nothing else to say.'

Once more the crackling of the radio-waves and a silence, a silence that lasted. The Captain did not stir. All I could see was his back and his rigid neck. Willsdorff's voice at last: 'I knew you were sick. I . . . no. You're right; there's nothing to say.'

A click: Willsdorff had cut off. The crackling of the empty ether, like a swell breaking on a distant beach. The Captain gave the microphone back to the fisheries officer. 'We are going home, gentlemen. '

A lookout burst in. 'Sir, they are signalling to us with the blinker.'

The *Damoclès* had put out her working-flares. All that could be seen in the darkness was her navigation-lights and a little beam that flashed off and on.

'G-O-O-D-B-Y-E,' spelt out the old gnome-faced boat-swain. 'G-O-O . . . goodbye: sir, he keeps repeating the same word, goodbye.'

'What is to be the reply, sir?' asked the fisheries officer.

'Signal *message received*: that's all.'

There: it was over.

The little winking beam went out. The *Damoclès* went about and we headed westwards. It was horribly cold on that bridge.

PART TWO

THE WINE

Give strong drink unto him that is ready to perish,
and wine unto those that be of heavy hearts.
Let him drink, and forget his poverty,
and remember his misery no more.

Proverbs XXXI, 6–7.

CHAPTER 19

————◆————

The Flesh

At 11.30 hours on Sunday, 18 December, with the Lofoten Islands on the beam, we saw the sun once more.

Towards the end of the afternoon I knocked at the Captain's door.

'Come in.' He was standing there, very straight, terribly thin in his severe uniform, his left hand resting on his desk. As usual, he had cut himself while shaving and the black blood made his wrinkles seem deeper still; his grey face had the look of the Sphinx, scraped and scoured by sandstorms. (I went to see the Sphinx in 1946, by moonlight – an enormous death's-head – when the *Pasteur* was in the canal: then I rejoined my friends in a squalid Cairo joint where fat women were doing the belly-dance.)

'I was expecting you.' His worn eyes challenged mine. He should have been sitting down: I knew the effort it needed for him to stand. He was in pain, but he let nothing show.

The silence became embarrassing: I could find nothing better to break it than the observation, 'The sun is setting, sir.'

He nodded. The *Eole* groaned, quivered, and suddenly lay over. It was hard for the Captain to keep upright; his living hand tightened on the corner of the desk.

'I think you can rest now,' I said gently. 'You've done what you wanted to do.'

'What have I done?' he asked in a cold, even voice.

'You've . . . you know perfectly well what I mean –

Willsdorff! You could confront him, confront him for this very last time, as upright as ever you were at the court-martial. You're full of pride. I almost believe you asked for the *Eole* just for that.'

His eyelids flickered: the gaze of his deep, cold eyes seemed to me strikingly remote. There were little drops of sweat on his upper lip and temples; they shone on the grey skin. He made no reply.

The distant rumble of the storm . . . The ticking of the chronometer in its mahogany box could just be heard: it was like the living, metallic gnawing of the white ants when you come close to certain dead trees in the jungle. Every second the hand jerked forward.

'*Omnes vulnerant, ultima necat,*'[1] said the Captain at last, with a musing irony. 'And that goes for you too, Doctor, ha, ha!'

His harsh, sad laugh was cut off suddenly by a spasm of pain; he needed an injection, but I knew he would not ask for it.

'Lie down, sir, and roll up your sleeve.'

'Thank you, Doctor.'

The drug had its effect; he relaxed and closed his eyes. I switched off the bedside light.

The trembling of the ship, the hiss of the sea, the chronometer's tick . . . inexorably the seconds-hand moved on in little jerks. It was 16.47 hours and 12 seconds . . . 13 seconds . . . 14.

As I was about to leave, his voice came out of the shadows, calmer, assuaged: 'I'll take this ship back to Lorient, Doctor.'

I went up on the bridge. Night was falling over the North Sea. The last yellow gleams – that special yellow one only seen at the end of a stormy day. The huge grim voice was howling. The helm clattered to and fro. The east was black, and the darkness swept on, covering the sky – the

[1] They all of them wound; the last kills.

darkness of the Crucifixion. And the huge voice grew louder still . . .

The propeller span (140 turns a minute, rather more than two a second). The earth revolved. Day was dawning on the river far over there, rising on the sentries deep in their holes, on the armies drawn up for battle. On my lost forest . . . Day was rising on Saigon; and on anxious, uneasy Phnom Penh . . . Night was falling on the North Sea.

Night fell; I did not bend to pick it up, said Alphonse Allais.

Night had fallen. A lookout was humming . . . Now it would be full daylight on the river, on the dead sentries and on those who were still alive, sheltering in their holes.

The Captain came out of the chart-room, sniffed the wind out on the wing, glanced at the compass (course 215), at the motometer (140 ahead, 12 knots), the radar-screen (echo on 172, 8 miles), the wind-gauge (55 knots, gusts of 60), at the chart under the red lamp and at the last cross marked on it by the officer of the watch; then he leant his forehead against the glass, both his elbows on the brass rail.

'Good evening, sir,' said the gnome-faced boatswain.

'Good evening.'

'It's over a glass of wine, red wine, that men come together in the evening, far, far from their wives, to laugh, tell stories, boast, to incite, warm and comfort one another . . . and to knock one another about – that's a great relief at times.' The Chief was expatiating on one of his favourite themes. 'As our old Rector used to say, "Maybe Peter's boast during the Last Supper – *Although all shall be offended, yet will not I* – was caused by the *gwin ru*." Being a fisherman, Peter loved red wine. And at the time he certainly believed what he was saying, poor Peter. Then after all he was the one who waved his sword and cut a fellow's ear off at the moment of the taking: to be sure, he had slept for a while on the hill instead of praying with Jesus when He was suffering, but there again, that was the effect of the wine! But then, do you see, there's always the morning after. The morning after is very rough on your drinker. He's weaker, more paltry than a little child. In the morning you hear the cock crow, and it's too late . . . Maybe Judas had had a drop too much as well. He could have dragged around the bars – he was the one who looked after the money of the Twelve. A drunkard's boast – "For thirty quid I'll undertake to give Him up to you." And the next day Judas hanged himself. Ha, ha, ha! What's the good of lying to yourself, if you're like that and can't be otherwise?'

'You always exaggerate,' said the sub-lieutenant. 'Not all men are drunkards.'

The Chief merely shrugged.

Later that night he showed me a game he had learnt from the American sailors in Barbados. A deeply stupid game. You had to cheat and lose to begin with if you wanted to win, or even to walk away on your own feet. A game of draughts, played on a squared cloth, with each piece representing a glass of whisky. ('In Barbados it was rum.') I did not cheat. I was winning, winning . . . I was the champion, the cleverest of them all . . . let the best man win!

The next morning my head ached, and I had a vague recollection of having lost the game into the bargain.

The sight of dawn had rejoiced my heart: but now I had the impression that green mould was gathering on the look-outs' faces, on the grey steel, on the clouds, and on the sea, lashed by a bitter wind; in my heart there was nothing but bitterness, and my mouth tasted as though I had been chewing ashes.

Amsterdam. A courtesy visit before proceeding to Lorient.

The pilot was waiting for us three miles off the great sluice. A grey dawn, the mingling of the land and sky, a drizzle that did not fall but that penetrated everything – all this was reminiscent of the Red River delta during the north-east monsoon. Below us, on the far side of the canal dykes, the flat country drifted past, drowned in melancholy: meadows, trees, little brick houses, blackened factory chimneys, long lines of cars on the roads, suburban trains. A little boy wrapped in a cloak with a cape sat on a milestone and watched us go by, sucking his thumb.

The Captain was in his chair, as grey and as sad as the landscape.

The first buildings of the town: depots, factories, cranes, shipyards, hulls of ships streaked with red lead – the bluish incandescence of the welders' torches – rows of identical dwellings, and beyond, hazy in the smoke and rain, the spires of Amsterdam.

That evening there was a reception at the Admiralty. There I met an elderly, grey-haired Dutch commodore and his Javanese wife from Surabaya; she was beautiful, with the profile of a Maya statue and a faultless amber-coloured face. And of course we talked about 'over there' – Djakarta, which the old commodore still called Batavia, just as I sometimes say Tourane instead of Danang. Tandjungpriok, the shipping district . . . One evening I saw more than three hundred Sulawesi schooners there, drawn up on the mud of the canals, looking like an eighteenth-century Dutch sea-piece and waiting for the monsoon to change in order to put to sea. The twilight was full of the smell of cloves, iodine, seaweed, and fish. The food-pedlars coming down from the town clashed their bamboos to attract custom. You could hear the laughter and the songs of the seamen as they sat round their fires. Voices said, *'We have fed the sea with our blood these thousands and thousands of years and yet she calls us still, still hungry . . .'* And there were others telling of storms, battles, pirates, islands, sharks, and pearls . . .

All remained dark until the rising of the moon.

In 1945 the commodore had taken part in the Allied reconquest of Borneo. 'The English had a maniac in those parts,' he told me, 'a red-headed Irishman. He gave us a

191

great deal of trouble . . . We had to buy him from the Dayaks; I believe the price was his own weight in salt. And then there was a Japanese colonel who was hanged later as a war-criminal. Between them they controlled the inland tribes. Madmen! I saw him once, the Irishman, and he didn't look anything so very extraordinary . . . except for his eyes. The English had shaved his head. They put him aboard a Liberty ship, and then . . .'

'I spent a night in prison because of him,' I said, interrupting. And I told him about my first call at Colombo in the *Pasteur*.

'Much later, towards the end of the 'sixties, I went to the Irishman's . . . kingdom. I travelled up the high Tunkalis and the Sembakung. In those days you could still find Japanese soldiers' heads hanging from the beams of the long-houses, covered with cobwebs. In the evening, when they were drinking ayak – an indifferent rice-wine – the drunken old sages would show them, laughing; and they would tell the legend of the Red Rajah, mingled with great epic poems from the *Time of the Adventures*. I found it very hard to separate fact from fiction; but one thing was certain – that man "with sea-grey eyes" had filled all the forest people with dreams . . .'

When I had managed to be put on half-pay – that was after my last meeting with Willsdorff in Haiphong – I lived with Maï Li, a young woman from Hué. I did not marry her, because of . . . I don't know . . . because of habit, because it did not seem to me necessary (to preserve the illusion of freedom?). I think it was the only thing she really wanted; and I did not give it to her – out of stupidity. I worked in clinics at Phnom Penh and Saigon; I felt free; I was waiting. A friend of mine, once an NCO in the expeditionary force, had a little tea-plantation on the Djiring road in the highland plateaux. He was a wonderful man: he had made friends with the neighbouring mountain people, the Maa,

192

a little-known tribe that refused almost all contact with the rest of the world. He had managed to win their esteem and their affection. He was always asking me to join him and settle down at his plantation. One evening, when my mind was full of the high country, the Hundred Thousand Hills and my astonishment at seeing them, I agreed. It was through him that I discovered the mountain people – their language, their ways, their legends. He took me with him, and together we made our way up the furious mountain streams to spend the night in villages where no white man had ever been, villages where we listened to interminable discussions and watched the sacrifice of buffaloes . . . With his help I wrote some articles on these subjects for the local papers. An ethnologist belonging to the School for Far Eastern Studies read them; he came to the plantation and showed us how to carry out a serious course of observation.

The origin of these proto-Malay mountain tribes is still an enigma, but it is known that the Indo-Chinese peninsula was traversed by the people who now live in Oceania. A single ethnic group inhabits the archipelagoes scattered over the widest expanse of ocean that the world contains, an expanse stretching from the shores of the China Sea to those of the Bay of Bengal and from Madagascar to Easter Island. Our ethnologist had his own theory about all this: according to him the American Indians belonged to the same stock, and they peopled their continent from the north, crossing the Bering Strait to Alaska. Later certain groups drifted over to Polynesia (*Kon Tiki*) and then pressed still farther west, thus coming back to where they had started from. I think he was slightly cracked, but he convinced us and he filled us with dreams. We would listen to him in the evenings as we sat on the verandah, drinking wine. (Sometimes the trumpeting of a wild elephant cut him short and we would have to wave torches towards the forest to protect our tea.) He had adopted Claude Lévi-Strauss's idea: 'We do not know what a race is; we do know what a culture is.' He said that a common cultural basis should be found in the myths and legends of all these scattered peoples, and that that basis should be the sea, even among those who lived deep in the forest far inland. Gradually arose the notion of a vast undertaking – a thesis, a broad study on the theme of the sea in the civilization of the forest dwellers. The ethnologist was to see to the assembling of the material, and he would set off for America and Polynesia. My friend would carry his researches into his own tribe even further – it was to serve as a point of reference. And for my part I was to go and see the Dayaks in Borneo, the Toradjas in the Celebes, the Bataks in Sumatra, the Sakai . . . ending up with the Nagas of Assam. (I did in fact find legends of the sea in all these places.) But then the war began again and every day it came nearer and nearer . . .

At present there is nothing whatsoever left of all that. The cracked ethnologist is dead, killed in a plane crash. My friend was seen for the last time in 1968, being taken away by Vietcong guerrillas: he was never heard of again. The Maï Li whom I did not marry – Maï Li is dead, murdered at Phnom Penh. A paper was left on her body: 'The Frenchman's whore'. Our notes and the chapters we had already written were burnt together with the plantation. Our Maa tribe, which dreamed of the sea without ever having seen it, no longer exists: some dazed women and children still survive, kept like animals in a reclassification centre; the men who did not die as coolies on the Ho Chi Minh trail are auxiliaries in the South Vietnamese army. Even the solitary elephant is dead, poisoned by defoliants. There is no civilization of the Indo-Chinese forest-peoples. It is at an end.

'The sea is changing . . . Everything changes, of course, but . . . I'm not so sure that it's for the better,' said the fisheries officer. Ha, ha! Innocent!

That same night the engineer and the young sub-lieutenant lured me into the red-light district. The uneven cobbles

194

gleamed under the street-lights and the revolving red neon signs. Sudden gusts of wind ruffled the black water of the canals and the puddles in the street. It was raining – a drizzle that swept over everything, but the *Eole*'s sailors, starved from months at sea, paid no attention: they prowled, filled with murky hope, sometimes alone, sometimes in little groups that gathered in front of the bawdy-house windows, elbowing the crowd, uttering nonsense that made them laugh, doing their best to look blasé. Their red pompons and their broad white collars added an astonishing note of youth and cheerfulness to the glum, dubious movement of the crowd.

The half-open doors of bars let out wafts of a drab, pathetic music that perfectly matched the atmosphere of these joyless streets. The glaring lights of the pornography shops lit tense faces; anxious eyes stared at the pictures of copulation. I had the feeling that I could actually see the uneasiness of men under the thrust of desire, the thirst for sensation raging in them – a thirst they were aware of sharing with animals on heat. (Another of our old limbic cortex's tricks!)

We let ourselves drift along on this wretched quest; we too stared at the women in their windows, all smiling the same dead, fixed smile that might have been painted on their mouths. We lost count of time; we wandered on and on, and perhaps deep down we had an unsophisticated, morbid desire to discover something horrible and unknown.

Thirst and the rain drove us into a bar. It was dark and warm in there, with a smell of drink, wet dog, and women. A black girl's splendidly feverish song heightened the silent expectation of the men drinking there, all facing a curtain lit up by two projectors – they were waiting for the women. All their eyes glowed in the dark, like those of animals in rut.

When the black singer had finished there was an almost painful silence. Then another record was put on and the customers uttered a growl of frustration. This collective desire, this kind of carnal fermentation, invaded us. Our eyes glowed too. We drank a great deal and it was as though nothing could be strong enough to cope with our nervous tension. Silence once more, a silence like a blow in the chest.

A drum-roll. The curtains parted to show an empty stage. The eyes of the audience grew desperate.

Another record: syncopated music, very slow. Then the women!

There were two of them. The first, young and graceful, hardly made up at all, with smooth fair hair, looked almost virginal. The second was larger and heavier, more vulgar; and she wore the placid smile of the whores in the windows. They danced together, each undressing, stroking and caressing the other. The glowing eyes followed their movements in a kind of heavy dazed stupidity.

Now they were naked. Their caresses grew more explicit. The young innocent-looking blonde was the more depraved, the more convincing; she uttered little cries and gasps and a blue flame showed in her pale eyes. Then two naked men came up on to the stage.

'Oh my God!' The Chief stood up and grasped the sub-lieutenant. 'Come on. Let's go.'

A band of sailors from the *Eole* made facetious remarks and suggestive noises. The two male performers seemed to be having some difficulty in carrying out their turn (like Mémette the Turk). The manager, who up until then had been standing behind the bar with the look of a sentry guarding a powder-magazine, rushed in, shouting in a kind of lingua-franca 'Shut up . . . Nix gut . . . Zilence . . . Pas pon . . . Nix lachen . . .' together with all the obscenities the Dutch language can encompass.

Outside it was still raining. The neon lights of the bars spread their red reflections on the wet pavement, and through these reflections the throng continued its sterile wandering. The Chief turned his face to the sky and breathed deeply. 'Forgive me,' he said, 'but . . . God above!'

He set off with long strides, his legs straddling wide. He was drunk, and he reminded me of Babourg running in the night.

We went back to the ship. As we reached the top of the gangway he said, 'I wish we had already sailed.'

The *Eole* did not sail until the next evening.

That afternoon, invited by the curator, I went to the Rijksmuseum with the Captain. At one point I followed his gaze. He had stopped in front of a Rembrandt self-portrait, full of strange shadows. He was leaning forward, motionless. Was he trying to understand the mystery of the rediscovered light and darkness?

And all at once I saw those faces again, those unknown faces craning towards the lit-up windows of the night before, the anxious eyes, the eyes gleaming in the bar . . . And I recognized the same despairing light in the Captain's eyes.

And I recognized it in Rembrandt's eyes, the eyes painted by Rembrandt himself.

CHAPTER 20

—◆—

Fear

Small white clouds in a pale sky. The grey cliffs of Dover. The jade-coloured sea. The *Eole*, making eighteen knots, was running up a long line of cargo merchant-ships bound for the Atlantic, the Indian Ocean, the Pacific ... In a week's time some of them would see the Southern Cross over the rim of the horizon. They were outward-bound and we were going home.

Each of us has his own private fear, his unconquerable, insuperable fear: for some it is the fear of death or of suffering, for others that of hunger and poverty. I was afraid of going home.

We were going home.

I leant on the rail of the starboard wing, watching the cliffs fade in the distance, and I felt a tension rising in me, a completely irrational uneasiness, accompanied by an oppressive sensation of guilt.

'*It's blowing!*

It's the sea-wind harrying us.'

Our old Captain was going home, too: and for good. He was fighting his last rearguard action. I went to see him in his cabin twice a day. He was in pain, but he never showed it. Except once: 'The beast within is still there,' he said with a smile that was more like a rictus, 'I feel the jerks.' He was grey and bloodless, always perfectly shaved (with black clotted blood showing the nicks). We talked. 'Are you afraid?' I asked.

He hesitated for a long while and I thought he did not intend to reply. 'No,' he said suddenly. 'No. Frankly it is not that . . . It's very ugly and it's going to be uglier still . . . Very ugly . . . And there's nothing to say. Absolutely nothing to be said . . . Nothing!'

He had his Bible beside him. 'Does that help you?' I asked, looking at it.

'No.'

'Then why do you read it?'

'I can't read anything else . . . My other books . . . don't interest me any more. You are too inquisitive, Doctor. There's nothing to say . . . It's a strictly private affair.'

He looked away and stared at the ceiling. (I thought of that night in Amsterdam and of Rembrandt's painted gaze.) 'I'm tired,' he said, to get rid of me.

Once I knew I was going to die, that I was going to be killed. It was the last year at the plantation, before it was burnt, and there had been fighting. In the darkness soldiers dressed all in black came to take me and they found two old American M1 rifles that we had kept for hunting. The soldiers grew very excited; they dragged me into the forest and searched me. In one of my pockets they found a notebook that was totally incomprehensible to them (the notes were written in a phonetic script invented by my NCO friend before we met the ethnologist, and it was designed to set down all the shades of pronunciation in the mountain-people's language). They thought it was a secret code and they became even more excited. They hit me with their rifle-butts and made me take off my clothes. I was naked; and I remember that I did not know what to do with my hands – protect my belly and at the same time call attention to it, or just let my arms hang, with no protection? Time seemed to have stopped. I was in a state of disconnection: the well-known phenomenon of double awareness – both a detached, mildly curious observer and at the same time a wild animal crouching in its hole, scarcely feeling blows: it is as though the mind dissociated itself from the body. I could feel my death coming, just as I could feel the black soldiers behind me, close behind me: the nape of my neck prickled. I hoped I might be killed from in front, because before dying I wanted to make some gesture, shout something. My mind searched frantically and found nothing to shout. Nothing! Well, yes: it did come up with the word *Shit*!

There were shots in the distance: explosions. An order, and the torches were stamped out. Someone came close up behind me and I could feel his hot breath on the back of my neck. He was smoking. He drew in a last pull, handed me the fag-end, wet with his saliva, and vanished. I was alone. I was naked but alive. I felt very tired. No cigarette ever gave me so much pleasure.

I had thought I was dealing with Death: in fact I was only dealing with men like myself, men of flesh and blood. It had all been very sudden and I think it had taken scarcely any time – like a car-accident avoided at the very last moment.

The Captain, for his part, really was dealing with Death. It was coming nearer calmly, step by step. There were no soldiers in black, no flaring torches or gleaming weapons. No blows from a rifle-butt, no furious glaring eyes, no shouting. There was not even the feeling of injustice . . . Death comes nearer calmly, step by step. The sun rises in the east. The sun sets in the west. Time passes. Death comes closer.

The bugle-call: *Action-stations! Action-stations!*

My station was the sick-bay, but I decided to go up on to the bridge. To train the crew, we had already had several alerts in the North Sea – the *Eole* was after all a warship – and each time the second-in-command had called the officers together to discuss the theme of the exercise: this evening it was unheralded; nothing had been decided in advance.

There was a slight mist. The sun hung very low over the water, like a vast blood-red disc. Not much swell. The *Eole* had increased speed to twenty-two knots and the rush of air was intensely exciting. Sometimes her bows scooped up a hatful of spray and it came whistling aft, so that the lookouts ducked behind the rail. The gunners raced along the deck and vanished into the turrets.

Detached voices in the loudspeaker:

'Radio command-post: all clear.'

'Right,' answered the officer of the watch.

'Gunnery command-post: all clear.'

'Right.'

Our old Captain was sitting in his chair, mute, grey, dead. I joined the fisheries officer on the starboard wing. 'Look at her,' he said. 'The dirty swine.'

A huge patch of oil, or more exactly a river of heavy oil three hundred yards wide: we were running along beside it at full speed.

'We came across it a mile back. And the dirty swine is still a good ten ahead of us.'

'Eight, sir,' said the boatswain. 'Sixteen knots. She's a big one, round about eighty thousand ton.'

'Right. It won't be long before we see her.'

'Is she damaged?' I asked.

The fisheries officer looked at me and laughed. 'She's pumping out, cleaning her tanks. It's forbidden at sea . . . but it saves money. We're going to get a sight of her. Report her. It won't be any use – she's sure to be under a flag of convenience. The Old Man wants us to put the wind up her.'

The Captain sent for the photographer on to the bridge. He was also in charge of entertainments, a somewhat anti-militarist, somewhat far-left-wing young man, the one who had taught Bongo Ba to read. He came without hurrying himself, looking rather offhand; but like many of the young men of his generation he was deeply concerned about ecology and as soon as he saw the oil-slick his attitude changed. ('They won me over, the monsters,' he said later, in his peculiar jargon.)

'*Sea Corona*, Panama,' called a lookout, putting down his binoculars.

We were in the tanker's wake, and she stood out sharply against the hazy sunset. The sea was clean again: on seeing us she had stopped pumping.

'Is there enough light to photograph her?'

'It's touch and go: I shouldn't like to make a botch of it: the dirty swine.'

'Switch on the searchlight.'

The white beam wavered, searched here and there, and settled on the tanker's stern. Her name and home port were now clearly visible. The foam churned up by her screw seemed phosphorescent. She was a very big tanker in ballast: we must have looked like a little grey mouse coming towards a big black tomcat.

'Captain, from radio-control.'

'Yes.'

'She's taking care not to answer us.'

'Right.'

The photographer was very excited. 'It's beautiful: the sun right along the line – a magnificent picture.'

The fisheries officer laughed. 'No aesthetic emotion. What we want is her name.'

'It'll be none the worse for being beautiful,' retorted the photographer.

'True enough. Why not?'

Suddenly the Captain stood up and leant against the screen. 'I take over,' he said to the officer of the watch. 'Full speed ahead: starboard fifteen.'

The old gnome instantly repeated in a voice of thunder, 'FULL SPEED AHEAD: STARBOARD FIFTEEN.'

'Take care, sir,' murmured the anxious fisheries officer. 'We are too close already. They'll send in a complaint.'

The Captain laughed bitterly. 'Where I'm going, no complaints will be forwarded . . . And I am the only officer responsible.'

For half an hour the *Eole* put on a splendid ballet performance in the twilight. At twenty-eight knots the spray flew high, taking on the redness of the sky. Our guns turned in every direction. A fantasia!

'Have the bugle sounded when we're to windward of her.'

And the officer of the watch had the bugle sounded. And the bugle sounded, sounded, with its pure, resonant, human voice. And the notes tore the darkening red sky. And all the lookouts stood motionless, like wooden figures.

Unperturbed, the tanker sailed straight on. Vast and black. A man appeared on the wing of her bridge and shook his fist at us several times.

'Captain, from radio-control.'

'Yes?' said the fisheries officer, after a moment's hesitation and a glance at our old Captain leaning motionless against his screen.

'She's screeching on all her wavelengths, even the distress frequencies, "A non-identified torpedo-boat is approaching us dangerously close in international waters. Guns are being pointed at us . . . Unjustifiable breach of the freedom of the seas . . . risk of collision . . ." And a good deal more. He's all worked up.'

'Very good.'

The Captain took a last look at the tanker. 'It's all over: we'll go home. Take over.' He returned to his chair, staggering a little. He closed his eyes. His face had that same translucent shade, grey and at the same time beige, that I had seen in Willsdorff and Mad-Head when they were let out of their Vietnamese camp.

'Doctor, come to my cabin with me, if you please.'

I helped him below. He was so thin that I could feel his more projecting bones in spite of the thickness of his pea-jacket.

'He won't make any complaint,' he said when he reached the cabin. 'You heard – non-identified torpedo-boat . . .

And what about our ensign, and our number! Those are the sort of people I hate ... an anonymous letter-box in Panama. Profit, profit . . . and when we're gone the world can go to hell. He'll start up again tonight, when we are far away.'

I gave him an injection. He looked at me and nodded. 'It's all over, Doctor. All over.'

Against all the rules the Captain handed over command of the *Eole* to the fisheries officer. 'I'll do all I can so that you may keep her for the Newfoundland cruise,' he told him. He also had kind words for the second-in-command.

We were going home.

My anxiety-neurosis, that kind of dread deep in my old cortex, grew so intense that I took refuge in the wardroom. I drank a bottle of wine with my friend the engineer and for the time being I recovered an artificial peace of mind.

'Why don't you come and spend your leave with me at Guenn-an-Avel, Doctor?'

The news:

Paris: Because of the economic crisis there are said to be already more than seven hundred thousand unemployed in France, and the situation is expected to worsen in the coming months.

Port Moresby (New Guinea): Papuan warriors belonging to two rival tribes have had a day-long battle, using axes, spears and arrows to wipe out an old debt of honour in blood. Five warriors were killed and hundreds of coffee-plants uprooted.

I could not sleep, so I went back to the bridge. In the west the sea and the sky were an inky black, dotted with the navigation-lights of the ships on the tramline. A huge moon was shining in the east, very low on the horizon. The sea was calm: almost no wind at all.

Someone climbed up on the wing by the outside ladder. 'Good evening . . . Captain,' said the lookout, after a slight hesitation.

'Good evening, Le Gall,' replied the fisheries officer. He glanced absently at the radar and leant against the screen, his forearms on the brass rail.

I went and stood next to our new commander. 'Pleasant weather for our return, don't you think, Doctor?' he said. And after a long silence he added more quietly, 'Do you think he did it because of him?'

'What do you mean?'

'The bugle – do you think it was because of . . . of your friend? The story you told us the first night: the charge on the river.'

'What do you think yourself?' I asked.

He did not answer but stared at the moon: it rose and fell gently in the doorway, keeping time with our easy roll. 'I've a friend who passed out with me,' he said suddenly, 'and he flies a Crusader in the *Foch*, the aircraft-carrier – he chose the fleet air arm. He told me once that . . . some nights, when he was on free-flight, he'd switch on his post-combustion and head for the moon . . . Mach 2.2. Straight at the moon!' He paused for a moment and went on, 'It seemed to him that it grew larger in his sights . . . Of course it comes to an end when you reach your ceiling – forty or fifty thousand feet, or something like that. He'd go back when he'd used up all his fuel.'

'Dien Cai Dau: Mad-Head,' I observed.

'Yes, that's it,' he said, laughing. 'Maybe the Old Man was something of a Mad-Head himself this afternoon.'

We were going home.

The Groix light. The radio picked up an SOS – a Spanish trawler in distress off Corunna . . .

The first beacon-buoys of the fairway. We ran in close to the villas of Larmor. I recognized the broad window I had seen when we were putting to sea. The room was lit up. The woman, dressed in black, was standing against the panes, alone. She watched us pass.

205

The arsenal. The big crane sharp against the sky. Dawn was breaking and the street-lamps turning pale. A train crossed the iron bridge with such a thunder that it drowned the murmur of the port. 'The Paris express,' said the sub-lieutenant, looking at his watch. 'Three minutes late.'

It was very dark that December morning of Christmas Eve. The liberty-men were lined up on the afterdeck in their best shore-going rig. The roll had been called over, but they did not move. And wholly taken up with the expectation of pleasure, they did not talk either. Only two or three of them passed furtively over the gangway and set off for the arsenal gates at a run, carrying their suitcases.

A thin, cold, penetrating, continual rain streamed down the grey steel. An Admiralty car drew up alongside.

The Captain was leaving. He was a mere ghost, but he held himself bolt upright. A little blood, diluted with rainwater, oozed from a cut on his cheek. The guard presented arms. All the officers were there. The whole crew: the liberty-men and the others in their working clothes. All of them: unmoving, set. I had not known that we liked him so much, that we had so much respect for him – a respect that could be seen in the pallor of those who looked at him and in the suppressed tears when he looked at us.

I knew he would not say a word. And it was very well so.

He passed slowly, stiff and upright. He saluted the guard. His black, gleaming claw quivered slightly.

The bosun's pipe.

The Captain stepped on to the gangway and stopped, facing aft, facing the ensign. Once again he saluted, a wide, slow sweep. Standing there . . . standing there. Thin and straight.

He crossed the gangway and got into the car: the door slammed. He had not turned round. He had not said a word.

As soon as the car had disappeared the liberty-men rushed over the side. There was a wild outbreak of shouts and laughter. A torrent of life. In the rain they ran to catch their trains or buses, full of hope and joy. It was Christmas Day tomorrow.

CHAPTER 21

The Renegade

Three days later the *Eole* went into dock to be heaved down. Two-thirds of the crew were quartered on shore or given long leave.

Nothing is more dismal than a laid-up ship. She is grey, dirty, and cold. The hull is streaked with red lead, like a salmon. The deck is littered with rubbish of every kind, tow, paint-pots, pieces of plating, mud, and strangers invade it, engineers and workmen. Tubes and cables everywhere. Welding and oxy-acetylene cutting go on in the midst of the din of hammers and compressors.

Bongo Ba came to say goodbye. His time was up. He was leaving for Fécamp to get in touch with the ship-owner and the maritime authorities and to wait for the *Damoclès* to come back (Willsdorff was still in the Barents Sea). Bongo Ba was slightly tipsy ('had to celebrate that with my ship-mates') and he absolutely insisted on having a drink with me. I fetched a bottle of wine from the wardroom. 'You have to have fun, Captain.' (He did not call me Doctor.) 'You have to have fun.' And he roared with laughter, a happy, vinous laugh.

On 29 December I received a telegram: it had my name on it, but the only address was *French Navy*. The Admiralty, having done a certain amount of research, had sent it on.

It read: ZANO MUCH SICK MAYBE DIE FELICITIES. PHUONG. Then came the name of a little street behind the Gare de Lyon in Paris.

Zano?

Why of course! Jean, Jeannot – Babourg's Christian name. And Phuong was his girl-friend: not very pretty, and possessed of a harsh, screaming voice. He had very nearly left her in 1950 when he was going back to France, but he got into a Chinese bus in Saigon at the last moment, without a word to anyone, and went back up the river to fetch her. He missed his boat, of course, and there was a good deal of trouble with the Navy. It was Willsdorff who smoothed things over. Babourg married the girl at top speed so as to be able to take her back with him by the next boat. I was his witness at the registry-office.

That evening I took the night-train for Paris.

Felicities: that turned out to mean the Ten Thousand Felicities, a little restaurant painted red, ox-blood red. Phuong worked there together with half a dozen other Vietnamese who were no doubt more or less related to her. She still had her screeching voice and in spite of all these years she still spoke pidgin French (the idiot Babourg had never troubled to teach her the language properly). 'Him always great nuisance for me . . . knock me. Look.' (She showed me old scars and a missing tooth.) 'Mad-head . . . Drink all him cash, drink all me cash too. Now him bugger off hospital.' A flood of passionate words.

Phuong set a bowl of Chinese soup down in front of me (delicious, with all the proper herbs). I asked her how she knew I had gone back to the Navy. 'Zano him say you not damn-fool like him; you sign on one time more . . . him and you drinking, too much drinking. Him weep after him seen you. Want smash everything . . . him much sod.'

Suddenly she began to sniff and her eyes filled with tears; she hurried off to the kitchen. Her relations gazed at me discreetly. She came back with dry eyes, carrying a plate of *banh cuon*.

Babourg's name was really Combourg ('You knowing good – Con Bouh, Zano Con Bouh') but I prefer to keep the name I have always used. A police-patrol had picked up Babourg lying in the street, dead drunk, and had taken him to the Saint-Antoine hospital. I got the house-physician on the telephone: 'Paraplegic . . . rotted by spirits . . . and every kind of excess. And the sequelae of a sickly time in the Far East too. Liver. Kidneys. He won't hold out much longer. He's done for.'

People were hurrying along the concrete corridors and stairs. Phuong and I were drawn into the current and swept along. When I saw Babourg in his hospital bed by a window my first impression was that the house-physician had exaggerated nothing.

It was very gloomy outside and they had lit those horrible neon lights that make even the healthiest look corpse-like. Babourg, exhausted and indifferent, was staring into emptiness. When he recognized us he made an effort and mumbled something incomprehensible. Phuong grasped his hand and squeezed it, moaning 'Zano, Zano, oh Zano . . .'

The doctor had let me bring a half-bottle of wine ('He's so far gone already . . . we'll pretend not to see') but I had forgotten the corkscrew.

'It's forbidden; don't let them catch you,' calmly observed an old woman knitting at the bedside of a little man in red satin pyjamas. Then she opened her bag and handed me a corkscrew.

Babourg's hand trembled so that he spilt some of the wine. We touched glasses and I proposed a toast: 'Your health, and a quick return to the Ten Thousand Felicities.' He looked at me intently and I was afraid that he was going to cry; but he controlled himself and shook his head.

The wine put a little life into him. He sat up, jerking. 'We . . . bloody hell, we were real men! Eh? Eh?'

The words were barely articulated: his speech too was paralysed. I nodded. He let himself slip back and closed his eyes; and now at last the tears flowed down his ill-shaved cheeks.

Yes, my poor old Babourg – my poor old Combourg – you

were a 'man' long ago, far away, on the river. You were a good seaman, a good soldier. And that is already a good deal, because . . . you talk, you talk, and it's all very fine; but when the bullets begin to whistle – crack, to be more precise – no one knows what he's going to find inside himself . . . You were brave. And on the landing-stage one morning you gave us all a lesson.

That particular morning was pure and clear, as though there were no war on. It was still cool. Cuc had made a whole pile of good things to eat and we were devouring them, drinking some commissariat wine that Babourg had somehow managed to lay his hands on ('better than their bloody beer'). The bugler Bocheau was no longer with us and our return had been less splendid than it was in his days; yet we were happy – the night-patrol had been a success. We had recovered several weapons and we had made a prisoner, a liaison-agent with a haversack stuffed with information. In the scuffle he had bitten a Vietnamese seaman in the calf; then he had twice tried to jump over-board; so as to have a little peace we had tied him up. (He must have been somewhat knocked about while it was being done.) He was now lying in the bottom of one of the sampans, mute and savage.

Cuc's peppery dishes, the wine, our fatigue and happiness kept us in a fine state of well-being. We laughed as we told each other about our sensations during the night. Monsieur Dégouzzi was purring: Willsdorff scratched his head.

'There's a gold-mine in that haversack of his,' said someone. 'And he must have a good deal to tell, too.'

We laughed, we agreed, we were happy. It was then that Babourg exclaimed, with his mouth full, 'Fucking hell! It's not so bleeding funny to be a prisoner; and if you have to give your mates away into the bargain . . .' He stood up and in a challenging voice he added, 'I know what I'm talking about: I've done time. Better kick the bucket straight away.'

Willsdorff knew – it was written down in Babourg's service record: he had stolen, 'borrowed' from his Picpus butcher's till – but we had had no idea. Babourg turned his back on us and walked to the far end of the pier. He jumped down into the sampan and opened his jack-knife. The helpless prisoner jerked about like an animal and for a moment an appalling terror showed in his eyes. Babourg calmly turned him over with one hand like a parcel, and cut the rope. Then he helped him climb up on to the landing-stage and sat him down on an empty stool next to me. The poor fellow, still dazed, rubbed his numbed hands to bring back the circulation. He looked so funny that we could not help laughing. Babourg was outraged at first, but in the end he too joined in the laughter.

'Come on now, mate: eat and drink – it's all on me,' he said, giving the prisoner a pair of chopsticks and a glass of wine.

The weariness, the wine, the pleasure of living – of being alive. We had after all gone through some ugly moments under fire that night. We felt full of affection for one another and for mankind in general. The little prisoner hesitated a while and then fell to with a hearty appetite; and that too delighted us.

'It'd go against the grain to give him up to those intelligence crabs,' muttered Babourg. (Like all the rest of us, he had adopted Willsdorff's way of speaking.)

Up until that point Willsdorff had said nothing. He watched first Babourg and then the prisoner, his eyes amused and crinkling at the corners. 'What's in the haver-sack ought to be enough for them,' he observed carelessly.

Babourg reacted instantly. 'Fucking hell! Do you think we could . . . Hell!'

'You were the one who caught him. Keep him. But watch out: he mustn't go jumping overboard again, eh? It's your responsibility. If all goes well, in a fortnight's time we'll sign him on properly. I don't think he'll go back to his friends: they'd take him for a traitor.'

'Hell!' Babourg gave his protégé a great enthusiastic slap on the back that made him jump with alarm. '*Tot lam, t tolam,* mate; drink up your wine – you won't get stuff like that every day of the week.'

The little prisoner gazed at us with his narrow, slanting, expressionless eyes: eyes like those of a cat, like Monsieur Dégouzzi's.

I took Phuong back to the Ten Thousand Felicities in a taxi. Night had fallen; it was raining. The street was black, deserted. The only lights were the two globes, one on each side of the restaurant door, and the steamy window, through which the dim forms of the customers could be made out. Phuong had not said a word during the journey. She opened the door of the taxi and asked, 'You eating?'

I shook my head. She got out, but still holding the door open she leant towards me: 'Him soon *chet*, no?'

'Yes: he's going to die.'

She said something else in a very low voice, a Vietnamese oath I think, but I am not sure because at that moment the roar of a train drowned her words. She slammed the door and ran through the rain; I could hear it pattering on the roof.

I took the cab on to the Champs-Elysées and got out at a brasserie. It was still raining. The west wind howled down the avenue, all ablaze with Christmas decorations, and rattled the awnings over the café terraces. It had crossed half the breadth of France, but it still had a slight smell of the sea. (There must have been an uncommonly deep depression off Ireland.)

I ordered a glass of beer. Through the windows covered with advertisements for Christmas and New Year festivities I watched the people running under the squalls. I looked at my neighbours: how was it that some of them could laugh with death printed clearly on their faces?

213

A man went from table to table, offering lottery-tickets: 'Today's your lucky day.' To attract attention he slapped the bundles of tickets against his hand like the food-pedlars of Tandjungpriok. Youths, clustered round a juke-box, were listening to an American girl beating out her lines.

I read the papers. Phnom Penh: The Khmers Rouges maintain their blockade. The Americans have set up an airlift to supply the town. The airfield has twice been hit by rockets.

Saigon: After hard fighting the South Vietnamese army had abandoned Ban Ho, a post in the highland plateaux to the north of Ban Me Thuot. (I knew Ban Ho. There used to be a very interesting Jorai tribe living there; they were not so shy as our Maa. Once I left my watch on a tree-trunk when I was bathing in the stream, and a monkey stole it.)

. . . Bomb in a Londonderry pub – seven dead . . . Oil crisis . . . Tension over the fate of hostages held by a Palestinian group . . .

My anxiety was there, crouching somewhere inside me, waiting. How I wished the ship had already sailed.

Babourg died on January 3, early in the morning, before the nurses' round.

Two weeping women came out of the morgue. I had to push Phuong to make her go in. The attendant pulled out a huge metal drawer and folded back the sheet covering the body. The room was cold. Under the neon glare, Combourg seemed to me calm and beautiful. His eyes were closed, but one of the lids was slightly raised. Phuong, deadly pale, kissed his forehead.

From the drawer the attendant took a parcel containing the dead man's shoes, trousers, a jacket coated with dried mud, and his last remaining little treasures – a ball-point pen, some papers, a crumpled photograph of his sampan with the landing-stage and the eating-house in the background . . .

'Sign here: it's a receipt for the administration.' Phuong let me lead her over. Laboriously she wrote her name.

The attendant drew up the sheet – the ridge of the nose stood out in relief – and pushed back the drawer; it closed with a sharp click.

I could not stay for the funeral; I had to go back to Lorient. There would only be the Vietnamians of the Ten Thousand Felicities to escort my friend to the graveyard.

The *Eole* was still in dock, dirtier, colder, and more cluttered than ever. The engineers and workmen were in complete control. I had a great deal of paper-work to attend to and I had to renew my stock of medicines for the Newfoundland cruise. I learnt that our old Captain was no longer in the naval hospital; he had already been taken to Villejuif as an urgent case. The chief medical officer gave me a dressing-down: 'You brought him back to us in a shocking condition. He did state that he had refused to let himself be examined, but you only had to look at his face . . .' The old crab had covered me as much as he could. 'He asked that you should be given this.'

A large parcel. His books: those that he had had on board. There was also an envelope containing a note for me: 'I do not need these any more. Keep them in . . .' The *in* had been crossed out but it was still legible. The few words that followed it were not. After them he had written in a firm hand, 'Thank you.'

The Bible was among the books. He no longer needed that, either.

To settle various arrangements I attended a meeting of deep-sea trawler owners in Bordeaux, and there I saw some of the skippers I had met in the north. Willsdorff was on the way home with four hundred and seventy tons of salted cod – not bad at all. Everyone was concerned by the slump in deep-frozen fish. The owners were pessimistic.

We received our new captain. (Alas for the fisheries officer, who had had great hopes of keeping his command.) He came to us straight from the Admiralty. I had met him once or twice in Haiphong in 1954, when he was a midshipman in the aircraft-carrier *Arromanches*. He had not changed too much – fewer curves, more hard lines – and he looked pretty good, but we should have to see him on the job.

In my damp cabin that evening, when the arsenal siren shrieked and the din of the pneumatic drills came to a sudden stop, a new chill came to mingle with my old anxiety: the certainty that I had been of no help to poor Babourg made me deeply uncomfortable. When we met that night, all I did was to discourage him a little more and send him faster on his downward course. I was angry, both with him and with myself.

The Chief took me home to spend the week-end with him at Guenn-an-Avel.

CHAPTER 22

The Sermon

'We'll go by way of the Montagnes Noires. It's very wild –
you'll see. And then it makes a change from the sea.' The
Chief had a very rusty Citroën 2CV. It was morning. The
damp air was almost warm: the grey sky somewhat overcast,
as the Breton sky so often is. We did not talk.

Quimperlé. We stopped for coffee at the Hôtel de la
Gare. The Chief knew the proprietress.

A small thin rain, a drizzle, began to fall, and it blurred
the melancholy countryside, the naked trees. At a crossroads
on the way to Guiscriff, a signpost: Lanvénégen.

'I'd like to go there.'

The Chief glanced at me and without a word he turned
the car around. The little town stood on the side of a hill. A
calvary, a saw-mill, small granite houses, a big square and
in the middle of it a fine church, whose slated roof looked
even blacker in the rain. It was cold. Nobody anywhere.
And everything was silent.

The war memorial: the classic soldier with his Lebel
rifle. There were close on a hundred and fifty names for the
1914–18 war; less than thirty for 1939–45. Next to these,
another plate – the Jewish or foreign names of those who had
been shot and then discovered in mass graves: some un-
identified. Korea: one name, and it had been chiselled out.
Indo-China: three names, and Romain Perron was the last.
Nothing for Algeria.

Drawing on his cigarette, the Chief gave me a questioning
look. 'A friend,' I said.

I was not going to tell him that I had only met Perron

once nor that the only words I ever heard him say were 'I'm thirsty'.

An old woman in black crossed the square under her umbrella. She looked at us. The Chief spoke to her in Breton and she came towards us, slightly uneasy. He must have found the right words to soothe her because she began to laugh. 'That was a queer fellow for you. Perron, Romain Perron! I was at school with him: one of his cousins is a baker – the other's a soldier too. He went to the Church secondary school. It was him who broke the . . .' She pointed at the soldier's rifle. Yes, the foresight was broken: I had not noticed it. '. . . . with a catapult, when he was aiming at a bird.' She laughed. 'How you make me go on . . . They say that now he's in the graveyard up there – ' she leant towards us – 'but it's not him. It's a Chinaman.' She was very pleased with the effect of her words.

'They found it out at the hospital at Brest, when they opened up. They shut the lid again and sent it all here, without saying a word. Monsieur le Maire's nephew, he works at the hospital . . . Still, we do put flowers on him at All-Saints.'

Sending the bodies home must have been a rather hurried job in Hanoi: it had to be done before the Viets came in. Poor Mad-Head was lying in a Tonkinese graveyard – and it was very well so. (Unless indeed they had sent him to an Algerian douar or an African village: who could tell?)

The Chief was profoundly amused. He loved stories of that kind. We went to see the baker in the higher town. He was a cheerful man: 'Well, and so you are a friend of Romain's . . . what'll you have, white or red? I never knew him much – always over there: that was the only thing he liked. Why, in the very last letter we had he asked for post-cards showing Breton women in coifs, because over there it seems the women wear coifs too, and he wanted to show them . . . And then a little while after that the gendarme came with the paper saying *reported missing, presumed captured...*'

We moved from the shop into the room behind so as to drink at our ease. On the wall, two good Japanese wash-drawings. The baker noticed my interest. 'No, that wasn't him; that was my other cousin, the major. They wrote his name on the monument too, did you see? Korea. Ha, ha, ha! Even the Chinese couldn't catch *him*. He did Indo-China too. And even in 1944 against the Germans, when he was quite a boy. And Algeria! He left the army after the ... the revolt. Lots of his comrades went to prison ... Yerc'h mad!'

We drank a pale, almost colourless muscadet that set one's teeth on edge. At last the Chief found a way of bringing up the business of the Chinaman in the graveyard. (A Vietnamese, without any sort of doubt.)

'There's no Chinaman at all,' said the baker decisively. 'Officially it's him. So for us it's him ... Anyhow, I talked about it with a big chap who'd come to look at his grave – they'd been friends over there. He laughed, and said, "It warms my heart to think that one of our little Tonkinese soldiers is in your cemetery. As for your cousin Perron, the Lord will know where to find him all right." He went and put some flowers ... and then there was a great to-do getting his cat back – this tall chap's cat. We had to send for the fire-brigade. He went up the ladder himself, because the poor thing wouldn't come down otherwise, on account of all the dogs that were barking.'

We travelled under the grey sky along little narrow lanes between green banks. Night was coming on. This was the deep melancholy of the Breton winter. Paths covered with moss and dead leaves; dark woods with water dripping slowly from branch to branch; the low white walls of lonely farms; sometimes crucifixes with arms outstretched, the naive Christs and the anguished thieves worn and eaten away by the centuries.

The countryside changed. A vast flat desert as far as eye could reach: arid wasteland, desolate hollows, marshes, withered reeds; stunted trees, stripped by the cold, twisted by the sea-wind – the western part of the ancient Bigouden. ('The chin of France,' as the Chief put it.) It looked like a sad and twilit landscape of the first ages of creation, a landscape wholly bare: the end and the beginning.

Empty hamlets, damp and austere, green with lichen. The occasional light, swinging in the wind. Old women in tall white coifs limping along the side of the road, like witches of the night.

Far away the Eckmühl light and the topped steeples of Penmarc'h showed faintly through a salty mist – the spray from the great Atlantic swell breaking on the rocks. A low sky. The twilight smelt of seaweed.

'My father's father used to say that in the old days the wolves came down here when the cold drove them out of the Montagnes Noires. You could hear them in the evening. Sometimes the old people said it was the ghosts of the dead. The dogs howled, and people crossed themselves and bolted the cottage doors,' said the Chief. And I believed him.

By the time we reached Guenn-an-Avel it was almost entirely dark. Sand crunched underfoot, and the sound mingled with the strong, elusive rumble of the sea, quite close at hand.

The western gale awoke me in the night. Rain struck hard against the window-panes. The turning beam of the Eckmühl light lit my room with its steady sweep.

In the morning the Chief brought me a bowl of coffee. He was wearing his uniform. 'It's Sunday. I must take my mother to Mass . . . it does please her so. I'll see you after.'

'No, I'll come with you.'

We walked along, one on each side of the old lady, in our uniforms. She resembled him; she had the same high-cheeked Mongol face and a yellow skin darkened by the criss-crossing wrinkles. Her hair, drawn tightly back, was wholly grey, the grey of ice. It was only her determined, searching eyes that age had been unable to overcome. She paced along, proud and straight in her traditional clothes, her coif quivering in the wind.

Men in navy blue; women in black, with white coifs. A grey sky. The little church with its slim granite steeple, gilded here and there by lichen: an enclosure filled with furze and graves. The sound of the sea. A heady wind that left the taste of salt in one's mouth. A few sailors took their wives as far as the porch and then walked off openly towards the bar.

The church was cold and as damp as a vault, all green with moss. Ex-votos everywhere: ships in bottles, little slabs of marble ('Thanks to Saint Ninnoc'h'), a large naive painting of a brig struggling in a prodigious storm, stone saints with big heads like gnomes, all lined up.

It was more than thirty years since I had been inside a church. I imitated my neighbours' movements, crossed myself awkwardly, knelt down, got up again, bowed my head . . . I no longer knew a single hymn nor a single prayer.

I was cold and numb; the bench was hard. A wicked wind moaned among the beams. We stood up again: a fine harsh sad Breton song. We sat down once more.

The priest, a big red-faced man, had a choirboy on either side of him, children in red robes and white surplices. He spoke but I was lost in my own thoughts and I did not attend.

And then, I cannot tell why, I found I was listening.

'We wander in the darkness, my brethren. And because we feel breath in us, because we are hungry and thirsty, because we turn ideas over in our minds, we think we are alive: whereas in fact we are dead.

'Nevertheless, we here in this church do believe that there is a sun . . . and a promise of everlasting life, even for the lowliest among us. This we believe, do we not?

'Around us we see those who have lost all hope, those who have turned towards drink to drown the terrors of the night, those who hold others answerable for their weaknesses and who would like to reshape the world so that it should become a lottery in which everyone would win at every turn, those who believe that good lies in the flesh and evil in that which dissuades them from fleshly acts, those who have once caught a glimpse of the light but who close their eyes saying, I saw nothing . . . But let us leave that to one side.

'We who are joined together in this church believe that somewhere there is a light.' For a moment the priest seemed overcome. He raised his head, and looking at the congregation he went on in a strong voice, 'How could we not believe it? What seaman, lost far offshore at night, does not know that there is a lighthouse somewhere along the coast to guide and save him?' He stretched out his hands like a Buddha in the un-fearing attitude. 'We, all of us here, must believe that there is a light. But have we seen it? Have we felt its kindly warmth? Have we gone away filled with joy and happiness?' He fell silent. A gust hurled itself against the door, and it seemed to shake the priest himself.

'No man can see God without dying, my brethren. A wealthy, intelligent young man named Saul was travelling along a road. He was going towards a distant city to continue his persecution and to increase it; he breathed out death and menaces against the followers of Our Lord Jesus. And all at once, as he was travelling, a light from heaven blazed around him. And he heard a voice saying, *Saul, Saul, why persecutest thou me? . . . it is hard for thee to kick against the pricks.* So much for Saul.

'The man who rose to his feet again was the apostle Paul, Saint Paul. Although his eyes were open, he saw nothing: they took him by the hand and led him to Damascus. He remained two days without sight, eating and drinking nothing.

'That is how our eternal Father acts, my stiff-necked brethren. He seizes a man and He flings him to the ground. He thrusts him through and through with His darts. He blinds . . . and He brings back to life.

'We are not the wealthy and intelligent Saul; we do not breathe out death and threats against the followers of the Lord. We are only humble fishermen and we work hard to gain our daily bread. Are we worthy of being flung to the ground like Saul, of being blinded . . . and of being brought back to life?' The last words were uttered in so low a voice that I do not think the whole of the congregation can have heard them. For a long while the priest remained silent, his head bowed, his face hidden in his hands. The choirboys looked at him apprehensively. When he stood up again he seemed to have recovered some of his convictions. 'The seaman lost by night in the open sea has something that will help him to find the lighthouse on the shore; something that will guide him, something that will save him. The compass! He sets his course and he keeps watch. He knows that in that direction there will be a light. He stares through the darkness and he waits. Let us be like the seaman. The Lord has given us a compass . . .' Slowly he raised his hand and let it fall heavily on the open Bible in front of him. 'Let us turn ourselves to the rites and observances of our Holy Mother Church; even if we do not understand, even if we doubt, let us compel ourselves so to do. Let us apply ourselves to our task like little children at school: let us pray, gaze into the darkness and wait. But above all do not let us ask for peace and a quietly sleeping mind; let us pray that we may be granted anxiety . . . and Glory. Alleluia!'

The wind was still blowing, bringing with it the smell of kelp and crab, a sharp low-tide tang. There was a real, almost a springtime sun in the pale sky; and very high and silent, an invisible aeroplane drew a long white condensation-trail. The lichen on the steeple glowed like brass.

Children were running about among the graves and their high piping laughter rose up to mingle with the cry of the gulls before the wind swept it away. In the west a luminous veil of spray and spindrift half hid the Eckmühl light and the metallic gleam of the truncated steeples of Penmarc'h and Saint-Guénolé.

After Mass it was the custom for everyone to visit the family graves. The Chief's mother stood, a living reproach, in front of the shell-encrusted cross that marked her husband's tomb. Her ample dress flapped like a black flag and with one hand she held on to her coif. 'He had a very weak mind,' she said severely.

A granite slab bore the name of the old Rector and these two lines:

Where is this man?
I do not know.

'It was he who wanted it like that,' explained the Chief's mother. 'He was a holy man, but his wits were not much good either. Why do men have to drink and make all this din instead of staying quietly in the corner the Lord has given them? I think they're mad.'

Gwen – the Gwenaël who was afraid of his own shadow – had his name inscribed on the plinth of the war memorial (a soldier and a rusty cast-iron cock) with the words 'Shot by the Germans'.

The village idiot watched us from afar, drooling; he was a little withered creature, rather like the big-headed stone saints: he laughed.

And there was I, who had thought the Chief made up all his stories.

In the evening we left the formidable old lady to her cats – there were seven of them. The Chief took me on a tour of Guenn-an-Avel's bars – there were five. It was a positive ritual: there was no question of going to any old bar at any old time; we had to observe a complex order, a hierarchic sequence known only to the initiated and one that would have charmed my cracked ethnologist – a sequence broken only by the summer visitors.

'That's how it is,' explained the Chief.

Bar after bar, round of red wine after round of red wine – the Chief had friends everywhere – and then came the uneasy time when the drinker grows withdrawn, darts challenging looks about him and drinks in silence without saying Yerc'h mad, as though he were containing a deep hatred.

At eight o'clock and at our fourth bar – our tenth or eleventh glass of wine perhaps – I turned towards the television to watch the news.

Strikes ... unemployment ... demonstrations ... hold-up with hostages taken ... Phnom Penh (I increased the sound): refugees were flowing into the already overcrowded town. Rockets fell. Planes were burning at Pochentong. Men ran, clutching their children in their arms (I recognized the great market-place). The driver of a cycle-rickshaw loaded a shattered corpse on to his machine. A man wept. Children were playing at soldiers with wooden rifles. Wounded soldiers, so young ... scarcely older than the children.

The village idiot laughed. An old man in navy blue gave me an angry look and muttered, 'Can't even hear each other. Not allowed to sit quiet with your drink.'

This was the dangerous time when the drinker stands swaying, his head low and his eyes set, when every now and then he speaks words aloud, as though he were talking to himself.

I ought to have left my old man alone – the Chief was making signs to me – but I had been drinking (I know, I know, at my age one should no longer do such things) and then these pictures had torn an old wound open. Like a fool I called out, 'You're quite safe in this hole of yours. You don't know a thing ... One of these days you'll be swept away too ...'

I was absurd. The idiot jerked convulsively. The old man stared at me sullenly, with the terrible solemnity of drunkenness. The Chief ordered a round for one and all.

Then happily there came the blessed moment when the drinker softens, grows loving, and gazes at his full glass with tear-filled eyes.

'Yerc'h mad.'

The old man told his story, and it needed four rounds before he reached the end. He was taken prisoner at Dunkirk in 1940 and sent to a camp in East Prussia. 'I told them I was a peasant . . . I'm a seaman. I told them peasant. I wanted to work on a farm. I don't like camps or . . . prisons. It's not right . . . They put me to a farm called Grandsk, not very far from Königsberg: potatoes and rye, and some cows too. Hard work . . . but you ate well. I had a Polish mate, name of Josef, and he scrounged me Red Cross cigarettes. Yerc'h mad.' (First round.)

Then came the Russian offensive of the winter of '44–45. 'Refugees everywhere, coming through half-frozen – twenty and thirty below. The farmer's wife, she still believed in Hitler's propaganda – no Russians in Prussia. Ha, ha! Josef and me, we harnessed the best horse, Jaromir, and loaded the cart with straw, blankets, something to eat, and schnapps. We had to lift the woman and her daughter in, crying and calling us out of our name. She said she'd have us shot as soon as we met with German soldiers. Poor woman . . . she was leaving a fine farm behind . . . and her cows. Yerc'h mad.' (Second round.)

They drove the cart west, but it was already too late, and they had to head northwards, in the direction of the Baltic . . .

'We weren't the only ones, oh no! And it was freezing . . . they were burying people in the frozen snow along the side of the road – little children mostly. I'd grasped what was up, but the woman, she kept wanting me to stop in the villages for a cup of coffee. Josef and I, we wouldn't let her. Then . . .

this is how it happened . . . a traffic-jam in a village. Click-clack, click-clack, click-clack – panzers! It's the Germans, said the woman. Germans? It was the Russians! They were smashing the carts, shouting, and firing in every direction. We got hold of the woman and Tulla, her daughter, and we hid in a cow-house. Yerc'h mad.' (Third round.)

'The Russians winkled us out . . . it was maybe fifteen of them had the woman – I didn't count. They even kept their guns hanging round their necks while they did it. And we could reckon ourselves lucky they didn't find our schnapps. Josef and I, we were up against a wall with our hands in the air and a Chinese-looking Russian in front of us who kept laughing all the time. "Franzouse, Franzouse, nixt Germansky." He laughed. "Franzouse kaput." And we could hear the farmer's wife. I had little Tulla with me. Too little, luckily for her. The Chinese-looking Russian laughed. It made him laugh. He wasn't wicked: he laughed – "Franzouse, kaput," and I laughed too, to please him. He took my boots and my watch . . . There must have been a little group of German soldiers retreating somewhere nearby, because all at once the fighting broke out. *"Davaï, davaï,"* and they all got into their tanks again. They smashed more horses, more people and sledges. Josef and me picked up the woman. Jaromir was still in the shafts. We drove across country, flogging and flogging him on – he was in a muck-sweat, poor Jaromir. He was steaming, and I nearly had my feet frozen off. Yerc'h mad.' (Fourth round.)

'The woman didn't talk any more; she just groaned. Maybe fifteen? I don't know. I didn't count. Then after that we had to cross the lake, the Frisches Haff, five miles wide, on the ice, at night, with their planes dropping flares to machine-gun us better . . . Some of the carts went into bomb-holes and disappeared under the water, horses, children and all . . . There were thousands of us on the ice. On the far side we saw German deserters hanging on the trees, and they swung there stiff with a placard round their

227

necks "I am a coward". The SS wanted to hang me too: said I was a deserter. And they didn't laugh like the Chinese-Russian; not them.'

The fifth and last bar, a lugubrious place that smelt of disinfectant and wine. We had taken the old man with us: he was our friend. The idiot had followed. Yerc'h mad.

A north-west wind had swept the clouds away. The rollers came in, curled and broke in a solemn rush of foam. A mist of spray rose above the black line of dunes, bringing the smell of seaweed. Every time the beam of the Eckmühl light touched it, a grey calvary emerged from the darkness, to fall back each time the beam passed on.

Now was the miraculous time when the drinker's soul wavers on the edge of the gulf . . . We set out, following the old man; he walked straight ahead, singing a hymn filled with love and joy and gratitude for I know not what or whom. 'Alleluia, allel aaalleeelu-ia, Alle-lu-ia!'

The idiot tripped several times, but not one of us fell down altogether.

The *Damoclès* had reached Fécamp.

CHAPTER 23

────◆────

The Solitary

'Will you go and see him at Fécamp, or will he come here?' the sub-lieutenant asked me shyly.

I looked at him with astonishment. 'Why?'

'I'd very much like to meet him,' he replied, blushing a little.

I spoke to Willsdorff on the telephone; he still had that off-hand tone he liked to assume. We should not be meeting this time either; I had to stand in for one of my colleagues at the naval hospital and he had too much work to be able to come to Lorient. 'At Saint-Pierre – we'll see one another at Saint-Pierre.'

The *Eole* left the dock. We went to take up a berth by the floating stage under the Admiralty light. It was our new captain who carried out the manœuvre. He came out of it quite well. He was far from having the mastery or the punctilious strictness of his predecessor. The atmosphere on the bridge was more easy-going – I was no longer aware of that icy tension nor that extremely sparing use of words that had so impressed me.

Normal life on board began again, and the crew were kept very busy restoring a little order and cleanliness.

The *Eole* went through her trials at the Glénans base. The Arsenal engineers were satisfied with the work that had been carried out. Our captain grew more sure of himself. We were ready for the Grand Banks cruise.

On 7 February the Chief had the television aerial unshipped, just after the midday news.

Phnom Penh is flooded with refugees. The airlift is at a stop; the last planes are burning. Every day rockets strike the town by scores; the hospitals are overwhelmed. A reporter interviewed one of the doctors of the French hospital. (I knew him; he was an old friend, and we had been together in Tonkin.) He launched a moving appeal: *Too many children are dying.*

My shipmates were taken up with the coming departure; they scarcely listened. *In South Vietnam the situation is growing worse. The Saigon government seems to be losing control of the highland plateaux . . .*

A bill concerning divorce . . . This summer will see the triumph of the G-string on the beaches . . . At this point my companions did look up; the bathing girls they showed us were utterly delightful.

At fifteen hours the *Eole* put to sea. The Captain took the port-pilot aboard. The weather was fine. (1020 millibars. Wind southerly, moderate: force 3 to 4. Sea calm.) The numbered buoys streamed along the side; the water was green with black reflections. A Panamanian was unloading tropical wood in the commercial port. Larmor. The villa I looked at each time seemed to be empty. A large notice was hanging from the balcony. Through my binoculars I read For Sale.

We headed west. The open sea. The outlines of two trawlers faded slowly eastwards. A few screaming gulls planed by on outstretched wings. It was quite warm. Little groups of men stood about on the afterdeck and one could hear laughter and snatches of conversation.

The dark-blue water of the Atlantic became grey, then black. Right ahead of us the sun sank lower: its shape altered, growing flatter . . . It was no more than a single blood-red point . . . Night! For a long while I leant there on the rail.

It was the *Tet*, the Vietnamese New Year. This was the

first day of the Year of the Cat. (That was something that should please Willsdorff, if he had not forgotten.)

The Captain invited me to lunch. 'Our fisheries officer was rather disappointed, I believe,' he said. 'The Old Man had made a very favourable report about him, but the Admiralty decided otherwise.'

'He's at Villejuif now,' I said.

'Yes . . . but not for long, I'm afraid. You didn't do much for him . . .'

I looked him straight in the eye and he lowered his head, pretending to look for his napkin. 'You were very nearly put ashore, Doctor. But the owners and the trawler-skippers made a fuss. The fishermen are very fond of you . . . Did he at least see him?' he added suddenly.

'No . . . he talked to him over the radio.'

'What did they say to one another?'

'Nothing . . . Goodbye.'

'Ah!'

While we drank our coffee we revived old memories: the atmosphere in Saigon during the battle of Dien Bien Phu, the *Arromanches*'s pilots who did not return from their flights over the basin . . . 'You remember What's-his-name? The one who let the nail on his little finger grow, like a mandarin . . .'

At that period Willsdorff was already a prisoner of war. 'I met him in Toulon in 1956,' said the Captain. 'After his adventures with the junk, the Navy wanted to call him to order: they stuck him aboard a cruiser. He was rather . . . excitable. He used to quote the Bible to us at every turn. He knew it better than the chaplain.'

'The Bible?'

'Yes. He'd learnt it by heart.'

I must have looked utterly amazed, because the Captain burst out laughing. 'It was the only thing he had left. He said it was a remarkable book, even for an agnostic.'

231

'Tell me about it,' I said.

'I first heard the story in Cyprus, after the Suez affair, He had run into a parachutist, a captain who had been a prisoner with him in Indo-China. The para was very bitter about it all – "We could have pitched our tents at the foot of the Pyramids!" He took us off to a little place in the Turkish quarter where you could smoke. Opium makes you talkative, as everybody knows . . . Willsdorff told us about being wrecked on the Yemen coast. There he was, soaked, sitting on the things he had managed to save with his cat on his knee and watching his junk go to pieces when the Bedouin appeared, took their sticks to him, tied him up, and seized all his belongings. Every time he protested a great brute of an Arab came and laid the edge of his knife across his throat, rolling his eyes and making horrible gargling noises; and then, it seems, all the others laughed like mad. Still, after the evening prayer they did untie him so that he could drink. He took the Bible out of his pocket, made signs to them to move farther off, knelt down and read where it chanced to open. "I did it just to irritate them – to provoke them," he told us, "because they annoyed me with their affected ways." '

'But where did he get his Bible from?' I asked.

'Out of his pocket . . . that is to say, he had come by it in the Maldives, after a cyclone. The captain of a warship made him a present of it, together with a new rudder and a drum of wine. So kneeling there facing the sea, he expected to be stoned, or at least to have his throat cut . . . But the astonished Bedouin let him carry on. At night they took him off, tied to the tail of a camel. The cat escaped when they tried to catch it.'

'It was a black cat.'

'Maybe . . . at all events he called it the Rat. In a mountain village they shut him up in a wooden cage – Willsdorff, not the rat – to show him to the women. After a while they put irons on his legs and he could walk about wherever he liked.

I believe he made kites for the children; there was a whole mob of them at his heels. He read the Bible because he had nothing else to read. "And while I was doing so they left me alone," he said. They used to send him to draw water for the women and by way of payment they would give him a crack with a stick or sometimes a little tobacco or that bitter drug they call *kat*. He hurried about in the dust with his chains clattering . . . The only real curse was the flies, he said. When a husband was beating his wife, he would run and laugh at the sight with everybody else. One day a thief had his hand cut off in front of the whole tribe: the hand was tied to a post and the executioner took it off with one stroke of his sword – summary justice, eh? The thief never uttered a sound and the hand stayed there hanging on the post, like an old glove. It was Willsdorff who looked after the poor chap; as I understand it, he cauterized the wound by plunging the stump into boiling butter . . . The tribe was more or less at war with its neighbours, and sometimes Willsdorff took part in their expeditions in the mountains as a coolie, carrying a water-skin on his back. He liked it well enough when the skin was not too full, because he could see the sea in the distance. The Bedouin were very cheerful, and they sang all the time. They didn't do much in the way of precautions – just a few men out in front and that was all. At the drop of a hat they'd amuse themselves by blazing away at the stones in the valley with their old 1898 Mausers. One day a fellow who'd been sniping at a stone without ever hitting it lent Willsdorff his rifle. At the first shot the stone skipped into the air, and they all began roaring "El . . . el something" – I don't remember the word. It meant the Half-wit, the Idiot, the Simpleton . . . it was the nickname they'd given him.'

'The Innocent,' I said.

'That's right: the Innocent! Willsdorff was vexed: he reloaded, picked another stone – it skipped into the air. He reloaded: another stone farther off – and again it skipped. At

233

the fourth, a man who was hiding behind the stone stood up and raced away, dropping his rifle. I don't know how the Bedouin recognized him as one of their enemies, but they did, and they started blazing away in every direction. The man ran like a hare. "He ran dead straight, the fool," said Willsdorff. "There he was right in my sights; he hadn't a ghost of a chance. Run, run, run, little man, I thought, and I even sent a round whistling past his moustache to make him run faster, just for the laugh." The Bedouin tore down the slope pell-mell to pick up the rifle. Willsdorff called them every name under the sun — the children had taught him their language, particularly the most horrible oaths — he put some order into their confusion and he made them manœuvre. The result was they flushed three or four men and captured five rifles. The chief was vexed, and maybe rather shocked by the oaths; he made them put the water-skin back on Willsdorff's shoulders and gave him a beating to teach him manners: but after the prayer that evening they made a place for him round the fire. They still called him the Idiot — the Innocent — but now they also said El Mansour, the Victorious. They let him have one of the rifles and they gave him back his rather damaged sextant. He became their military adviser. "With the Bible in my left hand, an 1898 Mauser in my right, and my sextant hanging round my neck," he told us, "I might have conquered the world; but then the Navy came to an agreement about my ransom. They did not bankrupt themselves — the price of four or five old rifles . . ." '

I made a feeble observation: 'Yes, he likes adventure.'

The Captain looked at me thoughtfully. 'An adventurer?' he went on. 'That's what we all thought when he chose the rebels' side . . . in Algeria. An adventurer! I'll tell you something. When he came out of prison I had lunch with him and a former shipmate of mine, a man who had left the Navy and taken to selling arms. My friend made him an offer: "In Africa there's an opening for good mercenary

234

officers . . . very well paid." Willsdorff looked at him hard, and then said, "Why do you think I behaved as I did? Just for the laugh?" And I assure you there was no laughter in his voice. The other man pressed him. Willsdorff stood up. "Fool," he said, and walked out. I have never seen him since.'

The glass was dropping. The sea was lumpish, uncomfortable, a dirty olive-green. Cirro-stratus made ominous haloes in the sky. The *Eole* was labouring and the officer of the watch suggested reducing speed to eight knots. The Captain nodded; his face was very pale and covered with sweat. He stepped aside to be discreetly sick over the rail and came back pressing his handkerchief to his mouth – a smell of eau de Cologne swept briskly away by the wind.

'Send for the weather-chart.'

'Yes, sir.'

The met office was just aft of the chart-room, a few steps away, but the Captain preferred staying on the bridge, where there was plenty of air. I understood him: my stomach too was somewhat queasy.

A petty-officer unrolled the chart. 'Received at 09.00 hours this morning, sir: all the stations give a gale-warning.'

'Excuse me.' Once again the Captain stepped aside and came back holding his handkerchief. The petty-officer carried on with his explanation.

Steadily the wind grew stronger. In an hour's time it was blowing furiously from the south-south-west, bringing huge masses of torn cloud. Pallid waves with an ugly white foam surged here and there in a total confusion, huge broken seas tumbling together – the chaos that comes before very dirty weather indeed.

Everything movable aboard was made fast. The wind increased and veered into the west. Gusts tore off the crests of the highest waves and sent them to leeward in a thick curtain of flying water. The lookouts took shelter, where for

235

a long while they kept rubbing their streaming eyes.

The Captain gave orders to reduce speed to three knots and to keep her head to the wind. He was no longer seasick, although the *Eole* was rolling so hard that one had to hang on with both hands to keep upright. Nobody was sick any more; the sight was too splendid, too enormously impressive. We all knew that we were aboard a strongly-built modern ship; we all knew that unless some unlikely human or mechanical error occurred the *Eole* was in no kind of danger; and all of us there on the bridge were filled with dread.

'No man can see God and live,' had said the Rector of Guenn-an-Avel.

This was not God; it was the wrath of God, of the cruel Old Testament Jehovah. We did not speak. We were alone, each one of us; isolated, crushed, clinging with both hands not to be carried away, filled with dread and awe . . .

The skipper of the *Colonel Mevel*, on his way to the Banks, radioed darkly, 'I've sailed the North Atlantic these fifteen years, and I've never seen the like.' On the coasts of Ireland, Cornwall and Finisterre thousands of ancient trees were uprooted, roofs carried away, concrete breakwaters torn loose. In the shelter of their harbours large ships parted their cables and went adrift. In the Channel four inshore fishing-boats and a German tramp were lost with all hands. At the Lizard the wind reached 112 miles an hour. And at Gris-Nez 119. The distress wavelengths were saturated: Mayday, Mayday, Mayday . . .

The *Eole* lay-to three days and three nights. We were rolled about, shaken, upset; we slid right and left and it was impossible to sleep in our bunks; fortunately there were the stanchions – you had to wedge yourself against them to close your eyes and get a little rest. Everywhere the drawers and lockers had flung out their contents and all these objects tumbled about in wild disorder, making a depressing noise. Frightful blows made the plating ring.

Once the *Eole* took such a lurch that it seemed she would never rise again. I seemed to be plucked up into the air and then I fell heavily against a bulkhead, my wits knocked out of me. I struggled in the midst of a heap of seaboots and jackets but neither my hands nor my feet could get a hold: I could not get up. My sick-bay attendant, flat on his back, stared at me with a completely idiotic expression on his face; he opened his mouth like a fish, but no sound came out, or at least none that I could hear. Then an enormous heave sent us both to the other side of the sick-bay, together with the boots and jackets.

I had many patients: a man from the engine-room with a broken arm, a badly burnt cook (they had to be lashed into their bunks), bruises and wounds, some serious, others less so.

On the fourth day the sun rose over a pale sea. The wind shifted north-west and then north-east, flattening the enormous western swell. The *Eole* was white with salt; she looked as if someone had taken a sledge-hammer to her – plating dented, bulwarks driven in, rails twisted, the bow-light torn away . . .

The Captain increased speed to seven knots and then, when the wind began to lose its fury, to ten. By noon we were back at our cruising-speed.

'Something two points on the port bow,' cried a lookout. 'I don't know what it is. Perhaps a wreck.'

'Right . . . Yes, I see it. No echo on the radar?'

'No, sir. Yes there is, though . . . very small. At . . . at six miles. On 252.'

The officer of the watch sent to tell the Captain, who was below in his cabin. (He had not left the bridge throughout the storm.)

'Steer for it. I'm coming.'

A heavy sea was still running, and the 'something' appeared and disappeared according to the swell. 'It looks like a boat,' said the lookout.

The Captain was obviously somewhat worn, but he had shaved and changed his uniform. 'There's been no ship in distress in our sector: I wonder . . .'

'It's a boat. There's even a scrap of sail,' said the lookout, who certainly had good eyes.

It was not a boat; it was a little eight- or nine-metre sloop, painted blue. Her mast had gone at the crosstrees. She was carrying a backed storm-jib and a little something aft, and she was lying-to with just a trifle of way on her, riding the swell happily. No one at the tiller. The sliding roof was shut.

'*Beatrice*, RWYC Plymouth,' said the lookout.

'Right,' said the Captain. 'I take over.'

He manœuvred cleverly so as to come up on the yacht without taking the wind out of her sails. (He was beginning to know his ship.) From the wing a lookout roared through the loud-hailer, 'Ahoy! *Beatrice* ahoy! Ahoy! Ahoy there, ahoy!'

Nothing.

The Captain brought the fog-horn into action.

Nothing.

Suddenly the cabin-door opened and a red-headed bearded man stuck out his head. There was no doubt that we had just woken him. Seeing us so close he gave a start. He waved his arms in vehement refusal. We could hear him shout, 'No, no! Go away . . . go away!'

He looked terrified. The Captain took the loud-hailer and called in English, 'Do you need some help?'

'No! No! . . . away . . . away.'

The bearded man was now right out of his cabin: he was furious, but it looked as though he were making polite bows in our direction as he leaned to and fro to keep his balance. The *Beatrice* dug her bows into a sea, and the soaking did nothing to pacify him. 'Go away . . . Trafalgar! Waterloo! Fashoda! . . . away, away.'

238

'I believe he is insulting us,' observed the Captain coldly.

The fisheries officer smiled. 'One of these solitary yachts-men,' he said. 'We have frightened him. Ever since one of our weather-ships ran into Chichester's *Gypsy Moth* on the grounds of asking after his health they have all been afraid of us.'

'Ran into him? Really?'

'Yes, sir. *France II*, a weather-ship: it was during the last single-handed transatlantic race. Chichester was already sick – no longer answering the radio. He had been through some heavy weather. *France II* found him and came rather too close . . . you can imagine the noise it made in England! And the ship was called *France*, into the bargain.'

The irascible red-head sat in his cockpit with his back turned. From time to time he glanced furtively over his shoulder.

'Presently, sir,' went on the fisheries officer, 'these people will be the last real sailors . . . I'd like . . . we might give him a little present. After this blow he certainly deserves a drink: I'd like to send him a few bottles.'

The Captain's reaction was surprising. He looked stern and scornful, but then suddenly, without transition, he burst out laughing. 'Your Englishman is mad. Ask the steward to find a bottle of cognac in my stores.'

'Thank you, sir.'

'Half a minute: you can enclose a little note – I'd like the brute to drink Bévisier's health. After all, we did win some battles against the English.'

The bosun's mate lashed the brandy and some bottles of claret to a little fluorescent buoy used to mark the targets during gunnery-practice. The *Eole* approached the *Beatrice*. When we were a little ahead of her and under her lee the Captain let go the package. The red-headed Englishman watched us, astonished. Then we saw him shift his head-sail, fill and heave-to again: he seized the buoy with a boathook. By now he was a good way off, but the Captain turned the

Eole to come up with him again. The Englishman seemed to be in a better temper. He raised one arm and called out in a ham actor's voice, 'Hail to thee that shalt be king hereafter!'

'Your Englishman is mad,' observed the Captain once more. 'Or else he has already started drinking. I don't understand a word he says.'

'I believe it is a quotation from Shakespeare,' said the fisheries officer. 'At all events he is hailing us as kings.'

'Much as I thought: and we are republicans. And I'll tell you something else. Sailors, real sailors, are the ones who earn their living, their daily bread, on the sea.'

To show that he could be well-mannered if he liked, the Englishman raised and dipped his ensign twice. And we answered in the same manner.

The next day the *Eole* ran into a thick fog-bank, and suddenly it was very cold. The sea was an ominous black. We had just left the blue water of the Gulf Stream and we were now in the Labrador current.

The fisheries officer got into touch with the trawler fleet. '*Eole* calling . . . Good morning to you all . . .'

The trawlers were widely scattered, from the Flemish Cap in the east right out to the edge of the ice-covered Artimon Bank, five hundred and fifty miles to the west. Others were in the Cabot Strait, off Port aux Basques. They had just arrived on the fishing-grounds, and the first hauls had been disappointing: the cod were hiding. The Portuguese, Spaniards, and Germans seemed no happier. The Japanese could not be understood, and the Russians were enigmatic. Although we were in the same latitude as Lorient the weather was as cold as it had been off Bear Island.

The *Mara* had a seriously wounded man aboard. (It is odd how some ships seem to have ill-luck: the *Mara* had lost a man before this, during the northern cruise.) She was fishing on the southern edge of the Trou de la Baleine.

The fog was so thick that the *Eole*'s forecastle could not be seen from the bridge. It was by radar that we found the trawler. The fisheries officer had a little radar-reflector set up in the dinghy and he guided us by radio, checking our course by the screen on board. A screeching of invisible gulls and a stench told us that the *Mara* was near – an uncommonly powerful stench of fuel-oil fumes, fish guts, burnt fat, tar, and paint, mixed with the salt smell of the fog. Then a few yards away a dark, hazy, slowly-moving mass. Voices hailed us.

The wounded man had a compound fracture of the thigh. He had lost a great deal of blood : I carried out a transfusion ...

We headed for Saint-Pierre. The Chief was delighted.

CHAPTER 24

Saint-Pierre

'As you'll see, Doctor, the people here are perhaps even harder-headed than the Bigoudens.'

The sub-lieutenant winked at me and went to fetch a bottle of whisky. He poured us out a stiff tot: 'Go on, Chief. Tell us.'

His Mongolian eyes narrowed and he began to laugh silently. 'They cut a man's head off once, in Saint-Pierre...'

'Ha!' interrupted the sub-lieutenant. 'I knew it would be another horrible story.'

'You don't know anything at all. Quite an amusing fellow he was; but he drank. He had murdered an old boy on the Ile aux Chiens: they call it the Ile aux Marins nowadays because the curé thought it sounded better – "My flock are not dogs; they are sailormen." The amusing type had cut the old boy into little pieces – disgusting! He was drunk: in those days – and I'm talking about the beginning of the century – they used to sell a rot-gut that sent you mad. You ought to see what they drink now – all the finest spirits in the world. And cheap! Anyhow, this amusing fellow, Neel by name, was brought up before the court and condemned to death. Fine. But still there was the question of bringing the guillotine to Saint-Pierre, together with Deibler, the executioner, to work it. Paris refused. Maybe Deibler had his work cut out for him there, ha, ha!' The Chief gazed at us, delighted with his joke. 'So would Neel have to be reprieved? No. An old quill-pusher in the ministry of justice searched the archives and found there was a guillotine at Martinique. They had it sent to Saint-Pierre with a note:

"To the executioner: take measures appropriate to the locality and read the instructions."

'Who wants to be an executioner? It calls for a certain taste for such things, ha, ha! Nobody could be found. Nobody! Not even in the punishment-squads, not even with the promise of money and a reduction of sentence . . . In the end the public prosecutor found a fisherman in prison – a man of France, as they say over there – a drunkard, a thief, a no-good bum and all the rest, up to the ears in debt. He agreed for five hundred francs and his freedom. And as an assistant he took on a mate no better than himself.

'The guillotine arrived from Martinique. It was an ancient machine dating from the time of the citizen who invented it – there was a rumour that it had been used for Marie-Antoinette – and the blade was held up by a line turned round a cleat. You cast it off and . . . clack, said the instructions. Still, it was better to have a trial run. Our two amateur executioners tied a little calf to the tip-plank – the creature bawled as if it had the colic – and let go the line. There was a squeaking and then . . . clack! Beheaded, but not entirely: instead of falling into the basket, the calf's head hung by a strip of flesh. Looking rather white about the gills, the prosecutor advised our two sods to bring their cod-knives the next time.'

'What did they do with the calf?' asked the practically-minded sub-lieutenant.

'Cut it up for the punishment-squad's soup. It seems they refused to eat it; though indeed it wasn't every day they had meat . . . You put me off my stroke with your side-issues. Give me a drink, because we're just reaching the dawn of . . . of the last day . . . Yerc'h mad.'

The Chief drank. 'A glass of rum, one last quid of tobacco, and Neel was carted off to the main square, where the two half-wits were waiting with their machine. Neel made a statement: said he was glad he had squandered the few sous his father had left him in drink. The chaplain held out a crucifix . . . Our two idiots spent an endless time strapping him down on the tip-plank. And then they stood there waiting, like the fools that they were. The prosecutor made little signs – go on, go on. They did not understand at all. There was Neel with his head in the hole, and he lashed about; he spat his quid out into the basket in front of him, and to encourage them he called out, "Get on with it, and don't you miss me."

'At last the two idiots recovered a little mother-wit and let go the line. There was a squeak . . . clack! Same thing as with the calf . . . fortunately they had brought their cod-knives.

'The prosecutor did not feel so good. Everyone was crying. The crowd moved off with bowed heads. Even the doctor who had asked for the body for an anatomy-lesson gave up the idea. Neel went straight to the graveyard.'

The Chief drank. 'That was only the prologue. Ha, ha, ha! Now for the real story. The amateur executioner was free: he had earned five hundred francs. But . . . nobody wanted to have anything to do with him any more. Nobody talked to him; nobody looked at him: it was as though he didn't exist. He couldn't find a job. He trailed about the town and everybody looked away. When he went into a bar the drinkers moved aside and stopped talking. He could drink, but he couldn't pay. Nobody wanted his money. He suggested paying back his debts and every time, without a word, his creditors gave him the bill with the word Paid written large across it. Nobody wanted his money. He was alone, quite alone . . .

'He was a very stupid man, but even so he understood: he asked to be sent back to France.'

'And what about the other one, the assistant?' asked the sub-lieutenant.

'He drank all day long, all by himself. As they wouldn't take his money either he said, "This is Heaven, this is Heaven." He was a philosopher, that fellow. One night he fell into the schooner-harbour. Splash!'

Newfoundland and Fortune Bay to the north . . . black rocks everywhere. L'Ile aux Vainqueurs, the Passe de la Normande, the Ile aux Pigeons . . .

The pilot was waiting for us near the Petit-Saint-Pierre light. Two Spanish trawlers – they call them oxen because they drag the trawl in pairs – lay in the roadstead, their crews breaking the thick coat of ice that covered them.

A pale, frigidly pure sky, cut in two by the white trail of a plane. The thin, transparent air, without the faintest trace of dust, was a delight to the eye.

L'Ile aux Marins, and its grey church and houses in the snow. I'Ile au Massacre . . . a black dog barking. Saint-Pierre: white hills with bluish shadows. The town: red, yellow, green. Dories pulled up on the beach. We berthed by the refrigerating station at Cap à l'Aigle.

I delivered my patients to the hospital and walked back, taking a roundabout way. I like wandering alone in an unknown town, staring about, heading in no particular direction.

Rue de la Liberté, rue Sadi-Carnot, rue de la République, place du Général-de-Gaulle. (That was where Neel was beheaded: at the time it was called place de l'Amiral-Courbet.) The frozen Barachois . . . La Pointe aux Canons . . . The new port, with big trawlers from Germany (Bremen) and Japan (Osaka). And still closing the horizon over the water, the grey church, the calvary and the deserted houses of the Ile aux Marins, the Ile aux Chiens.

Neak Luong, the last bastion on the river before Phnom Penh, has fallen. Soon it will all be over out there.

The Chief and the sub-lieutenant took me with them to the *Morue Joyeuse.* Our feet crunched in the snow. A fog-horn

245

startled the cormorants. A Japanese was leaving for the Banks. The beam of a lighthouse quivered on the Galantry hill.

A red neon bar-sign on the quay (a codfish wearing a sou'-wester and holding a glass in its fins). The landlord – the gendarme at Willsdorff's trial – had come to Saint-Pierre in 1965 to 'restore order'; he had met Madame, a Saint-Pierre girl 'as pretty as an English rose'; and when his time was up he came back to marry her. 'He has an Irish Black Bush twelve years old: the infant Jesus in velvet breeches,' said the Chief.

The room was full, every table taken, and we stayed at the counter. 'He wants to talk to you about your prisoner at the bar,' said the Chief as early as the first round.

'Prisoner at the bar?' The gendarme, a red-haired giant, rather overweight, scratched his head. 'Ah, the . . . I saw him again a couple of years ago. Deck-hand aboard the *Marie de Grâce*. He came in here with a whole crowd. I recognized him right away, because of his eyes. To begin with I said to myself it's just not possible. But it was him all right; I made a few inquiries . . . He danced with Madame – only waltzes. He held her rather closer than I cared for.' Madame looked modestly down. 'I kept my eye on him . . . I don't know whether he had recognized me, but I had the feeling he was making fun of me . . . in my position, you have to take care. His cat took advantage of my watching him to do it on the bar. Yes, sir, it pissed on the cloth I use to wipe the glasses, the filthy brute.'

'What about the trial?' asked the sub-lieutenant.

'It went off very well, monsieur . . . except for the way he always looked amused. As for me, I was certain he'd be guillotined.'

'Shot,' said I.

'No, guillotined. He was a civilian: he'd resigned before the failure of the putsch. They said so during the indictment. There were journalists outside, waiting for the verdict. They took photos when he got into the van for the Santé. I kept the article – you can see me very well in the photo. It was a woman who wrote it: "He passed in front of me with his cold killer's smile . . . like an SS man," and God knows how much more. And she said he ought to have been guillotined. Everybody thought so.'

An accordion-band playing a waltz on the gramophone: I asked Madame to dance.

'He was so sweet,' she murmured, as soon as we were well out on the floor, 'and well-mannered. He knows how to talk to ladies; I could tell he had a feeling for me.'

I could not help laughing: Willsdorff had told me that before every big party in the *Jeanne* the midshipmen used to put a torch of the proper size into their trouser-pocket 'so as to keep our reputation at its height without wearing ourselves out'. And these torches were appropriately nick-named 'feelings'.

My partner danced very properly, never attempting to find out whether I had a feeling of any kind for her. In any case I could sense the gendarme's eye firmly upon me.

'Last year he didn't come back to see me,' she said, sighing and coming a little closer. 'If you meet him at sea, tell him . . . that I've still got the key. He'll understand,' she added, in a whisper.

I looked at her: her eyes showed nothing but innocence and modesty.

At the bar the sub-lieutenant was listening to the gendarme. 'In the van, on the way to the court, he asked my colleague, Fougou Ernest, whether he'd ever been present at an execution. We aren't allowed to talk to them, but Fougou took out his cigarettes, gave him one, and said very quick, "It's best to empty your bladder first." After a moment the other one started to laugh. "Thank you," he said, "I'll remember that." Then he repeated, "It's quite right; it's absolutely right," and he laughed.'

247

The Mongol uttered his war-cry, 'Yerc'h mad!'

That was a memorable night. Even the Japanese who were quietly drinking their saké in a corner joined the mêlée in the end. A man who had belonged to the Free French corvette *Mimosa* drew the battle of the Atlantic on the bar, wrangling with a German he called Grand-Admiral Dönitz: they agreed on torpedoing a tanker of Black Bush and sharing the cargo.

At one point there was singing, too – Spanish, Turkish, Japanese. The gendarme and Madame topped up the glasses as you might re-prime a pump . . . Grand-Admiral Dönitz had disappeared.

'He's outside, in the hands of the Lord,' said a very dignified old gentleman wearing the Légion d'Honneur (his pale blue eyes seemed to see more than existed in the whole world).

Somebody told about the whisky days, when the Saint-Pierre docks were stuffed with spirits to be smuggled into the States. 'Once Al Capone came here; I saw him myself with his white hat.'

The corvette *Mimosa* was growing steadily more water-logged. The Japanese refused to take part in the battle of the Coral Sea. The old gentleman talked on: '. . . storm and fog – you could hear the Galantry siren because the wind was in the south. There were two American gangsters, there, at that table. Their speedboat full of spirits was lying in the Barachois because of the dirty weather. I'd helped in the loading and I'd drunk the heel-taps in the broken bottles. I was only a boy, and there I was, leaning against that very bar, sweating out my first real soak: I ought to have been in bed long before. There were some Spanish seamen too, with a woman. And the wind howling outside, and the Galantry siren . . . There I was, rather drunk, and the boss – he was Madame's father – knew it very well. "Aren't you ashamed of yourself, boy?" he said, and he gave

248

me some coffee. Then suddenly the door burst open, the two gangsters jumped up, their hands in their pistol-pockets . . .'

Coincidence? At that very moment the door opened and Grand-Admiral Dönitz surfaced again. (Pokriefke Joachim was his real name: second engineer in the trawler *Vogel*.) He at once engaged the corvette *Mimosa*, now listing heavily. The gendarme and Madame restored order by means of more Black Bush. The old gentleman continued with his tale: 'The door opened . . . a gust of wind? A seaman in black oilskins and boots walked in. Wringing wet, as if he had just come out of the water. He walked into the middle of the room and took off his soaking cap. The water made black snaking runnels on the floor. All at once it was very cold. The seaman said not a word but stood swaying as though he were amazed at being there. He looked sick: his face was deadly pale. The two gangsters had also become very white and the Spaniards fell silent in their corner. The Galantry siren outside . . .

' "You mustn't keep your wet clothes on," said Madame's father. "I'll lend you some dry things." "No, no," said the seaman, drawing back. "I must go. He's waiting for me." "You'll catch your death." The seaman only smiled, but it didn't make him look any the more cheerful. He looked at the clock behind the bar and gave a start. In those days it was a big marquetry clock that hung on the wall and chimed like Big Ben. I believe it was not far from midnight.

'The seaman went towards the Spaniards as though he wanted to talk to them; then he backed away and began the same thing with the gangsters. Maybe he was drunk. He looked desperate. Madame's father filled a big glass with rum and the seaman looked at him thankfully. The water was still running down his hair and his face and it seemed to me that he was crying. He was just next to me, horribly pale. He looked at me and murmured, "You can't say a thing." The clock started to strike and there was something like a huge voice outside. A call? Or was it perhaps only the wind and the Galantry siren?

'The seaman gripped my wrist – his hand was as cold as ice. He cried out, "You haven't the right to say anything, anything at all! But still, I've got to tell you this, boy: he exists! He exists!" He fell, as if he had been knocked down. He was even paler – the colour of death. I heard him groan, "All right: I'm coming, I'm coming." He got up and ran to the door. He looked at me again. "You have to know this, boy: he . . ." Then the huge voice once more . . . perhaps the wind and the Galantry siren?

'There was a man outside, waiting for him: the Spaniards saw him plain, through the window. A great big fellow in a big black oilskin under the street-lamp, casting a huge shadow. They saw him catch hold of the seaman's shoulder and run him off into the darkness. Where did they go? "*Madre de Dios, Madre de Dios* . . ." The Spaniards crossed themselves and ordered rum. The gangsters, deathly pale, soaked themselves in whisky . . . That's what I saw and that's what I heard. I was rather drunk, but Madame's father saw and heard it too.'

The gendarme had the brilliant idea of serving another round of Black Bush to dispel the gloom. 'All that's just a hallucination,' he said. 'These things happen sometimes, believe you me.'

The Japanese, who in any case did not understand a word of French, quietly gave up the struggle; and when they opened the door the screeching of the gulls outside bore witness to their faith in the transmigration of souls . . . Grand-Admiral Dönitz had finally lost the battle of the Atlantic. He was vainly trying to find his words and those that did come could not be pronounced – a few strangled efforts and then no more. His eyes had grown stupid. The corvette *Mimosa* watched him with pride and tried to celebrate the victory; but the glass fell from his hands.

At his post the gendarme was showing sings of exhaustion: no one listened to his endless flow. Madame was as trim as ever. The Turks and Spaniards croaked in their corner. The Mongol drank. The old gentleman with blue eyes talked: 'What did he mean? Why me? Perhaps the message was not meant for me at all. He was never seen again . . . Nor his companion either. Who were they? Still, there were a good many ships in the harbour and one couldn't know all the seamen. My dear sir, another glass. Madame, if you please: two fingers with no ice.'

Madame carried out the order.

'That same night,' he went on, 'a schooner was wrecked on the Pointe de Savoyard. No survivors were found. Only one corpse on the shingle of the little bay – a seaman in black oilskins and boots, wearing a cap. The rocks had scraped his face so that it was unrecognizable. I know because I saw him.' The old gentleman with the Légion d'Honneur did not speak for a long while. He drained his glass at one gulp, put it down on the bar and firmly seized my arm. 'My dear sir,' he said very politely, 'do you believe . . . do you believe that He exists?'

'The Devil? Certainly,' replied the Chief. 'The Other One? The Other . . . I don't know about him. Ha, ha, ha!'

'But it's terrible . . . terrible!'

Now came the fatal hour when the drinker bogs down, withdraws into himself, ruminating – alone. When his beard grows, leaving him a little older. When he must go home.

The night seemed peopled with things mute and unseen, things that moved noiselessly in the silence. The frozen air was still: an absolute and final stillness. In a world that had turned to stone, only the far-off Galantry light signalled its warning: 'Take care! . . . Take care! . . . Take care!'

The *Eole* put to sea, running through the Passe à Henry. Big black cormorants flew screaming from the Colombier. The low white coast of Miquelon, the tall cliffs of Langlade, the grey sky. The radio broadcast a special meteorological bulletin: 'Attention! Attention all shipping! Gale-warning...'

The *Damoclès* had reached the Banks. She had begun fishing northwards along the coast of Labrador.

Aircraft-carriers and destroyers of the American Seventh Fleet in the Gulf of Siam for the evacuation of US citizens from Cambodia. Thousands of refugees are still flooding into Phnom Penh.

Ban Me Thuot has fallen. The Saigon government has lost control of the highland plateaux. North Vietnamese offensive against Quang Tri and Hué.

Our old Captain had died. A signal from the Admiralty gave us the news.

Saint-Pierre Bank. Misaine Bank. Banquereau. The edge of the Goélettes. George Bank ... The *Eole* carried on with her mission. It was horribly cold when the wind was in the north-west. The temperature of the water was three degrees below zero and the spray froze immediately. The ice made us dangerously heavy, and hands were often brought on deck to break it off.

A courtesy visit to Halifax: the fisheries officer's cocktail-party.

Green Bank. The Eglefin Channel. The tail of the Grand Bank. Platier. The Bourrelet reef ...

Courtesy visit to St John's: cocktail-party.

The Americans are evacuating the whole of their embassy staff at Phnom Penh by helicopter. A company of Marines is covering the operation.

The Canadian television showed the ambassador laughing, running with the star-spangled banner rolled up in plastic under his arm. Phnom Penh was dying.

The North Vietnamese offensive: Quang Tri, Hué, and Danang have fallen without resistance.

252

Twenty-one degrees below zero. Persistent winds from the north-west, cold, dry winds that smelt of the vast snowy wastes of Canada – the call of the forest. The arctic waters of the Gulf of St Lawrence were as black as coal. The ice was coming south: it had already covered the Burgeo Bank, to the west of Saint-Pierre. The trawls froze and hardened as soon as they were hauled in over the stern-ramp. The cod were hiding, the fishermen gloomy. There was an enormous stock of unsold deep-frozen fish and the prices were falling . . . Life was hard on the Banks.

Retreat and rout of the Vietnamese army . . .

The Chief, to please me, fabricated a television aerial that could be worked by a direction-finder, and we picked up the Canadian and American stations. The Col des Nuages. Danang – which I would still sometimes call Tourane. Dead children, dead women: buzzing flies. Scenes of misery and panic. Faces. Flies everywhere: their buzzing in the microphone drowned the journalists' voices. A father dragging his child's body behind him in a plastic sack. He held a torn black umbrella to protect himself from the sun. He walked through sand-dunes covered with litter like a public rubbish-dump. He let go of his horrible bundle. He fell to his knees: he wept. Flies . . .

I drank the glass of whisky that my friend the Chief held out.

'Nobody loves us,' said President Thieu.

An American plane crashing into a marsh at the end of the Ton Son Nut runway: it was evacuating little Vietnamese orphans to the United States. Two hundred and fifty children dead. A Saigon soldier searching through the wreckage and darting a terrifying glance at the camera watching him: 'We still have others that you could take as souvenirs,' he said in English, as though he were spitting in our faces. More and more buzzing flies . . .

I drank whisky.

On the bridge. The numbing cold. The sea dead, black

and white, dead and frozen. The huge red heatless rayless sun: dead too. Two Portuguese oxen were drawing their trawl. Little men in yellow busy on deck. The gulls went mad; there were thousands and thousands of them screaming – a wildly confused, vehement, harsh and ugly din – as they dived on the rising net. They seemed to be fighting in their haste to snatch a scrap of fish. The little men staggered: they too seemed to be fighting one another or to be defending their catch against the seagulls' greed. The sun grew larger still.

The chief medical officer of the Saint-Pierre hospital fell sick: I was appointed to replace him for a while.

In the darkness and at the height of a snowstorm, the *Eole* took a pilot aboard in the green sector of the Petit-Saint-Pierre light. From time to time one caught a hint of the pulsing Galantry beam. The pilot did not like to bring us alongside the refrigerating centre of the Cap à l'Aigle. 'Better stay in the roadstead.'

We had a wounded man, and the Captain decided to move him into the pilot-boat. I drugged him a little so that he should not suffer too much and dropped into the boat with him. The fisheries officer gave me a knowing wink.

I became an important person and it amused me for a while. I was received by the governor, the *lycée* masters, the bishop of the Territories (another Alsatian), and by the head of the television station (known by one and all as the Sun King) and his pretty wife.

It was the Sun King who showed me Saint-Pierre and the people who lived there. They were happy, cheerful, hospitable, full of dreams and stories. They loved their rocks, their stunted trees, their storms; they loved hunting at Langlade and fishing in their dories. It was cold and we drank a great deal.

The German, Spanish, Japanese and Portuguese trawlers came and went. For a few hours their crews would fill the streets with life, and on Saturday evenings the whole town assembled to dance.

When my day's work was over I used to wander down to the *Morue Joyeuse* and drink Black Bush with the Sun King, the gendarme and Madame (as once I had drunk lukewarm beer with Cao Giao on the banks of the river). Sometimes I met the dignified old gentleman there: he told me about rum-running, chases, shipwrecks, crews blinded by the blizzard, cries in the night, a buried treasure on Miquelon... And we were thoroughly warm. And we drank our wonderful, mahogany-glinting Irish whiskey.

The Ile aux Marins was deserted; nobody had lived there for a long while. One of the Le Clinche brothers – the one they called the Devil because he was not pretty to look at (he had lost an eye, pierced by a fish-hook, and he wore a black band, a huge beard, and a red cap) – took me there in his dory. A black labrador guarded the place, hunting coots on the shore for its food. The weather-beaten houses were quite sound: there was the church with its ex-votos hanging from the arched roof (ships in bottles, model schooners, naive paintings), the café with a few glasses left standing on the counter, the little town-hall with a framed photograph of President Lebrun facing the bust of Marianne, the Church school with the last catechism lesson still chalked on the blackboard:

What is God?
God is a pure, infinitely perfect spirit, the maker of heaven and earth, the sovereign lord of all things . . .

The Devil told me that one foggy day an American yacht was wrecked on the other side of the island. A man and a woman swam ashore to fetch help. They ran wildly to the houses and knocked on all the doors, shouting 'Help! Help!' And nobody opened, of course; nobody answered. They heard nothing but the barking of the dog and the distant hooting of the Galantry siren.

'I think they went mad,' said the Devil. 'Anyhow, they

roared out like maniacs. I was fishing just off the Ile au Massacre and I heard them from there in spite of the fog – it muffles sound. I went to have a look. They had left all the doors open, squeaking and slamming in the wind. They weren't shouting any more, but I did hear a queer sort of dismal song . . . It's all very well not believing in . . . but when it's foggy you see things that aren't there and you hear noises you can't make out. It was the dog that led me to the church: there they were, on their knees both of them, praying and singing hymns. The woman let out a screech when she saw me. Stark raving mad. It was her who had made the man so frightened. She thought the whole world had died.'

Six hundred French subjects and foreigners have taken refuge in the French embassy at Phnom Penh. The Khmers Rouges have completely emptied the city; even the wounded and the patients in the hospitals have been sent away.

Three million people flung on to the roads. Where will they go? How many will survive? It was the south-west monsoon season. It was hot, but the rain was still keeping off. The deep humming of innumerable black flies. Phnom Penh was dead. Over there, too, was there one last question on a blackboard: *What is God?*

Hard fighting at Xuan Loc.

The last Southern soldiers were sacrificing their lives, for nothing, out of despair.

Refugees are still flooding into Saigon. Many deaths, many wounded, many sick. There are not enough doctors.

And I . . . I was here.

Certainly I had been expelled. To be perfectly honest, I had let myself be expelled. With a little urging I might have stayed . . . I had felt the disaster coming.

I said that I had chosen my people: and yet here was I in Saint-Pierre.

Over there the crowd was groaning, sobbing; there were

cries of fear and pain, calls for help . . .
But Peter followed him afar off . . .

On a day of thick, driving snow, the *Damoclès*, silent and ghostly, glided into the harbour. Her fog-horn sounded three times.

She vanished entirely, wiped out by a gust of snow that muffled all sound. Far away the Galantry siren, like the sad cry of some animal. A grey shadow . . . The bows of a ship, shouting, the mooring-lines thrown . . . A painted eye looking at me.

EPILOGUE

---◆---

THE SUNSET

Steer a ship on to the rocks,
Know that she is going there. Steer her there.
With unwavering hand.

Jean Chauvel: *D'une eau profonde.*

At sunset we were all gathered in the *Morue Joyeuse*. Big Le Clinche and his brother the Devil were there, so were the corvette *Mimosa*, the old gentleman whose pale blue eyes saw more things than existed in the whole world, the Sun King with one of his cameramen and a sound-engineer, and behind the bar the gendarme and Madame. The *Eole* was alongside the Cap à l'Aigle refrigerating centre – she had come to fetch me. The fisheries assistance cruise was over: we were going home. The Mongol, the young infantryman, the fisheries officer and the Captain – they had all come: we even had the gnome-faced old boatswain. We drank Black Bush. There were also some Portuguese, Spaniards, Japanese, Germans, and Turks – the usual set of customers. The sun had vanished behind the hills that mask the Pointe de Savoyard; the sky was red. Very high up an eastward-flying plane left a trail that shone like gold in the last rays of the sun. The Galantry light turned on. All bills were paid; all goodbyes had been said; we were going home.

'Have you seen him?' The *Eole* had scarcely made fast before the sub-lieutenant hailed me from the wing.

A little later I joined him and the Chief and the fisheries officer in the wardroom. The steward was wiping glasses with an air of unconcern; I could feel that he too was waiting.

'Well, Doctor, tell us about it.'

'Yes, I've seen him again . . .' What did they expect me to tell them? There was nothing to say. What were they hoping for?

Yes, I had seen Willsdorff again. He had not changed: tall and lean, a few white hairs in his thick curly thatch, the lines in his face deeper – the wrinkles at the corners of his eyes still gave him that mocking, happy look. He had perhaps lost that youthful air which had still been with him when last we met at Haiphong: his face, sharply drawn like those in some of Dürer's portraits, had at last caught up with his age.

He was in his cabin. He looked at me for a long while without a word; he searched my face, as I sometimes do myself, before my morning shave. It seemed to me that in each of my wrinkles he detected marks that showed the whole of my life – the acts of cowardice, the weaknesses, the betrayals, the drinking; and also that part of me I know to be the best.

He looked as though he were laughing. 'What a long, long road,' he said at last. His laugh was still the same.

Dien Cai Dau (Monsieur ma Conscience) was sitting on the desk, his tail curled round him: a black cat with a white bib (like Monsieur Dégouzzi and Mimi the Rat), very thin, almost skin and bone. (He must just have come back from one of his escapades.) He too stared at me, expressionless. His final verdict came: he turned his back on me.

I had seen Willsdorff again. Something had gone wrong with the *Damoclès*'s winch and she had to stay in Saint-Pierre for the repair: it took a week. We went fishing in the Le Clinches' dory; we went shooting in the snow at Langlade with the Sun King; we walked about together, just the two of us, on the Ile aux Marins, followed at a distance by the black labrador. We said nothing . . . Yet once I did speak about our old Captain: 'He's dead.' 'I know, I know.' Willsdorff did not choose to add any more.

In the evenings we went to the *Morue Joyeuse*. Madame was all blushes and the gendarme did not quite know how he liked it. I treated the whole crew – the two Tonkinese from Cat Ba, the three Algerian harkis, all the hands who had been aboard the *Marie de Grâce*, Bongo Ba, the nigger of the *Damoclès* – he often danced with Madame . . . Dien Cai Dau did not piss on the counter.

Yes, I had seen Willsdorff again!

The *Eole* came in to pick me up. The *Damoclès*, now repaired, was just about to put to sea for Labrador and Greenland. The fisheries officer wanted to arrange one of his cocktail-parties but Willsdorff could not spare the time to come aboard, so it was decided that we should all meet at the *Morue Joyeuse*. Willsdorff came with his Tonkinese and Bongo Ba, who wanted to have one last dance with Madame and to see his shipmates from the *Eole*. An evening of farewells, like so many others.

Through the din I suddenly heard the sub-lieutenant – he was as straight as a ramrod and rather flushed: he had gulped down his drink to give himself courage but there was a slight quaver in his diffident voice – I heard him ask, 'Sir, do you need a good first lieutenant?' Willsdorff looked at him; he seemed to be smiling, cruelly. 'I'd send in my papers . . . I'd like to . . . if you need a lieutenant, sir, I . . .'

He was still standing very straight but I saw that one hand was gripping the bar so hard that his fingers turned white. The Captain and the fisheries officer did not stir. The Mongol was laughing silently. A kind of emptiness formed around Willsdorff: he did not seem to be surprised by the sub-lieutenant's request; he looked at him without a word. The silence grew embarrassing.

No, he did not say to him, Follow me. I do not know what in fact he did say to him. Monsieur ma Conscience miaowed and I believe the gendarme started to laugh, stupidly – or else it was the Mongol or the gnome or the Devil and his brother, big Le Clinche: I just don't know. I couldn't hear what he said to him.

The Sun King and his team were very excited. 'We're going – we're going with you,' they cried. They wanted to make a documentary called *The Toilers of the Sea*, and Willsdorff had agreed to take them aboard.

'We're going, we're going!'

The sub-lieutenant was rather red – but perhaps it was the drink: Black Bush is a betrayer.

The sun had set. The pink trail of the aeroplane faded slowly in the east. A fog-horn sounded three times; the black dog of the Ile aux Marins answered with a howl.

'He's calling us, he's calling us. Goodbye,' cried the Sun King, and he ran out, followed by his team.

The Captain and the fisheries officer had gone, taking the sub-lieutenant with them. The Mongol was sitting with the foolish old man who had the Légion d'Honneur, telling him a story. He bored me, but nevertheless I listened.

'Three very drunken unbelievers were coming home across the Guenn-an-Avel moor: they were some way ahead of our worthy Rector – that night he too had been tempted by the *gwin ru*. When they reached the calvary, the cross the Eckmühl light touches every so often, a drunken notion came to one of the unbelievers: "I'll make him lose his faith." He told the other two he was going to get on to the cross and call out to the Rector when he came by. To make things look more real he took off his clothes, just keeping a cloth round his loins. The others had to tie him on, because he was too drunk – couldn't keep his arms out in a cross. "You hide yourselves; we're going to have a laugh . . ." '

A mad little flame showed in the old gentleman's pale blue eyes. The Mongol laughed. 'The innocent Rector came along, full of red wine and happiness. The unbeliever on the cross began to bawl, "There's no God, no heaven, no sin; it's all a pack of lies. There's nothing. Ha, ha, ha!" The poor old Rector dropped to his knees, rebuking himself for having made an ill use of the fruit of the vine and work of human hands. "There's nothing, ha, ha, ha! Nothing! Nothing!" shouted the drunk. The darkness, the wind, the startled, screaming gulls, the voice coming from the calvary, and this pale crucified form – it was enough to terrify the bravest man. "Go back, Satan . . . *Vade retro Satanas* . . ." "There's nothing. Nothing! Nothing, ha, ha!" The pious soul may have been a little tipsy, but he was no fool; he guessed someone was playing an ugly joke on him and he walked off. The unbeliever began to grow frightened: "Ahoy! Hallo! There's nothing, is there? Ahoy! Hallo! There's nothing!" Now his voice was full of dread. "There's nothing . . . Ahoy! Ahoy! Nothing . . . Help . . . help!"

The fog-horn. Night had almost fallen. The *Damoclès* glided along the wharf. I saw Bongo Ba on the forecastle; he waved his cap. There was also a figure on the wing, moving his arms – perhaps the Drummer-Crab or the Sun King – and I thought I heard a great shout. Was it Goodbye, Pierre? Goodbye Saint-Pierre? I don't know. The gulls screamed wildly and the dog on the Ile aux Marins howled.

'. . . It was the gendarmes who took him down next day, dead of cold and exhaustion. The wind had torn off his cloth and he had thrown up all his wine. His two mates had run away, terrified, leaving him in the darkness.'

I was drinking too much. The Galantry light throbbed: take care . . . take care . . . take care.

Willsdorff had given me a ship in a bottle, the corvette that the fisheries officer had admired so much. A Japanese wanted to buy it.

I drank. The Mongol watched me with his cat-like eyes.

He laughed. We both laughed. We drank. It was the saddest night of drunkenness. Outside the Galantry light throbbed on and on. It was cold.

On my way back to the ship I threw the bottle into the sea.

In the starlight I watched it drift away on the current. I was drunk.

The hell with it all!

We were going home.

And here was fear saying to me, 'Ha, ha! Now we will have it out together, just the two of us!'